"I don't want fritters."

Frowning, Molly regarded him. "Teacakes, then?"

"No. Something more." His grasp loosened, became more of a caress. His thumb stroked over the sensitive skin at the underside of her wrist. "Something…sweeter."

Molly trembled. Staunchly she made herself stop gawping at the lovely contrast between Marcus's big, sun-browned hand and her lace-trimmed gloves. He'd magically found the gap between those gloves and her long-sleeved dress, and he toyed with it even now. The sensation caused by his thumb against her bare skin made her want to close her eyes to savor it. Instead, she summoned all her will to address Marcus directly.

"Perhaps a dumpling, then? They're quite fresh."

So are you, Marcus's teasing expression said.

"No. Sweeter." He tugged her nearer.

It was true, then. He *did* have more in mind than mere delectables…

THE MATCHMAKER

BY

LISA PLUMLEY

MILLS & BOON®

First published in Great Britain 2007
by Mills & Boon, an imprint of Harlequin (UK) Limited,
Large Print edition 2011
Eton House, 18-24 Paradise Road, Richmond, Surrey TW9 1SR

© Lisa G. Plumley 2003

ISBN: 978 0 263 22385 9

Harlequin (UK) policy is to use papers that are natural, renewable and recyclable products and made from wood grown in sustainable forests. The logging and manufacturing process conform to the legal environmental regulations of the country of origin.

Printed and bound in Great Britain
by CPI Antony Rowe, Chippenham, Wiltshire

When she found herself living in modern-day Arizona Territory, **Lisa Plumley** decided to take advantage of it—by immersing herself in the state's fascinating history, visiting ghost towns and historical sites, and finding inspiration in the desert and mountains surrounding her. It didn't take long before she got busy creating light-hearted romances like this one, featuring strong-willed women, ruggedly intelligent men, and the unexpected situations that bring them together.

When she's not writing, Lisa loves to spend time with her husband and two children, travelling, hiking, watching classic movies, reading, and defending her trivia-game championship. She enjoys hearing from readers, and invites you to contact her via e-mail at lisa@lisaplumley.com, or visit her website at www.lisaplumley.com

To Melissa Endlich, with many thanks.
And to John Plumley, with all my love

Chapter One

Northern Arizona Territory September 1882

Change was afoot in Morrow Creek.

From the whispering ponderosa pines crowding the hills at the edge of town, to the false-fronted buildings lining Main Street and all the way to the shadowy interior of Murphy's saloon, things just weren't the way they were supposed to be. The way the bachelors of the town wanted them to be. Tonight, on this frost-tinged autumn evening, they'd gathered together to address the problem.

The problem of the mysterious meddling match-maker.

Marcus Copeland, running uncharacteristically late, made it into the meeting just as two of the bar-keeps broke apart from the crowd to bar the saloon doors. With a nod for both men, Marcus slipped inside and found an empty stool in the corner. From his position at the back of the room, he heard the heavy crossbar thud into place at the doors, sealing all the members of the Morrow Creek Men's Club inside for this, their third emergency meeting in as many weeks.

"Damnation! Somethin' has got to be done," old man Jeffries was saying. "It ain't right, what that matchmaker's been doin'. It just ain't right."

A round of nods and murmured voices greeted his pronouncement. Dusty boots stamped on the floor with enthusiasm, and several men raised their glasses of whiskey, lager and mescal in a show of support for Jeffries. If their combined grumblings and disgruntled expressions were anything to judge by, every last unmarried man in the territory felt equally beleaguered by the matchmaker's problematic meddling.

Marcus figured he had more vital things to worry about—like the set of ledgers from his lumber mill that still needed double-checking, and the schedule for next week's shipment that still needed to be assigned to one of his foremen. But as an upstanding member of the community, and a bachelor who'd been provoked just about as much as any other man there, he'd decided it was his duty to attend the meeting.

Whether he wanted to or not.

Near the saloon's bar, beneath Murphy's already-famous gilt-framed portrait of a scantily clad water nymph, another man rose. Marcus recognized him as O'Neil, the butcher. He clutched a pint of Levin's ale in a fist roughened by years of wielding a cleaver, and raised his voice to be heard over the other men.

"Jeffries is right!" he said. "This ruckus is getting out of hand. So are these forward-thinkin' ladies. Why just last week, Emmaline Jones turned up at my shop with—"

He paused, as though the truth of the matter were too awful to be admitted aloud.

"—with a yellow embroidered butcher's apron for me. The next day, she came back with a matching neckerchief. Seems the matchmaker told her I had a cold coming on, and would 'precciate the gesture."

"Was it embroidered, too?" yelled someone from beside the potbellied stove.

Guffaws filled the room.

"No." O'Neil hung his head. "But it smelled like rose petals. The fool woman wouldn't leave till I put it on. Now I ask you, how's a man s'posed to work wearin' a thing like that? Smellin' like *flowers?*"

The men's voices rose, loud with advice to O'Neil on the virtues of "smellin' pretty." Marcus cracked a grin and opened the first of the two ledgers he'd brought, scanning the rows of neatly penciled entries within. It looked as though it might be a while before the men's club came to any conclusions. He might as well get some work done.

"Quit yer bellyachin'," put in the tanner who kept his shop a short ways distant from the Copeland lumber mill. "That fool matchmaker's advice has the whole town in an uproar. It ain't just you. Hell, just this mornin' that little gal who just came to town gave me a pink knitted rifle cozy!"

Heads shook all around.

"Now I ask you," the tanner went on, "who the hell ever heard of a rifle cozy? My guns ain't cold, like a pot o' tea. What's a fella supposed to do with a thing like that?"

"Well," drawled the red-haired rancher from the west side of town, crossing his arms over his tobacco-stained vest, "you can't put it with my hand-sewed bullet carrier that Mary Jane Mayberry gave me two days ago."

"Why not?"

"'Cause mine's baby-blue." He paused. Spit. "Won't match."

Table-thumping laughter ensued. Marcus shook his head and turned another ledger page, blowing away the sawdust that clung to the paper. Compared to the rest of the bachelors in town, the matchmaker had taken things easy on him.

Sure, having his men come to work bleary-eyed and distracted from visits and letters and surprise gifts from hopeful brides-to-be hadn't helped his lumber mill any. In fact, it was downright dangerous having inattentive workers running the saws. But Marcus had handled those problems on an individual basis, by reassigning the affected men to less hazardous jobs. Where his personal life was concerned… well, the matchmaker's antics had left him relatively, and curiously, untouched.

"What about *this?*" Another man stood, holding a necktie aloft. It dangled from his fingertips like a limp, lace-frothed rattlesnake, remarkably ugly in shades of brown and green. "The matchmaker told the preacher's daughter to make this damn thing for me. Now, if she comes to my mercantile and I'm not wearing it, she gets all weepy on me." He shook his head. "I can't run a business with nonsense like that going on."

"Awww!" The men nearest him aimed nonsympathetic jabs at his ribs. One grabbed the necktie and slung it over the merchant's shoulders, then stepped back as though to study the effect. "I declare!" he exclaimed in a piercing falsetto voice. "You look just like a picture in Godey's."

They all laughed, good-naturedly slapping their friend on the back. The necktie was passed to a cowhand, who whirled it overhead like a lasso. At the sight of it, Marcus shuddered. A man had to draw the line somewhere. Ugly neckties—with *lace* of all things—seemed like a good place to start.

The worst he'd personally received had been a

tentative invitation to a "moonlit stroll with a lady admirer" in one of the matchmaker's personal advertisements. Printed in Adam Crabtree's *Pioneer Press* at irregular intervals, the advertisements were read with groans and expressions of resignation from the beleaguered men and eager giggles from the women. Of all the marriage-minded weapons in the matchmaker's arsenal, the advertisements were among the most powerful.

"Irene Posy wrote poetry about me," a bearded railroad man in the corner said. "And put it in the newspaper!"

"Alma Avondale follows me all the way to my mine claim every blasted morning, chattering on about the dance at the Chautauqua next month," another man complained. "She thinks I'd make a right fine partner for the quadrille, *if* I'd shine up my boots."

The miner's drinking companions huffed in indignation. Not a man among them would admit to getting gussied up for a mere female. Not in public, at least.

The shared complaints continued. Feeling increasingly fortunate, Marcus spent the next several minutes rechecking figures. Conversations swirled around him, punctuated with gulps of whiskey and streams of tobacco juice hitting—and missing—the spittoons. Growing warm in the mishmash of bodies filling the room, he peeled off his suit coat and laid it beneath his stack of ledgers. He loosened his starched collar, then went on working.

"That's nothing." A calm, authoritative voice broke into the melee, and Marcus glanced up to see that the saloon's owner, Morrow Creek newcomer Jack Murphy, had spoken.

"I won't give names, because the lady has a reputation to protect," he went on in his faint Irishman's brogue, spreading his hands to encourage quiet in the room. "But this morning, a lady claimed the matchmaker had sent her to find her one true love… here, inside my saloon."

A shocked silence fell over the men. For several moments, they contemplated this unthinkable piece of information. Even Marcus put down his pencil, frowning. If a woman would invade the sanctity of the saloon, what next? Females in britches? Ladies wearing face paint and powder and French perfume? Women who would take it in their heads to kiss a man *first,* without being courted?

Actually, upon reflection Marcus decided he liked the sound of that last notion. Quite a bit. But the rest…clearly, something had to be done.

The mysterious Morrow Creek matchmaker, whoever she was, had to be stopped. But how?

"Inside your saloon?" Old man Jeffries mopped his brow with a suspiciously doodad-embellished handkerchief, clearly done in by this new turn of events. *"Inside?"*

Jack nodded, looking somber. It was true, then. No place was safe any longer.

"Now, we all know there's no easy way out of this," Jack went on. Several men nodded. The creak of chairs shifting beneath bulky bodies as the men strained to see, and urgent whispers for quiet, were the only sounds in the room. "But between the lot of us, we ought to be able to come up with something."

"I already tried sayin' I wasn't keen on gettin' hitched," the sad-faced man beside Marcus said. "Leastwise, not to a woman who's not my own choosin'. But them gals get all fired up by the matchmaker. They don't pay no mind to reason."

Someone at the end of the bar laughed. "What woman does?"

A hum of agreement swelled upward, reaching to the raw-timber rafters that delineated the saloon space downstairs from whatever occupied the building's top floor. Thoughtfully, Marcus lifted his gaze, wondering if he could interest Jack Murphy in the purchase of a punched-tin ceiling from the lumber mill's assortment of building supplies. At three cents a linear foot, the profit on the new ceiling would be....

Another voice interrupted his musings. "Now hold

on. I reckon these womenfolk can be reasoned with," said Daniel McCabe, the town blacksmith. "That's what I did."

He raised his burly arm, chugged down an impressive quantity of mescal, then wiped his mouth with the sleeve of his plain white shirt. Tipping his chair back on two legs, he regarded the gathering with a self-satisfied smile. "That's all it takes."

"You don't say, McCabe." The butcher squinted, appearing to consider the notion. With a suddenly skeptical twist of his lips, he turned to Daniel again. "That made the ladies the matchmaker loosed on you quit comin' 'round and pesterin' you?"

"Hell, no." Daniel's grin widened. "But now they come 'round with things I *want* to have. A pair of new tongs from the mercantile, a bottle of lager on a hot day, a hank of sausage from your butcher shop—" He ticked off the items on his fingers, stopping only when interrupted by increasingly loud laughter.

Shrugging, Daniel hooked his arms in the braces holding up his soot-smudged pants. "You fellas just have to know how to handle a female, is all."

Only a few stools down from Daniel, Marcus accepted his customary evening meal—good ale, a plate of Murphy's tinned beans with bacon, and a hunk of brown bread—and counted out the coppers to pay for it. He began to eat, automatically scanning the day's recorded timber yield.

It was low, probably because of the slowdowns caused by the matchmaker's giggling, gaggling feminine disciples. They'd caused his men such distraction that both yields *and* profits were down. For now, the problem was small. But if it grew any more troublesome, Marcus's planned expansion of his lumber mill would be delayed.

Concerned by the realization, Marcus turned his attention to the conversation again. This was taking much too long to resolve. Wasn't anyone here capable of handling a passel of women?

"Why don't we speak to the matchmaker in her own language?" Marcus suggested, setting his beans and bread aside. "We can take out a personal advertisement of our own. Tell her the men of Morrow Creek want their lives back."

"And," O'Neil added, "that they'll do their courtin' on their own terms. With the women *they* choose."

Marcus nodded. Obviously, all this group needed was leadership. It was as true here as it was in his lumber mill all day long.

"Won't work." With a terse snap of his wrist, Jack Murphy finished wiping down the bar and flicked the wet cloth into the corner bucket. He spread his hands on the newly clean surface and leaned forward. "Adam Crabtree won't take personal advertisements from anybody but the matchmaker's private courier. Nobody knows who that is."

"Lord," the tanner groused. "She's got us sewn up tighter than Copeland's hold on his wallet."

Chortles abounded as heads turned toward Marcus. He laughed, too, as agreeable to the joke as anyone else. It was true that he kept a firm grasp on his money. He'd worked hard for it. There was no crime in wanting to secure a good future.

Especially after the things he'd gone through to get there.

All the same, Marcus wasn't so far off the mark that he couldn't appreciate the humor in a man who accounted for every last pine shaving at the lumber mill. A man who couldn't resist locking the door of his house when his neighbors did not. A man who'd stocked his pantry with enough tinned peaches, Arbuckle's coffee and bags of dried beans to last until he turned gray, and who never finished a meal without tucking away a portion of it for later...just in case.

A man like him.

"I'd say we've got the clue we need, then," he said, thinking back on what had been said about the matchmaker's personal advertisements—and the *Pioneer Press* editor's involvement in them. The man was known to be a radical thinker, espousing all sorts of eccentric ideas. "It sounds to me as though Adam Crabtree must be involved somehow."

"Or his daughters!" someone piped up. "Those

three are something else, again. Why, that Sarah Crabtree knows just about everyone in town, seeing as how she teaches all our children down at the schoolhouse. I'd say *she'd* have some definite ideas about who should be matched up."

"Now, hold on," interrupted Daniel McCabe, standing up so that his intimidating bulk loomed over the speaker. "I know Sarah, and there's no way in hell she—"

"You're right!" O'Neil said, breaking in before Daniel could finish. "There's something 'spicious about those Crabtree sisters. All three of 'em spinsters and busybodies are privy to half the town's secrets, between 'em. 'Specially that Grace Crabtree, with all her highfalutin 'ladies' clubs' and such. She must know every old biddy in Morrow Creek."

The men around him nodded vigorously. The buzz of conversation rose louder, enlivened by this new development. Jack Murphy weighed in with his opinion on Grace Crabtree, and Daniel McCabe rose again in defense of her sister Sarah. Talk turned to the third and youngest sister, Molly Crabtree. Amidst it all, Marcus worked on the ledgers and finished his beans and ale. Absentmindedly, he wrapped the remaining half of brown bread in his handkerchief and tucked the bundle into his coat pocket.

Suddenly, the tanner's voice came again: "You're

a thinking kind of man, Copeland. How 'bout that for a plan?"

Marcus blinked, unable to recall the multiple directions the conversation had taken after his suggestion that Adam Crabtree might be linked to the mysterious matchmaker.

"Yeah, Copeland. You're the one who thought up this idea," O'Neil said. "'Tis only fair you take on Molly."

"Molly?"

"Molly Crabtree," O'Neil explained. Inexplicably, his face reddened, as though the mere mention of the woman's name brought a blush to his face. Curious. "You must've seen her. Her little bakery shop—"

Titters erupted throughout the room, and were quickly stifled.

"—is just down the street from your place."

Marcus squinted, trying to recall what lay on the path between his modest house and the lumber mill he'd put into operation only two short years ago. He envisioned nothing. Most days, his walk to his office was filled with thoughts of the day to come—work crews to be assigned, timber to be felled, shipments to be hauled to the railway. He wasn't some kind of layabout, with time to gawk at the scenery he passed.

"I don't recall seeing her," he said. "I don't have time to—"

"Come on, Copeland," someone called from near the bar. "You must've seen her."

"She's a female." More laughter. "Remember those?"

"About so high—" one of the billiards players who frequented the newly opened saloon held his hand at chest height. "—with a fancy hat, a sweet swoosh of skirts, and a *very* important difference in the fit of her shirtwaist."

Everyone laughed. Irritated, Marcus slapped the second of his ledgers closed. He knew what a woman was! Hell, he'd done his share of warming up the long nights with someone soft and biddable and more than able to fill out the 'fit of her shirtwaist.' Granted, he hadn't had time for any of that for a while now…but that didn't mean he needed his friends and neighbors making him look the fool.

"Maybe we can draw a picture," teased the mercantile owner, "so Marcus here can locate the lady and find out if she's the matchmaker or not."

Ahh. So that was what the 'taking on' referred to by O'Neil was. The Morrow Creek Men's Club expected him to find a way to discover if the bakery-owning Crabtree sister was the matchmaker. Marcus frowned, raising his hand to forestall further discussion.

It didn't work.

"A picture! That's what he needs." Agreement was reached quickly. Jack Murphy winked and produced a finger's width of chalk from behind the bar, then tossed it to the man most likely to be able to render a recognizable likeness—Deputy Winston, from the sheriff's office. Hunkering down beside a nearby table, Winston examined the scarred wood surface, wearing the same expression he did while indulging in his favorite hobby: copying the images from the jailhouse's collection of wanted posters.

He drew. In no time flat, he straightened, revealing a bumpy, chalky likeness of a woman wearing a frothy dress, disproportionately huge bosoms, and an even huger bonnet. "There you go, Copeland. Have at 'er."

Tight featured, Marcus stood. For one long, silent moment, he stared down at the bawdy caricature. "Very well," he said at last. "I'll find out if Miss Crabtree is the matchmaker."

"And stop her!"

"Of course."

"Then we're all in agreement," Jack said from his place at the bar. "We find this matchmaker, we find whatever it takes to prove that she's behind the shenanigans, and we stop her. Marcus with Miss Molly, Daniel with Miss Sarah, and me—" he hesitated, seeming pained by the announcement "—with Miss Grace. All members in agreement?"

"Hell, yes!" cried the men. Hooting, stamping, clanking their glasses together in glee, they fell into clumps of four or five men each, ready to celebrate the impending downfall of the meddlesome matchmaker who had wrecked their peaceable lives.

"One more thing," Marcus said, raising his voice to be heard over the din. "The next man who treats a woman's likeness and reputation this way—" he thumped the chalk drawing on the table, bringing his gaze to bear on the roomful of men "—will have me to answer to."

A hush fell over the celebrants. Quickly the deputy stepped forward and rubbed away the image with his shirtsleeve. "Sorry," he muttered. "No offense meant, Copeland. I thought you didn't even know the gal."

"I don't." *But I will soon.* Marcus slung his suit coat over his arm and gathered his ledgers. "But I won't stand by and see a lady hurt. By anyone. For any reason."

He gave the crowd another warning gaze, then turned his back on them and headed for the barred doors. The two barkeeps hurried forward to remove the barrier designed to insure the Morrow Creek Men's Club's privacy. Wearing jointly chagrined expressions, they waved Marcus through.

Outside he paused, listening as the doors were barred shut again and the revelry resumed. Shaking his head, Marcus followed the moonlit path toward his house at the edge of town.

Cool, pine-scented air filled his lungs and restored his good humor. Before he'd walked very far, he was fairly champing at the bit to locate Miss Molly Crabtree tomorrow. If she *was* the matchmaker, stopping her activities would improve work at his lumber mill and fulfill his promise to the men's club, both. All he needed was a little ingenuity. A lot of patience. And a plan.

A plan to restore peace. A plan to set things right again, the way they should be. With a little effort, he decided, it shouldn't be all that difficult.

After all, Molly Crabtree was a woman. A woman engaged, oddly enough, in trade, but a woman nonetheless. How much trouble could she possibly be?

Whistling, Marcus went forward, feeling more than ready to meet the task that awaited him.

Chapter Two

Molly Crabtree just *knew* she could make a success of her new bakery business…if only she could get outside her family's front door and get to it.

But today, like nearly every day since she'd opened her shop, Molly was waylaid halfway across the parlor rug by a passel of well-meaning family members. Before long, escape seemed impossible.

Her mother entered the room first, clapping her hands together. "Wait just a minute, Molly May," she ordered.

Stifling a sigh, Molly turned. She hated it when anyone called her by her full name, as though she were a five-year-old in short skirts, instead of a fully grown woman of twenty-four.

"You're not seriously contemplating *walking* to your shop, are you? Alone?" Fiona Crabtree asked. Her upswept gray curls shivered with dismay, and her lips turned downward in a way that never failed to stir guilt, and exasperation, in Molly's heart.

"I am, Mama. It's not far, you know."

Fiona lowered her gaze to the wicker basket filled with cinnamon, a dozen eggs and a cone of fresh sugar that Molly had tucked beneath her arm. As though her youngest daughter had never spoken, she continued, "And with a heavy bundle like that, too? Why, it just won't do. I'll send for Ambrose to come drive you in the newspaper's wagon."

"Mama, thank you, but I—"

"Not while she's wearing that blue gingham of mine, I hope!" Out of breath, Sarah Crabtree hurried downstairs with an armload of schoolbooks for her students, eyeballing the gown Molly had filched from their shared bureau this morning. "Papa's wagon will make it filthy in no time. Do you know how difficult it is to wash out printer's ink?"

"I promise to take care of it, Sarah," Molly protested. "As for the wagon—" she faced her mother again, and was dismayed to find Fiona reaching toward her head with a gleam in her eyes— one Molly recognized perfectly well as an uncontrollable desire to redo the chignon she'd already set in her hair. "—please don't bother Ambrose. I don't mind walking."

"You'd best take a shawl, then." Grace Crabtree, pink cheeked from an early-morning bicycling jaunt with her ladies' group, paused at the parlor's entrance, then headed upstairs. Her new custom-made bicycling costume flounced cheerily all the way up the steps. "It's brisk outside this shortly after sunrise, Moll."

Molly sighed. A moment later, the family's cook bustled in from the kitchen at the rear of the house, carrying a napkin-wrapped piece of toasted bread.

She held it toward Molly. "You forgot your breakfast."

Exasperated, Molly stared at the strawberry jam gleaming atop the toasted bread. To be sure, she loved her family. But just once, she wanted to be treated as though she knew enough to dress properly, confront the weather appropriately, get herself to her shop efficiently…and eat when she needed to. Why couldn't anyone see that she was a capable woman in her own right?

It was as though she'd never grown up at all. Her family still treated Molly like the four-year-old who'd danced with an imaginary friend. Like the nine-year-old who'd lost countless gloves and hats during daydreaming walks to school. Like the fourteen-year-old who'd expressed an urgent desire to become a famous stage actress and had lost all her meager nest egg buying a talent potion from a persuasive drummer. It was true that Molly was sometimes given to flights of fancy. But that didn't mean she couldn't take care of herself, given the opportunity.

Now, though, despite her efforts, Molly had begun to wonder whether that opportunity would ever arrive.

"Thank you," she murmured, electing to take the bread rather than begin yet another battle she couldn't win. "Now, I really must be going. Good morning, everyone!"

Juggling her wicker basket of supplies under one arm and the unwanted breakfast in her other hand, Molly stepped toward the parlor doorway to retrieve her bonnet. Almost there. The carved oak of the front door beckoned her, promising escape to a world of her design, only a few feet away.

Her father's face popped into view as he rounded the banister and leapt from the staircase with his characteristic energy. Shrieking in surprise, Molly jumped. Her basket tumbled. The toasted bread flew upward, then came down again with a swiftness that defied even her father's speedy movements.

It landed on the shoulder of Adam Crabtree's favorite worsted wool suit coat. Jam side down.

It was just another typical morning in the Crabtree residence. Mayhem, meddling, flying bread, and all.

Molly was elbow deep in the first batch of her special-recipe cinnamon buns when the bell jangled above her shop door. She looked up, squinting against the early-morning sunlight. At the sight of the man standing on the threshold, her heartbeat quickened.

Goodness—a real live customer!

"Mornin', Miss Crabtree," he said politely, doffing his rolled-brim bowler.

Holding it between his restless hands, he looked around, taking in her shop's floral wallpapered walls, trim blue wainscoting, and shelves filled with napkin-lined wicker baskets waiting to be outfitted with cookies or tea cakes or lemon-raisin pies. From behind her work counter, Molly gave him her best, most welcoming smile. Considering that he was her first customer of the week, and it was already Thursday morning, she couldn't risk offending him with anything less.

"Come right on in," she said, inclining her head in what she hoped was a professional-seeming way. It was so hard to tell, when all she had was her father's own jocular example to go by.

He came inside, letting the door swing shut behind him.

Molly wiped her floury hands on her apron and gestured at the stools she'd optimistically arranged along the work counter. "What can I get you today? I have a small batch of cinnamon buns just about to go in the oven, if you'd care to wait a few minutes for a fresh one. I also have fig gems, apple fritters and a very nice batch of snickerdoodle cookies planned for this afternoon."

Tentatively he shuffled closer. "That sounds right fine. I ain't had a snickerdoodle since I left the States."

At the eager expression on his face, Molly could have kicked herself. She'd given the last three snickerdoodles to Ambrose this morning, for all his troubles in driving the wagon alongside her while she walked to the shop, and hadn't yet had time to make more. Because her business hadn't *quite* turned prosperous yet, it was necessary to make very, very, *small* batches of everything.

This man looked capable of devouring an entire dozen snickerdoodles, a feat that would have improved her fortunes for the day considerably. Hoping to cultivate his patronage, Molly smiled at him as she went on kneading her cinnamon bun dough.

"The fritters are quite good, too," she said. "Nobody else in town has baked goods quite like mine, Mr....?"

"Oh. Walter. Thomas Walter," the man stammered. His face flamed in colors vibrant enough to rival the changing oak leaves outside her window. "I—I'm sorry, Miss Crabtree, but I ain't come to buy anything today."

"You haven't?"

"No." He looked abashed, probably at her undoubtedly crestfallen expression. "I came because Mr. Copeland asked me to fetch you to the lumber mill this mornin'."

"Copeland's lumber mill? Why, I was planning on going out there later today as usual, but I—"

She stopped herself before she could admit the truth: Molly had almost decided to end her daily jaunts to the edge of town. More and more, the notion of selling her baked goods to the lumbermen who worked there seemed an impossible goal. Which was a shame, truly. More than half the men in town worked at Copeland's mill. Securing them as customers would give her bakeshop a reliable source of revenue. Or *would have,* if not for…

Marcus Copeland. The mill's owner—and *her* nemesis.

Molly meant that good-naturedly, of course. Truly, she did. But the man was a constant obstacle to her business goals for her bakery. Which was funny, really, because if anyone needed something sweet in his life, it was that stick-in-the-mud Marcus.

She'd discovered as much upon learning that he'd apparently given orders for his men not to leave the mill's premises until the workday was done. By then, all his men wanted was dinner, not sweets. Now, after all that, *he* wanted to see *her?* And hadn't even bothered to make the request himself, in person?

More than likely, the arrogant Mr. Copeland was

only summoning her now to order her to abandon her temporary, and hopeful, post outside the lumber mill. Once and for all. The very idea put Molly's back up—especially after the morning she'd just had.

"I was planning on going out there later today, as usual," she repeated to Mr. Walter sweetly. "But I would be delighted to visit earlier, instead. Just as soon as I finish this batch of cinnamon buns. Would you tell Mr. Copeland that, please?"

"Yes'm." Jerking his gaze from the front of her dress, Thomas Walter slapped on his hat and hurried out the door.

Left alone, Molly ducked her head. She examined the front of her borrowed, perfectly ordinary blue gingham dress. When she saw nothing there of interest—no wayward splatters of oil from fritter frying, no blobs of sticky date filling from gem making, merely the usual sprinkling of flour—she narrowed her gaze. Evidently the snickerdoodle-fancying Mr. Walter had an eye for more than sweets.

He had an eye for bosoms, too.

Not unlike many of the men in Morrow Creek, Molly had noticed to her chagrin. Wherever she went, the town bachelors seemed to glue their gazes to her bodice. Their appreciation might have moved her more had she not recognized it as completely superficial—not unlike the Crabtree sisters' admiration of a new hat they'd like to own or a pair of buttoned-up brogans they'd like to possess.

Being equated with a desirable possession did not appeal to Molly—however much the men in town seemed oblivious to her feelings on the matter.

She wanted to find a beau who appreciated *all* of her. Fortunately, her mother and father understood that. They hadn't pressed her into taking up with the occasional would-be beaus who'd called on her. Adam and Fiona Crabtree's sometimes-radical views offered all their daughters the freedom to wait for a loving marriage, not a union spurred by bosomy interest. Unfortunately, the men inclined toward such an arrangement did not appear to live in Morrow Creek, at least in Molly's experience.

It was lucky, she decided as she hastened to roll out the springy, yeast-scented dough, that the matchmaker was working so diligently to pair up the men with suitable wives.

Very lucky, indeed.

Rapidly Molly spread the dough's surface with softened butter. She sprinkled on brown sugar and cinnamon, then added her special secret ingredient, making plans for her encounter with Mr. Copeland all the while. When a strategy finally occurred to her, she smiled.

After all, Molly reminded herself, there was no call to be cowardly. Marcus Copeland was only a man. A man, oddly enough, who seemed immune to her dresses' allure, but a man nonetheless. Once she'd dealt with him face-to-face, how much trouble could he possibly be?

As Marcus might have expected of a woman, she was late.

Annoyed despite his determination not to be, he turned away from the edge of the lumber mill yard, where he'd been watching for Molly Crabtree to arrive. According to Thomas, one of his longtime buckers, she had agreed to come to the lumber mill nearly two hours ago. Where was she?

Two men walked past, carrying a crosscut saw between them. This was the third trip they'd made across the yard, Marcus knew. Other men loitered nearby, some bearing double-blade axes or sledge-hammers and others propping their weight against the springboards they should have been using to work with. Instead, far too many of his men were spending their time waiting for Miss Crabtree to arrive.

Just like him.

Damnation.

Marcus couldn't put his plan into motion until Molly Crabtree got there. It required the coopera-tion of his men, which was why they loitered about when the sun was nearly overhead. For the tenth time that day, Marcus removed his hat, shoved his hand through his hair and wished he'd never agreed to help the Morrow Creek Men's Club discover the identity of the matchmaker.

If he'd known it would take this much time from his day, he'd never have swallowed the notion at all.

"There's the signal, boss!" one of the sawyers yelled, pointing down the well-tended dirt path leading toward town. "She must be comin'!"

Sure enough, Marcus glimpsed a red bandanna being waved wildly between the swaying pine tree boughs. At the sight of the signal he'd instructed his foreman to use once he spotted Miss Crabtree headed their way, his belly lurched with something very close to excitement.

Impatience, he told himself sternly. It was impatience he felt to have this chowder-headed business behind him, not excitement.

Marcus was still reminding himself of that fact when the woman came into view, wearing a close-fitting dress and a bonnet nearly as enormous as the one Deputy Winston had drawn on the caricature at the saloon last night. For an instant, his thoughts lingered on the other, rounder, softer and equally impressive attributes he'd given Miss Crabtree in the picture. Marcus wondered if as little exaggeration was involved there as had been involved with her hat.

Shoving that enticing mystery aside, he turned to give his men the second signal. Marcus raised his hand, prepared to gesture with it…and realized that not one of his men was looking at him. They all stood with stupid, eager grins, slack jawed and glassy-eyed, watching Molly's feminine, side-to-side swish as she made her way down the path toward the lumber mill.

They were hopeless.

So was Marcus, by the time she recognized him and ran the last few steps toward him. Lord, but the woman was a sight to behold.

Her face was alight with good humor, pink cheeked and delicately shaped beneath the brim of her flower-bedecked hat. A few tendrils of honey-colored hair had escaped its confines to tease her lips, drawing his attention to their tempting fullness. Sucking in a deep breath, Marcus took an instant to prepare, then treated himself to an up-close view of her fine woman's figure in that waist-hugging dress.

No wonder his men had gone slack jawed.

For the life of him, in that moment Marcus couldn't imagine a single reason why Molly Crabtree, as delightful looking a female as he'd ever seen, had grown into a spinster. How, he wondered to himself, could it be that no man had ever stuck a ring on her finger and made her his own?

Then…she opened her mouth.

"Morning, Mr. Copeland," she said brightly. "Beautiful day, isn't it? I'm so glad we've finally had this chance to meet face-to-face. Why, I don't think we've ever said two words to each other, and that's after you've been living here in Morrow Creek for the past *two* years! Can you imagine that? I guess we've just never had a moment to spare, what with you working on your lumber mill, and me working on my various ventures. Busy, busy, busy. That's us."

She paused for breath. For an instant, Marcus believed her chatter had come to an end. But then she looped her arm companionably in his, started walking them both toward the two-story lumber mill behind them, and just went on.

"I'm so happy you invited me here today. I just know we can come to an agreeable arrangement. My baked goods are unlike any others in town, you know. They're positively unique."

Marcus nodded, too distracted by the pleasurable feel of her slender arm cradled in his to offer much more to the conversation. She smelled spicy, he thought, and sweet. Like pumpkin pie, or gingerbread. Cinnamon, Marcus identified after a moment. Cinnamon and sugar.

Mmm.

He had a sudden impossible yet wholly irresistible image of himself together with Miss Molly. Alone. In his imagination, Marcus unfastened the first tiny pearled buttons on her dress. As he opened her gown, he kissed the warm, creamy skin he'd revealed at her neck. She tasted of spices as delicious as any he'd sampled...and of some, more exotic still.

Transfixed, Marcus let himself be led toward the shade of a stand of pine trees a few feet from the mill's main entrance. Beside him, Molly struggled with the covered wicker basket she'd brought. Marcus chivalrously helped her lower it to a ponderosa stump.

Freed of her burden, she rummaged through its contents. Her movements sent her blue-checked skirts swishing against her legs, and the clump of men who'd followed them pushed closer. As one, their combined gazes dropped to her stocking-clad ankles.

A stern glance from Marcus had them all busily examining axes, tightening suspender straps and looking purposefully toward the towering pines beyond. With a shake of his head, Marcus dismissed them to await the next phase of his plan.

"I'm glad you could come on such short notice," he told Molly when they were alone again. "I don't often do things without planning first, but I—"

"Oh, but you should! The things you don't plan for are often the most enjoyable of all."

The very notion made Marcus frown. Fail to plan? Unthinkable. "Be that as it may, I did have some ideas in mind for us today."

She quit fussing with the basket she'd brought and looked up. Her eyes were blue, he noticed inanely. As though that mattered a whit to discovering if she was really the secret matchmaker.

"You do?" Molly asked.

"Yes."

"Well, then." She smiled up at him, and turned so they faced each other fully. "I guess you'd better tell me what you have in mind. For us to do together, I mean."

Together. Suddenly, all manner of unified activities occurred to Marcus. Things they could do together—very close together. As though guessing his thoughts, Molly lowered her gaze coquettishly, encouraging him to lower his gaze, too…all the way to those remarkable feminine curves of hers. Lord Almighty. Was Molly Crabtree flirting with him? It would seem so.

'Twould be fitting, if she were truly the matchmaker.

The matchmaker. Reminded of his mission, Marcus smiled back at her. He was no mere boy, to be dumbfounded by a feminine smile and a handful of enticing words.

Was he?

Hell, no. With new determination, Marcus cleared his throat and got on with his plan. "I couldn't help but notice you outside the lumber mill yard these past weeks," he began.

It wasn't strictly true. His foreman, Smith, had enlightened Marcus about Molly's continued vigil outside the mill yard, and the rest of his plan had sprung from there. Looking at her now, though, Marcus couldn't imagine how he'd missed the sight of her.

Had business success turned him blind to the appeal of a pretty woman? Suddenly ill at ease, he wondered if his friends in the men's club were right, and he needed to socialize more.

"If you mean to make me leave that spot," Molly interrupted, turning back to her basket with shoulders gone suddenly stiff and defensive, "I'll have you know that the road is public land, and so is its edge. You can't force me away from there. Why, the whole town would probably be in an uproar if you so much as tried."

"Hold on. There's no call to get riled up. I never said I was asking you to leave, Miss Crabtree—"

"Molly, please." Her shoulders relaxed, slim and

delicately curved beneath the blue checked fabric of her dress.

"Molly." He liked the sound of it. The intimacy of it.

"Friends ought to call each other by their first names, don't you think so?" She rose, holding a napkin-wrapped bundle in her small, elegant-looking hands.

"Uh." He experienced an unprecedented urge to take those hands in his and slowly pull her closer. With a frown of confusion, Marcus wrestled down that impulse and settled for answering her question instead. "Yes, I do. Especially if you agree to the proposition I have in mind."

"Proposition?"

She raised her eyebrows, looking intrigued and not half as offended as she might have been, had Molly guessed at the kind of bawdy thoughts that had been going through his mind.

"Yes. I want you to bring some of your baked goods to my lumber mill each day—at a time we agree on, of course—for sale to my men. It seems they've noticed your post outside the yard, too. To a man, they all clamored to have your sweets."

A smile even more dazzling than her earlier one lit Molly's face. "Truly?" she whispered.

"Truly." *Liar,* his conscience jabbed. This was no more than a ploy, and Marcus knew it. *It's for a good cause,* he reminded himself, and went on. "So I agreed."

"Why, Mr. Copeland!"

"Marcus," he insisted. Being on friendly terms with her could only improve his chances of discovering if she was the matchmaker, he reasoned. And of ending all this pretense quickly.

"Marcus, then. You're just a big old softie at heart, aren't you? That's so sweet! My word, I'd never have guessed that a man so…well, so very businesslike as you would treat his men so finely. I'm impressed, truly I am."

Her constant chatter made his head throb. Putting a hand to his temple, Marcus said gruffly, "My men fell more timber when they're treated fairly. It's just good business."

Molly's impish grin told him she believed not a word of it. "So was calling out Nellie Baxter, so you could sample *her* baked goods, I reckon," she said, naming the owner of Morrow Creek's other, more established bakery. "I passed by her on the road on my way here. Nothing else lies out this way except your lumber mill."

Marcus tried to look abashed. He made a mental note to pay Smith a bonus for his suggestion that they pretend to consider the other bakery, lest Molly become suspicious of his sudden summons. "Well, now. Every man likes to do a little sampling, before deciding what's right for him."

Her eyes narrowed, fixed on the bundle she held as she unwrapped the napkin. "According to the matchmaker, it's thinking like that that gets a man into trouble."

Interest sparked inside him. "The matchmaker?"

"Surely you've heard of the matchmaker. The whole town's abuzz with news of all that's been accomplished." As though that fact were of little consequence, Molly finished her unwrapping, revealing a plump, golden-brown cinnamon bun. Crystals of sugar sparkled in the sunlight. "But all that aside, you've asked me here to discuss business, and that's what I intend to do."

"Certainly." *And when we're finished, I intend to ask you all about the matchmaker.* More and more, it seemed as though Molly knew something about the subject. Something she wasn't telling...

"Here." She offered him the cinnamon bun, along with an encouraging smile. "Once you try my goodies, you'll never even think about anyone else's."

Marcus nearly groaned. Did the woman have no sense of what ribald words like that could do to a man?

Evidently, she did not. Neither did she realize what he was truly up to. It was all the luckier for him,

Marcus told himself. He'd be finished with this business and back to work in no time.

Putting one hand behind his back as he leaned forward to accept the cinnamon bun, he signaled for his men to begin the next step of his plan. Like magic, lumbermen of all ages and sizes surged forward. They encircled him and Molly, waving fistfuls of money and declaring raging hunger that only her baked goods could assuage.

In the midst of it all, a startled-looking Molly gazed in wonder at the ruckus surrounding her. Then, with a beaming smile, she began selling napkin-wrapped bundles identical to the one she'd given Marcus.

In no time at all, she was left with an empty basket, a fistful of money and an expression of gratitude that, when she turned it on Marcus, made his heart lurch painfully.

"Same time tomorrow?" he made himself ask.

"Yes, indeed!" Molly replied. Still seeming slightly bedazzled, she gathered her things, bade him goodbye and made her way back down the path toward town.

She was hooked.

Indisputably.

But it was Marcus, to his consternation, who felt as though he'd been walloped over the head unawares. Something told him that proving Molly Crabtree was the matchmaker wouldn't be as simple a process as he'd expected…and neither would making sure he didn't fall prey to her charms, in the process.

Chapter Three

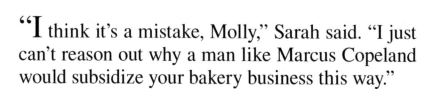

"I think it's a mistake, Molly," Sarah said. "I just can't reason out why a man like Marcus Copeland would subsidize your bakery business this way."

"Maybe he has a sweet tooth," Molly countered.

"Somehow, I doubt it."

"Perhaps he regrets ignoring my efforts till now."

"Not hardly."

"I suppose he may have heard of my baked goods," Molly mused, "and wanted to try them for himself?"

"Well…" Sarah hesitated, then appeared to think better of disagreeing. "Perhaps. My point is, I think you should be careful. There must be more here than meets the eye."

Sighing over her sister's skepticism, Molly put down the square of corn bread she'd been eating. True, Marcus's abrupt change of heart had seemed a little suspicious at first. But his offer had simply been too good to pass up. Molly was all for anything that helped her bakeshop. It was her pride and joy—or would be, once she made a success of it.

Besides, she generally thought the best of people. Surely Marcus was a good man, or would be, once he let himself be.

She gazed out over the schoolyard filled with laughing, running, playing children, then tapped her heels restlessly against the schoolhouse steps where she and Sarah had met for lunch, bothered by conflicting feelings. Why couldn't Sarah just be happy for her?

For the past week, Molly had been making daily treks to the Copeland lumber mill, each time with an increasingly heavy basket. Those lumbermen—now *those* were some fellows with a sweet tooth! They had a surprising quantity of money with which to indulge it, too. It was a plain stroke of luck that Marcus had loosened his stance against letting her sell her baked goods to his men. Whatever his motives had been, she'd be forever grateful to him for setting her on the road toward making a success of her newly launched business.

A brisk September breeze swept over the schoolyard, ruffling the hems of her green worsted gown and Sarah's yellow calico. Beneath their feet, fallen leaves danced across the white-painted steps, pushed by the wind. Molly shivered and looked again at Sarah.

"Why can't you just be happy for me?" she asked quietly. "Why can't you believe in me, and accept that maybe I'm capable of accomplishing something on my own?"

"Of course you're capable," Sarah began. She broke off to tell little Wally Brownlee not to capture the girls he was chasing by yanking on their pigtails. More seriously, she said, "I'm just concerned about you, that's all. We all are. Mama and Papa, and Grace, too. You're the youngest. You have an impulsive streak. There's no denying that. I'm afraid it will get you into trouble someday."

"I'm managing just fine," Molly told her. *All except for the fluttery feeling I get whenever Marcus Copeland comes near.* She raised her chin. "I don't begrudge you your happiness over teaching here at the schoolhouse, nor even all the acclaim you'll likely get when you manage the Chautauqua next month."

Sarah blushed at Molly's mention of the highly anticipated annual event, featuring orators, a concert, plays and picnics, which she had volunteered to organize. If Molly were fortunate, she'd be allowed to host a booth of her own at the pavilion, featuring her baked goods. Participation required approval by the town leaders, but she was hopeful.

Especially now, when she had the patronage of a well-respected businessman like Marcus to rely upon.

But that didn't mean she cared any less about her family's opinion. Resuming her earlier argument, Molly said, "Furthermore, I don't caution Grace about all *she's* doing, even though—"

"Nobody cautions Grace about anything," Sarah broke in.

They shared a laugh. Their older sister was notoriously well-known for taking charge of things—and accepting no arguments, while she did.

"—even though," Molly continued doggedly, "she must be involved in every women's group, lecture series and ladies' aid organization in Morrow Creek." Drawing in a deep breath, she hoped with all her heart that Sarah would understand the dreams she held so closely. "All I'm asking for is a chance to do something...just once...all on my own."

At the end of her impassioned plea, Molly looked at her sister. Beside her, Sarah sat, chin in hand, looking at the false-fronted buildings that stood in the distance along Main Street. She sighed. The sound was filled with longing—a soul-deep, romantic kind of longing Molly had never once suspected her sensible bluestocking of a sister might be vulnerable to.

"Why, Sarah! You're not even listening to me."

Sarah jerked. She pulled her gaze back to Molly, then picked up the fried chicken drumstick that was all that remained of her lunch. "Of course I'm listening."

"No, you're not."

"I am." She nodded, took a bite of chicken and chewed vigorously. But still her gaze wandered in the direction of town. "Truly."

"Humph."

Curious now, Molly leaned sideways, the better to figure out what held her sister so enraptured. All she could see were the same old buildings—the back side of the mercantile, the church steeple, the various saloons and shops along Main Street…and the blacksmith shop, where a tall, powerfully built man stood beside a water barrel, sluicing its contents over his face and bare chest. Squinting, Molly just managed to make out the dark hair and strong features of Daniel McCabe, a moment before he shook his head and went back to work.

"I don't believe my eyes," she murmured.

"Hmm?" Vigorously working away at her drumstick, Sarah didn't look up. So engrossed was she, in fact, that she failed to notice the wide grin spreading across her sister's face. "Whatever do you mean?"

"You're sweet on Daniel McCabe," Molly said, shaking her head over the sheer obviousness of it.

After all, Sarah and Daniel had been friends since their days running up and down the same schoolhouse steps the two women now sat upon. "It's only fitting, I suppose," she went on, "considering how close you two have been for all these years. But still—Daniel McCabe? Surely you don't think a rowdy type like him would be best for—"

"He's not like that," Sarah interrupted. "Not on the inside."

"You know what the matchmaker says—a man's a man, all the way through, and nothing's going to change him."

"Pshaw. I don't want to change him."

"I hope not."

"I don't want to hear anything else about the matchmaker, either!" Furtively Sarah glanced around the schoolyard to make sure they hadn't been overheard discussing the subject, then rapidly tucked the remainder of her lunch back into its box. "You know we've all agreed not to discuss...*the matchmaker...* in public."

"You're right." Unable to take the smile from her face at the knowledge that Sarah fancied a beau—especially one so brawny as Daniel McCabe—Molly put away her lunch, as well. They both stood. "I won't mention you-know-who again."

"Thank you," Sarah said primly.

"No matter how much," Molly continued, "you might need matchmaking services."

Still smiling, she skipped down the last few steps, looked speculatively toward the blacksmith shop, and then waved goodbye to her sister. It looked as though the Morrow Creek matchmaker might have some very busy days ahead, indeed.

At the mill, Marcus walked between stacks of neatly piled lumber with Smith, his foreman, trying mightily to direct his thoughts toward the business he'd worked so hard to build…and away from a certain blue-eyed baker who was due to arrive at any minute. It wasn't easy. Ever since Molly Crabtree had begun selling her cookies, tea cakes and cinnamon buns at the mill each day, he'd found himself less and less able to concentrate.

No doubt his inattentiveness was an example of the disruption she caused among his men, Marcus told himself firmly. Once he'd found the proof he needed of her matchmaking activities, his life would return to normal.

He hoped.

Unfortunately, just having Molly nearby had produced inadequate evidence in his investigation. He hadn't detected any obvious matchmaking activities or inclinations in her. Not so much as a flirtatious glance had passed between Molly and his men as she'd doled out their sweets. If he was to discover her secret matchmaking activities, Marcus realized, he would clearly have to take things a step further… engage her more closely.

Setting that intriguing notion aside for now, Marcus nodded toward a stack of rough-hewn pine ties to his right. "You say this batch is ready to be bundled for the railroad?"

"Sure is, boss," Smith told him. "Fifteen hundred railway ties for the new express line going down between here and Prescott, exactly as ordered."

"Good work." Satisfied, Marcus moved on to the next waiting assortment of lumber, just around the corner. As he did, he reached up to thump the stacked wood. The solid feel of sawed lumber beneath his hand never failed to make the success of his mill feel twice as real. Twice as enduring.

Twice as secure.

The pine boards shifted at the motion. One slid sideways, and something fell from beneath it to the floor below. It rolled, then struck Marcus's boot.

Frowning, he bent to pick it up. About the size of the baseballs used in the new Morrow Creek league, the object was dense and light brown in color. Marcus raised it higher. Just as Smith paused and turned to see what had delayed his boss, Marcus realized what it was.

A cinnamon bun.

Undoubtedly from Molly's bakery.

What was it doing rammed amongst the railroad tie shipment?

"Uh, sorry 'bout that, boss." Smith edged nearer. "Can't reckon how that got there."

He grabbed for the cinnamon bun. Marcus held firm.

"Never mind," he said, scooping up the plain white napkin that had fluttered to the floor alongside the sweet. He wrapped the cinnamon bun inside it and shoved the bundle into his suit coat pocket. Better there than here in the main work area. If the stale bun had fallen from a greater height, it might have brained a man. "How are the sharpeners you hired coming along?"

On the way to their work area, Smith shared a few details about the recently hired men. Just around the corner from where the sharpeners labored to hone the various axes and saws used by the loggers, Marcus spied something else. He stopped. Frowned.

Yes, he'd guessed correctly, he saw as he pried out another napkin-wrapped bundle from between two freshly peeled logs. Another cinnamon bun.

With a disapproving glare around the room, Marcus stowed the rocklike bundle in his pocket alongside the first, then went on with his daily inspection.

"I think the new equipment is working out just fine," Smith remarked a short while later. They stood side by side, watching thoughtfully as two men directed logs into the splitter Marcus had had shipped in by rail from back East over the summer. "Real nice."

"Yes." Burdened by a worrisome feeling he didn't understand and didn't much like, Marcus fiddled with the wrapped bundles of cinnamon buns—and a few tea cakes—lining his pockets. By now, his suit was filled fair to bulging with the abandoned sweets. "It's fine. What about the shipment that came in last week? Jack Murphy might be in the market for some of those pressed-tin ceiling forms for his saloon."

"Ain't many of 'em left," Smith said. Outside, they walked together through the shade of the pines clustered around the lumber mill building, then entered the main work area again. "I reckon we could get some fair quick, though."

"Good."

With a distracted feeling, Marcus examined the building and its furnishings. The men all appeared to be working as usual—with the exception of the pair near one of the muley saws. The two bearded mill hands hadn't noticed Marcus in their midst, which probably explained the fact that one of them was juggling.

Marcus's frown deepened. Here was proof that letting down his guard—and letting a female into his place of business—had been a mistake. Now the men thought they had leave to indulge in frivolous behavior at *all* hours. Why had he agreed to join the damned matchmaker search in the first place?

He silenced Smith's questions about the new work schedules Marcus had been working on, then stalked toward the juggler. Halfway there, he realized the man was not juggling rocks or dirt clumps or any of the other things he'd assumed…he was juggling an assortment of Molly's molasses cookies.

If she caught wind of this, she'd never be back. He'd never uncover her secrets. With new determination, Marcus crossed the remaining distance between him and the laggard worker.

"I understand," he said, snatching the cookies from midair as they fell, one by one, from the startled man's hands, "that you have a pile of logs waiting to be peeled before lunchtime. Isn't that right, Jameson?"

"Y-yes, sir." Caught, the man backed up, his mouth agape.

"Then I suggest you cease these childish games. Unless you relish the notion of peeling those logs with your bare teeth, and eating the bark for your noontime meal."

Jameson clapped his mouth shut. He nodded and, with a mumbled apology, sped toward his usual post with his companion in tow. Ramming the cookies into his pocket along with everything else, Marcus turned to see Smith hurrying to meet him.

"You can make the men buy 'em," he said, looking dour, "but God's own angels couldn't make them eat 'em."

Marcus glared toward the departing men's backs. "I paid the men good money to buy these sweets. Money out of my own pocket, damn it! Why won't they eat them?"

Smith shook his head, as though remembering the plan Marcus had struck upon to bring Molly Crabtree to the lumber mill each day—and deciding upon its foolhardiness, once and for all.

"Have *you* tried 'em, sir?" he asked.

That was beside the point, Marcus thought in frustration. He needed regular contact with Molly to find out if she was the matchmaker the men's club members sought. Bringing her to his mill—by whatever means possible—had been the most efficient way to accomplish that. But it wasn't enough.

"She is a professional baker," he reminded his foreman. "Surely the sweets aren't that bad."

"Hmm." Sadly, Smith shook his head. Into Marcus's hand, he pressed a napkin-wrapped bundle he'd confiscated somewhere between the mill's back door and its center work area, then released its petrified weight. "I reckon you'd better try some yourself."

* * *

For a man who spent his working days surrounded by rough-hewn loggers, Marcus Copeland was a surprisingly well-mannered man, Molly decided on her seventh day visiting the mill. She'd finished selling her basketful of baked goods within minutes of arriving there, and was now being given a tour of the business at Marcus's side.

"That's where the skidders drop each load when it's ready to be milled," he said, pointing toward a stack of logs waiting to be taken inside.

"My goodness!" Shading her eyes from the noontime sun, Molly looked toward the neatly piled stack. "Look at the size of those logs! You could drive a wagon right over top of that one on the right."

"Or down the middle, if it was hollow."

"It must be quite a challenge, cutting all those down. However do your men manage it?"

Marcus shrugged. "Hard work. Teamwork. It's their job, just like baking is yours."

Molly couldn't help but brighten at his words. At last! Here was someone who took her and her ambitions seriously. That Marcus respected her business aspirations encouraged her greatly, even as she struggled more each day to see *him* strictly as a professional associate.

He was, after all, a very fine-looking and personable man.

He had not, apparently, noticed similarly appealing qualities in her. How had it happened, Molly wondered, that the one man in years she might not have *minded* admiring her bosoms seemed oblivious to them?

Marcus hadn't done anything more forward than take her elbow to help her over a patch of rough ground. She hadn't the faintest idea how to flirt openly so that he might understand how her feelings toward him were broadening. The whole situation was confusing.

She hadn't felt this out of her depth since she'd decided to become a circus acrobat by reading an illustrated book on the subject. No matter how much she'd concentrated on the pages, her limbs simply hadn't *bent* in the proper ways. Now, it seemed, neither did her thoughts. Perhaps, in all her daring endeavors, she'd damaged her feminine wiles somehow.

It was a worrisome notion.

"I'm so glad to hear you say that," she told him, shoving aside her concerns along with her enjoyment of his steady grasp. "Most people don't understand why a woman would want to become involved in trade."

"Especially one like you, I'm sure."

"Like me? What do you mean?"

"Nothing terrible." Marcus grinned, undoubtedly at the suspicious expression Molly felt puckering her face. He paused, taking her arm to help her across the gnarled tree roots in their path, then said, "Only that it must come as a surprise to folks that a pretty lady like yourself has time to run a business. Between fending off beaux, and all."

"Beaux?" Molly laughed, unreasonably delighted by his image of her as the belle of Morrow Creek. The only beaux she had were the unwanted bosom fanciers, who'd chased her since she'd reached womanhood. They hardly counted. "You're incorrigible, Mr. Copeland."

"Marcus," he reminded her.

The warmth in his brown-eyed gaze gave her the same kind of fluttery feelings she'd been beset with ever since their first meeting. Biting her lip, Molly dared a second glance at him as he strode along beside her. Yes, she was definitely smitten with Marcus Copeland.

Smitten, for the first time in her life.

What, she wondered, would the matchmaker advise?

"Very well. Marcus." She smiled, liking the sound of it. "But what makes a bachelor like yourself think I have so very many beaux, I wonder? It's not as though I could count *you* among them."

"You could." He stopped, still holding her arm. Slowly he slid his hand down past her elbow, over her forearm, and all the way to her hand. "If you'd allow me to call on you."

Marcus linked his fingers with hers. For one wild instant, Molly wished away her stylish braid-trimmed gloves. She wished to feel his skin against hers, to measure its warmth and texture, to marvel at the novel sensation of a man's hand—so much larger and stronger than hers—holding hers closely. But then his words pushed through her thoughts. Their implications went much further than a simple meeting of hands.

"Would you, Molly?" Marcus asked. With a smile that appeared surpassingly devilish for a man as respected as Marcus, he moved closer. "I'm sure the matchmaker would approve."

"Pshaw. *I'm* not worried about the matchmaker."

But she was. A little. Given what she knew about the matchmaker's activities, she'd vowed never to… no, Molly decided. She wouldn't worry about that now.

"Then you'll let me call on you?"

"I don't know if I should. I'm a businesswoman, after all. A businesswoman who's engaged in trade here at your lumber mill with your permission. It's possible that your calling on me will only muddy the waters of our business relationship."

His smile flashed again. "Surely even businesswomen need beaux."

Molly wrinkled her nose. "Strictly speaking, I'm not sure they do. According to my parents, a woman who builds an independent life for herself is free to choose a beau. Or not, as she pleases."

"Or not?" Marcus pretended shock. "That can't be your fate. Please, Molly. Twice daily visits to the mill. A Sunday walk. Whatever you choose. I want to see you. I *must* see you."

His persistence—his *urgency*—was flattering, if a little unexpected. Something Sarah had said, about Molly being too inexperienced to deal successfully with a man like Marcus, edged into her thoughts. It was possible her sister was right. But how else to *gain* experience? Letting herself see more of Marcus might be exactly what she needed, Molly decided.

"Very well," she told him. "In that case...I have an idea. It will keep things on a businesslike footing between us, too."

Marcus raised his eyebrows.

Molly went on. "I've heard you eat all your meals at Jack Murphy's saloon. This seems as good an opportunity as any to protest that, in the name of all that's edible."

"Murphy's grub is edible."

"All right, in the name of all that's fit to spend time eating, then. If you agree, I'll use my expertise to tutor you in basic cooking and housekeeping skills. *That's* how we'll see more of each other."

Marcus looked skeptical. "I'm a bachelor. The last time I tried cooking anything, it was my socks as I boiled them clean."

Oh, dear. "These lessons will be bachelor-proofed," Molly promised. "We can meet in the evenings after your mill and my shop are closed. Say, twice a week?"

"A man needs to eat *seven* days a week," he reminded her.

"I might be able to manage four days a week." She pretended reticence.

"Then there's the fact that there are *three* meals in each day, which adds up to—"

"Very well, six days a week! Excepting Sundays," Molly acquiesced. Reluctantly she withdrew her hand from his to retrieve her basket, then straightened. As she did so, the satisfied expression on his face came into view. She couldn't prevent a smile. "You drive a hard bargain, Mr. Copeland."

"Marcus. And driving a hard bargain is the way I've built my business. These maneuverings between us have been gentle."

She looked him over, seeing him in a new and unexpectedly dangerous light. This was a man who got what he wanted, Molly realized all at once. Marcus Copeland, for all his fine suits and good manners, was as strong as any man she'd encountered.

She'd better be on her guard, lest he someday

maneuver her into offering things she wasn't prepared to give. Like her independence. Her sense of propriety.

Her untouched heart.

"Of course, if I'm to forfeit five of my evenings a week, plus Saturday mornings before my shop opens, I'll need a commensurate sacrifice from you," she said, suddenly driven to take a stand of her own. "Say, help with my accounting practices?" Bookkeeping was, indeed, one of her least favorite tasks.

"You're a quick study in this bargaining business." He nodded and delivered her a final smile. "I'll do it."

"We're in agreement, then." To seal the deal, Molly put forth her hand. "Prepare for a unique learning experience."

"The same could be said for you," Marcus told her as he accepted her handshake. "I'll wager this arrangement might deliver some new experiences to you, too."

Did he have to look so...masculine when he said that? It was as though Marcus's words offered a promise she didn't understand...but might, soon.

"Until tomorrow, then," Molly agreed, nodding. She adjusted her basket, her hat, and her skirts, taking refuge in the motions as an excuse to avoid the unsettlingly anticipatory light that had brightened Marcus's dark eyes. What, she wondered, did he know that she did not?

He escorted her to the front entrance. As their time together drew to a close in the same uneventful fashion it usually did, Molly felt reassured. Surely this new arrangement wouldn't change things between them, she decided.

Then Marcus stopped her as she prepared to leave.

"Be sure to bring your baking supplies and plenty of sugar tomorrow," he said. His gaze caught hers and held. His rascally grin somehow managed to warm her clean through. "The first thing I'll be wanting from you is something nice and *sweet*."

Oh, my. This arrangement was changing things already.

"I will," she choked out, then fled to town as fast as was possible without actually seeming to run away.

Thankfully her skirts hid her rapid strides. From a distance Marcus couldn't hear her breath come faster as it squeezed from beneath her stays. Not for anything would Molly have given him the satisfaction of thinking he'd gained the upper hand with her. The last thing she needed was someone *else* who thought they knew what was best for her.

Someone else who'd view her dreams with skepticism.

No matter what, Molly vowed, she'd deal with

Marcus on her own terms. Sensibly. Rationally. Definitely *not* impulsively.

Never mind the fact that, if her family could have heard her thoughts, they'd have been laughing their heads off already. Starting tomorrow, she'd show everyone exactly what she was made of. Marcus included!

Chapter Four

Marcus awakened on Saturday morning to a knocking on his front door—and a sense of confusion. He'd been dreaming of Molly Crabtree, dreaming of sugar and spice and enormous flowery hats, and he wanted those dreams to go on. In them, Molly whispered sweetly to him. She moved closer, took his hand, smiled into his eyes as she puckered her lips and…

Tap, tap, tap.

Groaning, Marcus flung back the blankets. His bare feet struck the chilly pine plank floor. For economy's sake, he banked his woodstove at night. The resultant coals didn't do much to warm the frosty September morning. Dragging on a flannel shirt and wool britches over his undershirt and drawers, he went to the door.

"One minute. I'm coming."

If this was one of his men, here to nag him about timber assignments or supplies—both of which were overseen by his designated foremen now—Marcus would have his head. It had been months since he'd handled all the mill's details himself. Delegating those jobs hadn't been easy, but he'd done it.

He wrenched open the door, scowling. *"What?"*

To his surprise, Molly Crabtree waited there. She backed up a step, as though his question had blasted her. Her eyes widened.

Hell. He'd scared her. In his sleep-fogged state, he wasn't sure what she was doing there at all, but the last thing Marcus wanted to do was frighten her. Jabbing a hand through his rumpled hair, he started to apologize.

Before he'd gotten very far, Molly's grasp tightened on the basket she carried. Her chin came up. "Good morning to you, too, Mr. Copeland. You passed a late night, I see. Along with the rest of the men in town. My father excluded, of course. He never attends the men's club meetings."

She squeezed past him, her eyes bright and her manner brisk. Marcus was too startled by her arrival to protest. In a businesslike fashion, Molly stepped into his house. With a comment about the chill in the room, she maneuvered unerringly past the parlor toward the kitchen. Marcus tried to intercept her— the gentleman in him demanded he carry her basket for her—but she only continued onward, talking all the while.

"In Papa's opinion, gender-exclusive organizations rarely offer more than shared commiseration and, in the case of the Morrow Creek Men's Club, shared lager."

She sniffed suspiciously, as though expecting the tang of liquor to cling to him now, hours later.

Marcus figured it probably did.

"And there's not a gathering of any sort in this town that goes unnoticed by my sister Grace. If she didn't organize it, she is at least informed about it. In this case, we ladies could hardly fail to notice the mass exodus of our men to Jack Murphy's saloon."

She raised her brows inquiringly.

"There was an emergency meeting last night," Marcus explained. "Emmaline Jones turned up at O'Neil's butcher shop yesterday with a Bloomingdale Brothers mail-order catalog in one hand and a pencil in the other. She refused to leave unless O'Neil gave her his opinion on the wedding dresses."

"But why? Emmaline hardly knows Mr. O'Neil."

The matchmaker was to blame, of course. But Marcus only shrugged, not ready to broach the subject. "Apparently, she admires the way he wields a cleaver."

And Molly admired the way Marcus answered a door, he realized. She'd been staring, transfixed, at him ever since putting down her basket on the kitchen table. She looked utterly proper as she stood there, buttoned up and begloved, with a jaunty hat on her head. But there was something wonderfully... *speculative* in the way her gaze roved along the gap left by his unbuttoned flannel shirt.

He found himself liking it. Perhaps he *had* been too long without feminine company.

"You're not prepared for me, Mr. Copeland," she accused, taking off her gloves.

"I hadn't expected you so early," Marcus said, finally remembering their meeting. Molly intended to begin teaching him cooking and housekeeping skills today. "But I assure you—I *am* prepared for you."

He smiled, reminded of his dream. "Quite prepared," he added.

Her eyes narrowed. "You sound as though you're expecting something far more delightful from me than a simple cooking lesson."

"From you?" He leaned against the door frame. "I am."

She seemed to consider that. "Good. Because I have a lot to offer. More than people in this town seem to realize."

Molly probably meant she had a lot to offer regarding her business ventures, misguided though they were. Marcus knew full well that a woman in trade was an anomaly. Didn't Molly's terrible baking confirm that fact?

In all likelihood, Marcus reasoned, her bakeshop

was merely a cover for her matchmaking activities. Her shop couldn't possibly mean as much to Molly as, say, his lumber mill meant to him.

"I don't doubt you have much to offer," he said. "You seem a very talented woman to me."

She paused amidst unpacking supplies from her basket. Something in her expression changed. Molly slanted him a sideways glance. "You needn't flatter me, Mr. Copeland."

"Marcus."

"Marcus. I'll receive my end of our bargain later, when you help me with my shop's bookkeeping. This is purely business between us, remember?"

"I remember." He levered from the door frame and stepped nearer. Why not achieve two goals with these meetings of theirs? Uncovering the matchmaker *and* renewing his dealings with the fairer sex could both happen at once. "But that could change."

Molly eyed him. "Not hardly."

She turned away. He felt unaccountably wounded by her dismissal. He felt even more put out by the way she chose that moment to examine his dusty cast-iron cookstove. Was a hunk of unused black iron more interesting to her than he was?

Impossible.

"You can't be sure," Marcus coaxed. "You never know—"

"Oh, I know." Molly kicked the edge of the stove.

She lifted the blackened teakettle. Frowned. "I'm very certain of my feelings."

"Feminine feelings change. Like the wind."

"Not mine."

"I've heard otherwise. Some say you're *especially* changeable."

At that, she pursed her lips. Still all but ignoring him, Molly seized the stove handle and opened the oven door to peer inside. "I'd suggest you clean yourself up as befits a proper business meeting. It will take me a while to get this stove ready."

Marcus frowned. She was issuing orders to him? This couldn't be happening. He was the man. He was in charge of these proceedings. He would retain the upper hand.

Molly reached into the cold oven. She fished out an old leather boot, then passed it to him with an air of utter disdain. "I believe this is yours?"

"So *that's* where it got off to!" Marcus marveled, momentarily diverted. "I stepped in a puddle after that rainstorm last month. I put it in there to dry out."

"Any longer and it would have become boot jerky."

She waggled it, giving him a pointed look.

Marcus snatched it. At the motion, Molly's gaze fluttered over his improper attire and disheveled hair—again. She frowned.

Had he imagined she enjoyed the way he looked? He must have, because now Molly seemed entirely disapproving of him. Doubtless, this matchmaker search was addling his thoughts.

He had to stay the course, Marcus reminded himself. The sooner he uncovered the matchmaker's identity, the sooner he could have this done. The sooner he could be finished with Molly Crabtree.

He must have been mad to think this bossy, independent-minded woman might be the one to lure him away from his lumber mill and back toward the nonsense of courting, socializing and other ways to waste time. He would do better, Marcus told himself, to find a more amenable, less difficult, woman for that. Molly Crabtree couldn't have been more wrong for him.

No matter how appealing she seemed, brightening his kitchen with soft pastels and the sweet swoosh of skirts.

Disgruntled, he turned to do as she'd asked.

"Remember to shave," Molly called after him cheerfully. "And a suit like the ones you usually wear wouldn't be untoward for our lesson today. It would set the correct tone for the proceedings between us."

Now she presumed to dress him? Marcus paused. This, he decided, was the final straw. Molly was far too opinionated for her own good. Far too talkative, and far too mannishly industrious. She deserved a lesson in proper feminine behavior. Marcus vowed, right then and there, that he would be the one to offer it to her.

Before he'd finished with her, bullheaded Molly Crabtree—secret matchmaker or not—would learn that a woman did *not* belong in business, but in a man's arms. In a man's life. That was the natural course for females. Setting Molly straight was the least he could do. For the good of men everywhere, Marcus had to take a stand.

Otherwise, who knew what unfortunate knucklehead would someday be blinded by Molly's beauty, and find himself trapped with a wife who'd rather tally accounts than raise children? With a wife who brought in her own funds? With a wife who *commanded her husband to shave?*

A female's natural place was as the light of the home, as the appreciative recipient of her husband's labors. Marcus could imagine nothing worse than a wife who didn't *need* him. He wasn't ready to fit himself with a marriage noose now, but someday, when he was, he wanted a woman he could pamper. A woman who would wait for him at home, and who would delight in her husband's attention. Didn't every man?

Honestly, clarifying this point for Molly would be for her own good.

"Don't worry," he told her, pausing near the hallway that led from the kitchen to the second-floor stairwell beyond. A mischievous grin burbled up from someplace inside him. Marcus managed to stifle it. "I know *exactly* how to handle these proceedings between us. Just wait and see."

Molly stood by, stiff as a freshly laundered shirtwaist, while Marcus delivered his parting comment. She held her head high as he strode down the hallway out of sight. She felt her hands tremble at the sound of his footsteps on the stairs, followed by the heavy clunk of a second-floor door closing.

She sagged with relief.

What had she gotten involved with? Seeing Marcus this morning, so casually and so *intimately,* had nearly been her undoing. Molly hadn't expected to find one of the most proper men in all of Morrow Creek still abed so long after sunrise—much less to find him answering his front door clad in...well, practically nothing!

She was *certain* his trousers hadn't been completely fastened. In the gap at the top of Marcus's waistband, she'd caught a scandalous glimpse of knit underdrawers. And of course, that glimpse had led all the way to a full-on view of his undershirt, plainly visible beneath his open flannel shirt. He hadn't even had the decency to choose a modest undershirt, one that wouldn't hug the muscles of his chest quite so closely.

Plainly Marcus Copeland possessed no modesty at all, at least not outside his lumber mill office. It seemed downright unbelievable, but it was true. She would have to be on her guard, lest she find his bachelor influence having an unseemly effect on her. As it was, she knew she might still be blushing.

It wasn't strictly proper for Molly to be here, after all. An unmarried woman, alone with an unmarried man? Why, if theirs *hadn't* been a business arrangement, it would have been quite outrageous. Fortunately, Adam and Fiona Crabtree possessed liberal views, and an abundance of faith in their daughters' good natures. Had they known about Molly's mission, they'd doubtless have sent her off to it with their blessings.

She'd left early, though, gathering up her basket of supplies and tiptoeing out before her venture with Marcus could become an issue. Just to be on the safe side.

For all she knew, her family would react to this the same way they had to Molly's intentions of becoming a cardsharper at the age of twelve—with laughter, jokes and a tip to Deputy Winston about the "gambler" in their midst. After that, Molly had been unable to practice so much as a riverboat-style two-handed double-deal without calling undue attention to herself. Shortly afterward, she'd decided to become a poetess instead, and that had been that.

Pushing aside those memories, Molly prepared to get down to work. She finished unpacking the flour, butter and leavenings she'd brought and arrayed them on the worktable near the sink and water pump. She set a covered pitcher of milk beside them, then carefully removed her hat and placed it atop her basket for safekeeping. She tied on her favorite apron.

All the while, Marcus thumped and bumped upstairs. Water splashed; doors and drawers clunked shut. Once Molly could have sworn she heard the husky melody of a ribald drinking song wafting downstairs. Surely she was imagining things. Marcus Copeland was one of the most upstanding citizens in town. Despite his improper appearance this morning, he wouldn't dare sing such a tune, especially in the near-presence of a lady.

Would he?

Perhaps she didn't know Marcus Copeland as well as she thought she did. It was rumored he had experienced all sorts of things while living in an eastern city in the States, before he'd made his way westward to the territory two years ago. Despite his businesslike demeanor, was it possible he possessed hidden qualities no one in Morrow Creek knew about?

Booted footsteps sounded on the stairs. Hurriedly

Molly quit gawping at the ceiling. She pretended to be engrossed in searching for a biscuit pan.

"Your home is quite wonderful," she said conversationally, knowing Marcus would see her industriousness as he entered the kitchen. "So expansive. All the most modern amenities, too."

She gestured toward the indoor water pump, the grand, if dusty, stove, and the expanse of marble-topped worktable meant to be used for pastry. She didn't have anything nearly so fine at her bakeshop. Everything in Marcus's home was covered in the bits and pieces of bachelor life, of course, but that was to be expected with a man like him. It was obvious he needed her help to learn about civilized living.

Boot jerky, after all, was not an appropriate table-top centerpiece.

Molly averted her gaze from the offending footwear, propped on the worktable where he'd left it, and turned her attention instead upon Marcus.

Shall we get started? she intended to ask. The words faltered on her lips, though, at her first sight of him.

He looked magnificent.

"Do I pass muster?" he asked from the doorway, spreading his arms to indicate his newly clad self. "Or perhaps you'll want to inspect me at closer range before we begin."

As though to help her in that regard, he strode

nearer. His boots rang against the plank floor. Although his tone had been perfectly solicitous, Molly couldn't help but find it distinctly at odds with the mischievous expression on his face. Nervously she stepped backward.

How had he accomplished so appealing a demeanor? And so quickly, too? His hair was combed, thick and dark to his collar. His jaw was clean shaven, his clothes…

Molly shook her head. "That, Mr. Copeland, is *not* a suit."

It was instead, she saw to her chagrin, an ensemble nearly as revealing as the one he'd answered the door in. A knit Henley-style shirt stretched across his broad shoulders and strong chest, and was crossed in the appropriate places by the braces that held up his trousers. Those, Molly noticed, were the same risqué pair from their earlier encounter.

Holding her breath, she dared to peek.

His britches were fully buttoned.

Sweet heaven. What had gotten into her?

Biting her lip, Molly hurriedly shifted her gaze. Of all the things she'd aspired to become, a loose woman had not been among them.

"I must protest. That, Mr. Copeland, is not proper business attire."

He grinned. "It's proper enough for today."

"I strongly disagree!" Where had all those muscles

in his arms and chest come from? The fineness of his physique had certainly never been apparent beneath his customary tailored wool worsted suits and waistcoats. "You look like a lumberman!"

"I *was* a lumberman. How do you think I began my mill?"

That was neither here nor there. Flustered, Molly tried not to gawk as his smile widened.

"I'm sure you were a wonderful lumberman," she told him firmly, "but for today, a suit would have been better. Much better. You have such lovely suits."

Please, put one on, she begged silently. Dressed like this, he seemed much too...*not stick-in-the-mud*...to her. Like this, Marcus seemed a different man. An approachable, wholly masculine man, unbuffered by formal clothes and the decorous attitude that usually came with them. He seemed very much *not* like the man who'd been her unwitting nemesis for the past several months...and very much *like* a man who could make ladies everywhere titter and swoon.

Including Molly, if she weren't careful.

With shocking casualness, Marcus propped his hip on the tabletop. He regarded her. "I don't wear suits on Saturday."

He seemed regretful. Molly was positive that regret was feigned. Behind Marcus's warm brown eyes, a certain teasing lurked. A smile tugged at the edge of his mouth.

"You shall, for our meetings!" she blurted. "I insist!"

"I'm afraid, Molly, that you're in no position to insist."

Lazily, Marcus straightened. An audacious tilt cocked his brow as he came closer.

At his advance, the room seemed to cozy in upon them. Molly found herself stepping backward again. Her bustle squashed against the tabletop, bringing her up short. An instant later, Marcus halted his booted feet mere inches from her own. The warmth of his body reached out to her, along with an unidentifiable fragrance. Soap, surely. And something more?

"Now…are you?" he murmured.

She swallowed, looking upward. "Am I…what?"

"In a position to give orders." He sent his gaze over her face, seeming to savor the sight of her. "Especially to me."

Oh, my. Her whole being quivered with a nonsensical urge to agree. To nod her head, to blurt her assent and be done with it. In the shadow of Marcus's imposing form and surprising force of will, Molly could barely remember what they'd been talking about.

"I'll wear what I like," he assured her.

His tone, deep and sure, somehow signified that

something greater than mere wardrobe was at stake. Alerted by that tone, Molly felt her usual backbone return.

Time to be brave. Businesslike. Unimpeachably proper.

"Perhaps a hat, then?" she ventured.

He laughed out loud, stepping back a pace. Something akin to respect glimmered in his eyes. "You don't give in, I'll credit you that."

"I do not," Molly agreed. "Is that a yes?"

"To the question of a hat? No."

Disappointed, Molly frowned. But she *had* made progress, she was sure. It was almost as though by standing up to Marcus, she'd passed a test of some sort. Things between them had shifted subtly.

They shifted again when Marcus next looked at her. Speculation enlivened his expression. "All this talk of suits has me thinking of work. But I'm not expected at the mill until noon, and until then the place is in capable hands with my foreman Smith. Why don't we use this time to take a walk together instead? These things can wait."

The sweep of his hand indicated the baking supplies Molly had prepared. Dumbly she stared at them, then at Marcus's broad palm. His hands looked capable, she thought inanely. Masculine. Unreasonably enthralling. She wondered how one of them would feel clasping one of hers.

"You don't really want to think about a boring business venture like ours, do you?" he went on, his tone persuasive. "Not when the sun is shining and there is leisure to be had."

His smile coaxed her to agree. Lulled by it, Molly almost nodded. It *would* be nice to take a stroll, to enjoy the changing colors of the oak leaves outside. Especially with someone whose company she enjoyed by her side.

At times, she did grow lonely in Morrow Creek, where the townsfolk only thought of her as flighty Molly Crabtree, liable to embark on a silly quest at any moment. They didn't understand that she'd only been searching for something all this time... something that would make her feel whole.

"Your expression says you agree," Marcus said, breaking into her thoughts. "Excellent."

He grasped her hand. His fingers, strong and slightly callused, entwined with hers as he tugged her away from the kitchen. The sensation was every bit as enthralling as she'd imagined. Surprised, Molly let herself be led for a moment, her only protest a backward glance at the flour, sugar and milk assembled in a tidy row.

The supplies seemed to offer a silent rebuke. *Are you here for a pleasurable stroll?* they asked. *Or a businesslike arrangement?*

She couldn't very well expect Marcus to help with

her dreaded bookkeeping, she realized abruptly, if she didn't hold up her end of their bargain.

"Wait! You haven't eaten yet," Molly said. "I'd planned biscuits with honey for breakfast. The fire is stoked and the oven should be ready soon. Aren't you hungry?"

"Hungry?" Marcus repeated. As though taken aback by the question, he examined her.

In the process, his regard changed. At first rather hurried, it mellowed into a leisurely perusal that caught Molly by surprise. He *did* look hungry, she thought—and with a multitude of appetites. Not all of them, Molly expected, could be satisfied with her baked goods. Again she remembered her sisters' cautioning words.

She may have been a bit…reckless in thinking she could deal successfully with a man like Marcus. Particularly given her unexpected, *untoward* interest in him.

"Let me worry about that," he finally said, freeing her from his heated gaze. "Get your hat."

"No."

He looked perplexed. On him, the expression seemed a poor fit. Perhaps it didn't get used often.

"What?" he asked.

"No," she repeated, pulling her hand from his. She straightened her spine. "I'll not get my hat."

He frowned, obviously displeased at her refusal.

But why? Surely a walk wasn't so urgent as all that. Yet Marcus seemed quite put out that she…no. There was something else afoot here. Suddenly Molly was sure of it.

"But the outdoors awaits," Marcus urged again.

Beyond the glass-paned window he gestured toward, ponderosa pines crowded the small house's yard. Mixed between them, the slender-trunked oak trees common to the northern parts of the territory brandished multiple-colored leaves. Molly could almost smell the fresh scents she knew the trees carried.

Marcus didn't glance longingly at the landscape at all, she noticed. It was then that she realized the truth.

"You're afraid!" She turned in wonderment to face him. She crossed her arms with the conviction of her revelation. "You're trying to divert me from our tasks because you're afraid. I can't believe it!"

"I'm not afraid of anything."

"You're afraid of baking."

"Ha! Ridiculous." He ran a hand through his hair. "You women and your outlandish ideas."

"Identify the flour," Molly challenged, sweeping her arm toward the supplies at the other end of the room. "I dare you."

"Don't be childish."

"He said, glowering," she teased.

"This is a very unbecoming side of you. Do you think I'm so helpless I can't pinpoint something so basic as flour?"

Silently she waited. The flour, salt and baking powder were in identical canvas sacks, perhaps eleven inches high and eight inches wide. Molly had sewn them herself, specifically for transporting baking provisions today.

"I think you're afraid to try," she said. "Don't worry. Everyone is uncertain at the beginning."

"I am *never* uncertain."

"That's something we have in common, then."

Her pronouncement seemed to goad him into action. With one final, exasperated look, Marcus went to the worktable. He jabbed his finger toward one of the sacks. "This is the flour."

"Are you sure?"

"Of course."

"Then we'll begin the biscuits with two cups of that." Molly joined him at the opposite side of the worktable and pointed to the teacup she'd found for measuring. "Go ahead and measure some out, then pour it into that bowl I prepared."

Marcus blanched.

"Afraid you've guessed wrong?"

He scoffed and grasped the teacup. It looked ridiculously fragile in his hand as he scowled into its bowl. He drew in a deep breath, then thrust the teacup into the opened sack he'd chosen.

White powder billowed upward. Molly hoped he liked sour biscuits. She could tell from this distance that the substance held suspended in a stream of sunlight was far too fine to be the rather coarse milled flour she'd purchased at the mercantile. Sugar didn't waft in a cloud like that. Neither did salt. Marcus had chosen the baking powder.

She waited for him to admit his mistake. He did not.

Instead, he peered skeptically at the teacup, now overflowing with baking powder. His drawn-together brows were frosted with white. The sight might have been humorous, if not for the earnest concentration on the features below them.

Marcus snagged the rim of the earthenware bowl. He dragged it closer. He held the baking powder above it and prepared to empty the teacup.

"Wait!" Molly cried. "I can't let you do it."

He gave her a bland, cocksure look. Without taking his gaze from her face, he overturned the cup. Baking powder landed in the bowl with a muffled whump.

Oh, no. This was worse than she'd thought, Molly realized. There would be no reasoning with a man who believed himself capable of *everything*. She hurried around the table to Marcus's side.

"That's baking powder," she protested, staring aghast into the bowl.

"And...?"

"You don't need a whole cup of baking powder for this recipe. Unless you're making biscuits for two hundred people."

He squinted. "We'll need a much larger bowl."

"No, we won't. We'll need to start over."

Marcus gave the bowl an accusing look. "You see? We should have taken that walk I suggested."

"No, we should have begun at the beginning." She refused to be swayed. Because Marcus was otherwise so capable, Molly had credited him with too much kitchen competence. But that didn't mean she intended to give up, or let herself be distracted from her mission. "I can see now that I should have begun with something simpler for you. Something like..."

"Like a walk."

"Like toasted bread," she decided.

"I prefer biscuits," he said stubbornly. "I have biscuits every morning at the Lorndorff Hotel."

"Every morning?"

He nodded. "Coffee, eggs, an edition of the *Pioneer Press,* and biscuits."

"What if you fancy griddle cakes one day?"

"I prefer biscuits," he said firmly.

Evidently Marcus Copeland was a creature of habit.

That masculine trait could work to her advantage, Molly decided, if she handled things correctly between them. She'd simply have to train him properly, and she'd succeed. Magnificently.

"Then it's biscuits you shall have today," she acquiesced with a smile. Molly scooped the baking powder from the bowl. She returned it to its sack, then dusted her hands clean. "The eggs and coffee will have to wait for another lesson. But you must agree to do everything I say. To follow my every direction. In this, I'm your instructor. You are my pupil."

"You are enjoying this far too much."

"Nonsense." She hid a smile. "I'm merely doing my part to make our business arrangement work. You'll find I'm a very determined woman."

"You'll find I'm a very poor pupil." Marcus stared at their baking supplies, hands on hips in a disgruntled pose. "What I've learned I've learned on my own. I don't take kindly to being told what to do."

"Then why did you agree to our arrangement?"

For a moment, Marcus only went on with what he'd been doing—frowning the baking powder into submission. Then he shifted his gaze to her face. He shrugged. "I have my reasons," he said.

Leaving Molly to wonder, for all the rest of that day, exactly *what* those "reasons" of his really were.

Chapter Five

Molly Crabtree was a singularly confounding woman, Marcus decided after a morning in her company. She chattered nonstop, but never seemed to reach any kind of conclusion. She smiled reassuringly at him when he made mistakes, yet looked discomfited when he performed his unfamiliar tasks correctly. She gazed at him often, touched him occasionally, and nearly drove him mad with the way she held the tip of her tongue between her teeth while concentrating...but somehow managed to sidestep every flirtatious advance Marcus made.

This last put a serious splinter in his plans. He'd come downstairs that morning intending to use everything at his disposal to end Molly's cautiousness, win her confidence and extract the truth about the matchmaker from her. He'd expected her to crumble beneath his charm. He'd expected to have her babbling by noon. Instead, he'd survived three hours of biscuit tutorials, with nary a sign of weakening on Molly's part.

Was it possible he'd found the only person in Morrow Creek who possessed as much stubbornness as he did?

Marcus didn't think so. After all, it was widely known that women were indecisive creatures, prone to flights of fancy and changing interests. All he had to do was figure out Molly Crabtree, and he'd have this task completed. How difficult could it be, he asked himself, to reckon out one woman's true nature?

He'd have her tallied by sundown, Marcus vowed. He'd have the matchmaker's secret delivered to the members of the Morrow Creek Men's Club by moonrise. Tonight, the rafters of Murphy's saloon would shake in celebration.

The only trouble was—and Marcus was certain it was but a minor glitch—that she'd put him completely off balance. He could find no logical excuses for Molly's behavior at all. No matter how he tried, he could not anticipate her actions. She was a puzzle to him.

He should have realized the challenge that lay before him from the first. What kind of woman bypassed a leisurely stroll in favor of work? What kind of woman nattered on about her bakeshop with as much zeal as some ladies discussed quilting? Only Molly.

As the morning wore on, Marcus became uncomfortably certain that, had he waved an issue of Godey's Lady's Book in front of Molly's face, she'd have used it to flatten biscuit dough. She was singular. Confusing. And, he had to admit—however begrudgingly—fascinating to him.

He wanted to figure her out. And then, to best her. Marcus refused to believe there might be any more to his interest in her than that.

"Watch this," he told her, brandishing a round copper biscuit cutter. "The third time's the charm."

"Very well. Have at it."

Molly gestured toward the flour-dusted rectangle of biscuit dough before them on the worktable. It was their latest batch. The first had yielded breadstuff so tough it had nearly chipped his tooth; the second, flat mounds too brittle to do anything but crumble when touched. Molly had proclaimed herself mystified at the biscuits' failure. Marcus knew that her lamentable baking skills were likely at fault.

He brought down the biscuit cutter.

"Push straight down," Molly instructed, laying her hand atop his wrist. "Don't twist the cutter. The biscuits won't be able to rise properly."

"If you continue touching me that way, I won't be able to concentrate properly."

"Oh!" She snatched her hand away. "I'm sorry."

"Don't be." Marcus glanced at her. "I'd rather have your touch than another batch of baked goods any day."

As he'd expected, she looked flustered. Her cheeks brightened with a blush. Her hands fluttered.

"Honestly, Mr. Copeland—"

"Marcus, remember?" He paused amidst delivering his first few biscuit rounds to the waiting skillet that would serve as a baking pan. "We've been as close as dancers waltzing these past few hours. Surely you can call me Marcus. And remember to do so from here on, too."

Molly shook her head. "I truly shouldn't. The matchmaker says that using given names is a sign of inappropriate familiarity between unengaged men and women."

Aha. Finally his patience had been rewarded with the opportunity he needed. He'd been right to wait for Molly to bring up the scourge that had been bedeviling the men. This way, she wouldn't become suspicious about his interest in the subject.

"The matchmaker?" Marcus scoffed, baiting his trap. "I don't believe the matchmaker exists."

"*Of course* the matchmaker exists!"

"I believe the women in town invented her. To have an excuse for pursuing the men the way they have been."

"That's outrageous!"

He shrugged. "The truth sometimes is."

With careful leisure, he arranged the final biscuits in the pan. Surveying them, he experienced an undeniable and ridiculous feeling of pride. Marcus dusted his floury hands.

"Your theory is *not* the truth," Molly protested. "The matchmaker *does* exist. I know it."

"You do?" Excitement simmered inside him. That, and a strong sense of impending victory. He had to tread carefully now. "Exactly how do you 'know it'?"

"I—I merely do. That's all."

He tsk-tsked as he lifted the biscuits toward the oven. "Feminine logic. It's as unassailable as a boat with a hole in the bottom."

Molly shot him an aggravated look. "How do you know the matchmaker *doesn't* exist?"

"I don't." Marcus grasped the oven door handle with a cloth to shield his hand, slid the biscuits inside and said a small prayer. If these were inedible, he didn't think he could survive baking another batch.

"It's possible she exists," he said with a careless gesture. "It's possible I will wake up next week and find myself one of her hapless victims."

Molly grumbled something incomprehensible. It

was probably just as well Marcus couldn't understand the words, given her expression.

"It's possible," he continued nonchalantly, "that Murphy's dog will begin talking to him tomorrow."

"Ooh! This is all a joke to you, then?" Crossing her arms over her chest, Molly followed him to the stove. "The women in town merely wish to make matches with suitable husbands, and you find that *humorous?*"

He pretended innocence. "Are you suggesting I shouldn't?"

"Of course you shouldn't. There's nothing funny about women making their own decisions, seizing their own destinies—"

"Seizing any man within reach—"

"Not any man! *Particular* men," Molly disagreed. "Men whom the matchmaker has deemed appropriate. Haven't you seen the matchmaker's personal advertisements in my father's newspaper? Even the blind advertisements are very precise."

"Precise?" Marcus echoed, setting aside his cloth. "Those advertisements are fiction. They're about as believable as a dime novel."

She tilted her chin. "I happen to like dime novels."

"You would."

She gave a strangled exclamation and whirled around, then set to work cleaning bits of dough from their work surface with jerky motions. The exertion pinkened her cheeks, or maybe it was aggravation that lent her that particular glow. Marcus found it becoming, if a little alarming. Did she have to scrub the table with such…vigor?

"Those advertisements," he said, pushing a little further, "are obviously fabricated. They're more proof that the matchmaker doesn't exist."

"The matchmaker *does* exist," Molly said tightly.

"I'll never believe it."

Fisting her hand on her cleaning cloth, Molly glared at him. Marcus tried to look as dubious as possible. She exhaled and went back to cleaning. She was close to revealing what she knew. He was certain. If nothing else, he figured, Molly would not be able to withstand being thought wrong about something. Anything.

They were alike in that regard.

"Women are not, by nature, pursuers of men," Marcus told her, ladling hyperbole into his trap. "Their aggressive behavior demands an excuse. A scapegoat, if you wish. Hence, the make-believe matchmaker."

"The matchmaker is not make-believe," Molly said from between her teeth. "And you know nothing of women if you do not believe they can pursue what-ever they wish, whenever they wish to. I started a business! I—"

"Ah, but that is commerce, not romance. Between

men and women, there can be only one pursuer." He pointed to himself. "Men."

"Nonsense. These are enlightened times. Women can pursue whatever and whomever they wish."

He feigned regret, shaking his head. "If only the women in Morrow Creek believed that were true. Then they'd have no need of this matchmaker pretense."

Molly gritted her teeth. She flung down her cloth and faced him, hands on hips. "If I chose to, I could *prove* to you that the matchmaker exists."

Marcus scoffed. "Next you'll tell me *you* are the matchmaker."

A tense moment stretched between them. Marcus hardly dared breathe, lest he destroy the fragile momentum he'd created. Any moment now, Molly would tell him the truth.

Once she did, he realized, they'd be done with their meetings. The notion saddened him. Thanks to Molly's frequent visits to his lumber mill, and now their tutoring sessions, he'd begun looking forward to their time together. In Molly's chaotic company, he felt nearly lighthearted. It was an uncommon sensation—and a surprisingly welcome one, too.

But Marcus had a mission to complete, and he intended to do so. The members of the men's club were counting on him. Several of them believed Molly herself might be the matchmaker. Were they right?

Her gaze met his. He was certain he detected secrets there.

"We have gotten ourselves off course," Molly announced.

She untied her apron with a few practiced tugs and removed it. Before Marcus could so much as blink, she'd traversed the short distance to her basket and tossed the garment inside it.

"I have other things to do today," she said. "Other chores to perform, and much of my own baking to do. We'll meet again as we agreed, on Monday evening after your mill and my shop close."

"But the biscuits—they're not done yet." It was a pathetic attempt to make her stay, yet Marcus's determination demanded it. Success had been so close! "Stay," he coaxed. "At least until they're out of the oven."

Molly shook her head. "Never fear. You'll know when they're done. You're a quicker study than you seem."

His protestations to the contrary were useless. Marcus could not make her stay. Moments later, Molly's supplies were packed, her gloves and hat were on, and she was on her way out the door.

"Well. This has been…invigorating," she said.

She offered him a handshake. It was brief, businesslike and, for Marcus, deeply frustrating. He had the unexpected feeling Molly had beaten him today, without even knowing it. It had seemed impossible that she might elude his questioning, and yet she had.

Clearly he needed another strategy. But what?

"Thank you," he said. "For everything."

"Everything?"

"The baking lessons. The company. I enjoyed it."

She smiled. It was then, seeing her smile, that Marcus's next tactic occurred to him. It was a little risky—mostly to him—but if it resulted in unveiling the matchmaker sooner, it would be worth it.

Molly might not know that she had beaten him, but he would know for certain when he finally bested her, Marcus vowed. His victory in this was imperative, for the sake of the men's club, for the sanity of the town, and for the restored sanctity of life as it was meant to be: calm, predictable and constant.

"I'll see you on Monday," he promised, then bid her goodbye, the better to give himself time to plan during his ritual walk to the lumber mill.

"I believe Marcus Copeland knows something about the matchmaker," Molly said to her sister Grace that afternoon.

"Why do you say that?" Grace asked.

Hesitating, Molly shifted the sign she'd been carrying down Morrow Creek's main street. Emblazoned with a slogan in favor of women's suffrage, it was identical in sentiment to the sign carried by her elder sister. Grace was a staunch supporter of the work of Elizabeth Cady Stanton and Susan B. Anthony, and spent part of every Saturday, when the farmers' wives often came to town, spreading the word about the women's campaign.

"He insists the matchmaker doesn't exist," Molly said. "Quite adamantly, too. I'm certain he's been trying to goad me into revealing something."

"It's possible. Men sometimes use bullying techniques to get what they want."

Remembering the way she'd felt in Marcus's presence—alive, challenged, *eager*—Molly shook her head. "It wasn't like that. He didn't *force* me to reveal anything."

"Force comes in many forms." Grace waved her sign toward a group of cigar-smoking men outside the mercantile. They hooted in an ill-mannered way, but she only continued on, head held high. "Sometimes the merest persuasion is a kind of force. Particularly when wielded by skilled hands."

Marcus's hands were skilled. Molly pictured them, recalling his strong, gentle grip as he'd urged her outside for a walk. She'd enjoyed his touch. But she doubted that was what her sister had in mind.

"Have you given away our secret?" Grace asked sharply.

"No." Molly was offended that her sister could

even suspect as much. "I won't, either. You know we promised to keep it close, between ourselves."

"I know. But this is too important to let slip, and you're more liable to weaken than Sarah or I."

"I am not! Just because I'm the youngest—"

"Doesn't mean you're the least capable. I know, I know." Grace gave a weary sigh, adjusting her grasp on her sign. "You keep telling us that. But honestly, Molly, it does. You haven't the experience *or* the critical nature to recognize when you're being led astray."

Molly rolled her gaze skyward. "Pardon me for not being a cynical old cow."

"Heavens," Grace said sweetly. "Shall I begin mooing now, or only when Mr. Copeland appears?"

"Now. Please," Molly returned in an equally sugary coo, helpless to prevent a smile. It was impossible to insult her opinionated sister. Truly, it was.

"Perhaps I will," Grace mused, far too seriously for Molly's peace of mind. Her sister gazed directly ahead. "There's Mayor Wallace, now. Conceivably, if he thinks I'm addled he'll humor me by listening to my views on temperance."

"Either that or he'll lock you up and provide you with the perfect opportunity to lecture inmates on the evils of liquor."

It had been a jest. Molly might have known her sister wouldn't see it that way.

"You know," Grace said, "you may be right."

Oh, dear.

Grace's expression turned thoughtful. She trained her attention on the mayor's lanky form as he strolled toward the town's favorite meeting place, Murphy's saloon.

"Those criminals *could* use a word or two," Grace said.

Recognizing one of her sister's impassioned outbursts in the brewing, Molly grabbed her just in time.

"Oh, no, you don't," she cried. "Not again."

"Molly, let me go!"

"You'll not embarrass us all by harassing the mayor," Molly said from behind her women's rights sign. She waved to a few local ladies passing by, then addressed her sister again. Sternly. "Especially if doing so involves invading Mr. Murphy's saloon. Promise me you won't go in there."

"Pshaw. I won't embarrass anyone."

"That's what you claimed last month. Before you and the members of your Ladies' Literature group chained yourselves to the awning of Mr. Nickerson's Book Depot and News Emporium."

"He refused to stock the works of Jane Austen."

"I know. But I doubt Papa was thinking of the glories of literature when Deputy Winston carted you home."

With a disgruntled frown, Grace freed her sleeve from Molly's hand. She glared at the saloon's elaborate facade as they continued walking but, to Molly's immense relief, did not veer toward it again. The promise of good behavior she'd asked for, however, was not forthcoming. Predictably so.

Instead, Grace hurled a parting scowl over her shoulder and said, "In my opinion, Jack Murphy deserves all the trouble he gets in that saloon of his."

"Grace!"

"He does. The man has pestered me to no end lately. He is insufferable."

"I've heard said he's charming. That lilting accent, those sky-colored eyes, that wondrous dark hair—"

"That arrogant manner, those archaic opinions, that insistence on pure entertainment as a worthwhile pastime," Grace interrupted with evident disgust. She tightened her grip on her sign and raised it defiantly higher. "The man doesn't seem to realize that the twentieth century is nearly upon us! Some women may find those things charming, but I certainly do not."

"Mr. Murphy is frivolous, then?"

"Utterly."

Grace confirmed this truth with the air of a woman

who'd glimpsed something horrible. Horsehair pantaloons, perhaps. Or a bonnet made entirely of mud.

"He is utterly frivolous," she repeated, "and completely thrilled with the fact of it. He is also nosy, persistent and altogether too sure of himself for polite company."

"It could be said," Molly remarked offhandedly, "that a woman like you *needs* a little frivolity in her life."

"Frivolity? *Frivolity? No one* needs frivolity."

Privately Molly thought her sister did. Grace was far too serious-minded. Surely the happiness she needed couldn't penetrate so sober a disposition. Could it?

"Mark my words, Molly, and be on guard," Grace said, tidily proving her point. "The men in this town cannot be trusted. They are up to something—Jack Murphy and Marcus Copeland included. They're behaving entirely too sneakily. I imagine it has to do with those meetings they've been having at the saloon. Until I can be certain, you must be careful."

"A conspiracy?" Molly shook her head. "Surely that's not possible. I can't quite envisage the men engaged in—"

"I realize they don't seem capable of it," Grace interrupted knowingly, "with their pints of ale and their constant gambling. Not to mention their inability to communicate without grunting. But despite all that, they seem to have united. And thus united, well, you know I believe integrated effort is the key to many things. Thus united, the men may actually be able to enact some changes in this town."

"What kind of changes?"

"Never mind that now." They reached the end of the street and pivoted for their final parade homeward. "Just promise me you'll exercise caution. Given what you've told me of Mr. Copeland—and what I already know of Jack Murphy—they may well be on the hunt for the matchmaker."

Molly felt her eyes widen. "I *knew* it!"

"I knew it first." With a trace of sisterly smugness, Grace reached out to straighten Molly's suffrage sign. "Given the matchmaker's striking success, the men were bound to become suspicious eventually. But," she warned, "I don't want *you* to be the first to reveal our secret."

Molly wouldn't be. She swore it to herself, then and there. No matter what Marcus did, no matter what devious or tempting strategies he tried, she would be ready for him. And she would prove to her sisters that when it came to keeping a secret, *she* was the one who could be relied upon.

Guaranteed.

* * *

In the day and a half remaining until he next met with his "tutor," Marcus worked harder than ever at his lumber mill, and spent the rest of his time finding out everything he could discover about Molly Crabtree.

She was, it seemed, a bundle of contradictions. As a youngest daughter, she'd never kowtowed to her older sisters. As a businesswoman, she'd never sought advice or funding. As a friend, she'd never stopped searching for more company, more conviviality, more enjoyment from life. She baked but burned the bread; lived in a journalist's household, but rarely took time to read. She found interests in many areas, but had yet to stick through to the end with a single one.

It was this last that intrigued Marcus the most. If Molly constantly changed passions, then it was likely her stint as the matchmaker—if she were, indeed, that mysterious, meddlesome creature—would be short-lived. Inevitably Molly would tire of pairing men and women in Morrow Creek, and would move on to something else. With luck, and Marcus's guidance, her next venture would be something vastly more suitable.

Like knitting, perhaps. Or darning socks.

Women were well fitted to such pursuits. They probably found them fulfilling, he reasoned, much as he found running a successful lumber mill fulfilling. Given Molly's unconventional upbringing, she'd simply gotten the misguided notion that other activities might satisfy her better. To wit: archery, poetry, watercolor painting, astronomy, "professional" billiards, circus performing and millinery—all of which she'd attempted with greater or lesser success in the past.

Molly's enthusiasm was endearing, Marcus thought, and her capacity for hard work was admirable. That was something—*another thing, a tiny part of him prompted*—they had in common. Molly did not stint in her efforts, but pursued whatever her current goals were with distinct passion.

Much the way he did.

Heaven help the man whom she decided to snag for a husband, though, he considered as he strode homeward after a wearisome Sabbath of visiting and talking. Faced with Molly's inimitable zeal, the poor knuck wouldn't stand a chance. He'd find himself hog-tied and glassy-eyed, overcome by the ardor that Molly undoubtedly brought to everything she did. Poor, pitiable man.

It was fortunate he, himself, wasn't susceptible to her.

Whistling with good cheer, comforted by the notion that he was finally getting things well in hand, Marcus entered his blessedly silent house.

He chucked his suit coat and hat, laid a fire and assembled all the accoutrements for his usual Sunday routine—a ledger, a rationed inch of penny candy and a lantern. By the time he'd turned the first page of his account book, Marcus knew that tomorrow would bring him victory at last.

That, he reckoned, or another rock-hard cinnamon bun. A man couldn't ask for the world, all at once.

Chapter Six

Marcus's plans began unraveling the moment he stepped outside his front door on Monday morning, only to trip over the gift of a blank clothbound ledger—decorated with *ribbons!*—propped outside his front door. He picked up the monstrosity, wincing as the pastel grosgrain affixed to its cover fluttered in the breeze.

From a most sincere admirer, the accompanying note read.

For an instant, he paused. An admirer. Could it be Molly?

No, Marcus decided instantly. This kind of frou-frou fancywork went beyond her capabilities. For that matter, so did this kind of inane schoolgirlishness.

No, the fault for this exploit had to lie with the damnable matchmaker. She'd undoubtedly gotten some unmarried female worked into a state with one of her personal advertisements in the *Pioneer Press.* This time Marcus was the hapless victim.

Scowling, he held the ledger by his fingertips and opened his front door again. He flung the beribboned thing inside, wiped his hands and set out on his way.

Along the path to the mill, he discovered still more signs of the matchmaker's mischief. A miner walked by reading a perfumed letter, the fragrance wafting from the paper so strong it made Marcus's eyes water. The tanner opened his shop, surrounded by two brazen women who seemed determined to knit their way into the man's heart with a pair of redesigned rifle cozies.

"It ain't that the old one didn't work," the tanner told them as Marcus passed. "It's just that…aw, hell. Do ya' have to look so blasted *hopeful?*"

The tanner caught Marcus's eye. The pleading in his gaze would have been funny—if not for the very real chance that Marcus might find himself with a knit *ledger* cozy at any moment. He hurried onward.

At the edge of town, a gaggle of women gathered over a kettle of frothy gray liquid, making soap. As they worked, snatches of their conversation drifted to Marcus.

"If he thinks he's getting away from me that easy, he's mistaken!" one of the women said, stirring. "We're ideal for each other. The matchmaker says so. He just can't see it yet."

"Sounds like my Horace," another woman agreed. "No matter how many times I point out how well we suit, he won't agree. It's plain I'll have to try harder. Specially with the dance at the Chautauqua coming up next month."

"The dance!" another exclaimed. "How will we *ever* make these menfolk of ours look nice for the dance? My George won't even scrape the mud from his shoes, much less shine them."

Marcus glanced down at his own dusty boots, the same pair Molly had fished from the oven. They were old, familiar and comfortable. Exactly the way he liked them. Why would he want to waste time making them shiny? Muddy or gleaming, they'd still fit the same on the inside.

Sometimes he just didn't see the sense in female logic.

Shrugging, he continued on. At least he had the sanctuary of the mill to look forward to, Marcus told himself as he rounded the bend. There, men were men, and women weren't allowed. Voices were raucous, jokes were ribald, and the only fragrances were of cut lumber, fresh pine needles and honest sweat. Perfume didn't waft amongst the axes and crosscut saws. Inane chatter and polite manners didn't muck up the work to be done. And no one bothered to gussy up the workaday surroundings with ribbons and bows.

By the time Marcus arrived—customarily early—the work crews would already be setting off with blades and springboards and steel wedges for back-cutting. They'd have their lunches in tin buckets and their oil cans ready for cleaning pitch from their saw blades. Without a care for feminine niceties or social nonsense, they'd turn swearing into a language all its own as they tromped into the woods, discussing the workday to come.

It was a coarse world, to be sure. But it was a world Marcus was comfortable in. A world he loved. A world he'd come from, beginning as a lowly skid greaser—working in tandem with a bull whacker to haul logs to their ship points—and fighting his way up to hooktender, sharpener and faller. He knew and understood every job at his mill. Marcus never assigned a man to a task he wouldn't have been willing to do himself. That was his philosophy, and he'd never wavered from it.

Not even while finding the success he had here, in the old-growth ponderosa forests of the northern Arizona Territory.

Embraced now by one of those forests, Marcus continued down the narrow logging road. His ledger—his customary, nonembellished ledger—swung easily in his grasp. The rustle of birds and squirrels in the underbrush followed his progress, and the rising sun winked between the tree trunks alongside him.

Tomorrow he might bring out his own well-used pair of corked shoes, embedded with steel spikes in the soles and heels, and head out with one of his logging crews. It would do him good to remember what it felt like to bite the ax into an undercut, to sledgehammer bits into a backcut, to try again the solitary bucker's job of sawing the felled lumber into manageable pieces. He'd swap stories with the men. Trade curse words and jokes. Labor until his arms ached, and…see pink ribbons up ahead on the lumber mill?

Marcus blinked. They remained, billowing at least six feet long on a smoke-scented breeze. The wood smoke, he knew, came from the heating stove in the mill's offices. But the ribbons, attached as they appeared to be to one edge of the mill's eaves? Those were new. And unwelcome.

He stared at them as he stalked closer. Not only had they been somehow attached to the eaves, but a four-foot-long *thing* had been constructed beneath them. As he neared it, pushing his way through the crowd of lumbermen assembled there, Marcus realized it reminded him of nothing so strongly as a marketplace stall. It was nestled smack up against the outside wall of the mill, looking for all the world as though it had sprung there overnight like a particularly gaudy mushroom.

Molly Crabtree stood inside it, beaming with delight. She hadn't spotted him yet—which probably explained the carefree expression on her pert, pretty face—because she was thoroughly occupied with handing out baked goods to his men. They lined up four deep to obtain her dyspepsia-causing disasters, grinning like idiots all the while.

But how could that be? This was Monday. The day Marcus customarily doled out money to the men, money meant for exactly this purpose.

It hadn't seemed fair to force them to spend their hard-earned funds on inedible fripperies, all so Marcus could interrogate Molly about the matchmaker on his own convenient terms. Today, though, he hadn't equipped them yet. How, then, were they paying? Were they using their own coppers for those sticky snickerdoodles, petrified cakes and lackluster pies?

Marcus spotted one man seated on a lumber pile nearby. He'd propped his ankle on his knee and now peered at his shoe critically. As Marcus watched, the man hefted a cinnamon bun. He aimed his gaze at the sole of his shoe, spied the loose nail that had doubtless been troubling him then hammered it cleanly in with the iced roll in his hand.

Aw, hell. Clearly Molly's baking hadn't miraculously improved. Unable to prevent a wince, Marcus looked away.

No, he most *assuredly* couldn't ask his men to

spend their own money on these "goodies." He'd have to pay them back for their purchases the minute Molly left, and be more careful about doling out their weekly baked-goods funds in the future, too.

Nearby two men filed snags from their fingernails with the edges of small cakes. Beside them, another man slipped a snickerdoodle into his boot, smiled as the cookie filled in a hole in the sole, then happily sauntered away. Marcus fought an urge to cover his eyes against this disaster. If the men became any more inventive in their nonedible uses for Molly's baked goods, he might find himself with an outhouse of pasted-together pastry "bricks," glued immovably with cinnamon-apple mortar.

It was time to put a stop to this. Frowning, Marcus commanded his way to the head of the crowd. He stopped in front of Molly, enraptured for the barest moment by the curve of her cheek as she glanced downward to wrap a pile of cookies in paraffin-coated paper.

Then he came to his senses. He cleared his throat. "What the hell are you doing here?" he demanded.

Molly jerked, startled from her careful wrapping by the sound of Marcus's irate voice. She looked up...straight into his narrow-eyed gaze.

My, you look handsome today, a traitorous part of her whispered. She squelched it cleanly. After all, the man *was* presently glaring at her. It wouldn't do to swoon over him.

Defiantly she stood up taller.

"I'm selling my baked goods to your workers, of course." With dignity, Molly handed over the snickerdoodles to the lumberman who waited for them. "Just as we agreed. And by the way, your profanity is unwelcome here, Mr. Copeland. You really ought to consider setting a better example for your men. I doubt they appreciate their avowed leader using such language. Especially in the presence of a lady."

Muffled guffaws could be heard. Molly didn't think she imagined the slight tinge of purple that entered Marcus's clean-shaven complexion. Nevertheless, she went on.

"Be that as it may," she told him gaily, "I'm glad you're here. I wanted to show you the new stall the men surprised me with today." She spread out her hands, showcasing the small sales booth they'd built for her. Constructed of unpainted lumber, it featured a plain face, a work surface and hidden shelves behind. "With these twin beams on each side, which very intelligently affix the whole works to the eaves of the lumber mill building—" at this, she rewarded the men with a proud smile "—it almost looks as though it was always meant to be here. Doesn't it?"

Her smile widened with delight. Truly, the lumbermen's gesture had been too kind. They had made her feel welcome here. Molly was grateful for that.

"And to embellish the structure with these pink ribbons?" she went on enthusiastically, catching the tip of one with her fingertips. "Absolutely wonderful! Why, they must have worked for hours to build this for me. I have to tell you, Mr. Copeland. It makes me feel downright at home here."

The men lingering nearby looked abashed. A few waved; more kicked their boots shyly in the dirt. Marcus's frown deepened.

"I am surprised, though, at your late arrival. I felt sure you would beat me here by several hours at least." She cocked her head thoughtfully, momentarily pausing in her baked goods sales to examine him teasingly. "Was I mistaken in believing you arose at sunrise, worked till moonrise, and only bothered to rest on alternate Sundays when rain prevented the mill from running?"

"Rain," he said tightly, "doesn't prevent the mill from running."

"See then? That makes it all the more remarkable. I've beaten the hardest-working man in town to his job. Imagine that!"

Molly smiled, hoping to jolly him into good humor.

She did not succeed. Marcus bared his teeth, then rounded the edge of her stall. He muscled his way into the cramped space with all his usual authority.

"Stop!" she protested, trying to shove him back out again. "We've already discussed this. No one is allowed inside my baked goods stall except me. Right, Mr. Smith?"

Molly glanced rapidly about for the mill's main foreman. At the same moment, Marcus grabbed her elbow. He steered her backward, the better to sandwich her between the wall and his broad chest.

"Mr. Smith?" she tried again, rising on tiptoes to locate the foreman. Marcus's wide shoulders blocked her view. "We agreed. Mr. Smith!"

There came a tentative murmur.

"Shut up, Smith." Marcus didn't so much as look over his shoulder to be assured the man obeyed. Doubtless, he didn't need to. "And *you,* Miss Crabtree. What business do you have arriving at my mill before I do? Your customary sales time is two hours from now."

"Why are you being so persnickety? Honestly, I don't see what difference it—"

"We have a routine here, *Miss Crabtree.*"

Once again he used her proper address—deliberately, no doubt. Probably to assure his men they should do the same. Molly felt pleased that her proper-manners tutorial had taken effect so quickly. But Marcus was still going on.

"A routine that has never altered in the two years I've owned this mill. Neither you nor anyone else is going to change that. There are…*things* that need to take place before your arrival."

"I merely meant to get a head start on my day," she explained. "I have calls to pay this afternoon, visits to make to the townspeople who are heading the Chautauqua committee. My sister Sarah has warned me that I must impress them if I'm to have a booth for my bakeshop this year."

"Are they impressed by impertinence?"

"Obviously not. And don't be silly. You're clearly trying to bait me." Molly remembered her conversation with Grace, and resolved to be strong. "But it won't work. You imply that I'm being impertinent now, which in this case would be impossible. Since I am not in any way subservient to *you*."

Marcus gawped, clearly outdone by her logic.

To prove her theory, she wrenched her arm free and addressed the next man in line. "What can I get for you today, Oswald?"

Marcus elbowed forward. "A path to the forest to start work?" he suggested in a growl.

The man's jaw dropped. "I'll get my cakes later," he mumbled, then hurried away.

Other men followed. Molly watched them leave with dismay.

"See? See what letting you into my booth has done?" She jabbed Marcus in the ribs with her elbow, feeling boundlessly provoked. "You're chasing away my customers."

"How?"

Not even humoring her by rubbing his side, he pretended innocence...poorly, she thought.

"It isn't my fault if the men who want to retain their jobs are leaving to go to work," he said.

"This is hardly a function of our business arrangement," Molly pointed out. She folded her arms and regarded Marcus indignantly. "You are reneging, Mr. Copeland. It's very poorly done of you. How can I be expected to satisfy your men if I'm not allowed to service them?"

His lower lip twitched. A hint of amusement brightened his eyes, then spread all the way to the rest of his face. From one moment to the next, Marcus's entire countenance changed. Molly had no idea why. His sparkling eyes and barely stifled mirth aggravated her to no end.

"What is the matter with you?" she demanded. "I insist upon servicing your men!"

A few lumbermen paused in their retreat. They glanced over their shoulders with palpable hopefulness—probably, Molly reasoned, still hankering for sweets. Feeling justified in her pique, she surveyed her nemesis, Marcus.

He was bent nearly double, his shoulders shaking

with laughter. If that was his answer, he deserved no further discussion.

Molly grabbed her basket. She hastened after the departing men. "Wait! Who wants more sweets? Don't listen to Mr. Copeland. He *severely* underestimates my determination to satisfy your cravings."

More men stopped. Heartened, Molly beckoned them closer. Three paced nearer. Then their eyes widened, their expressions changed, and they bolted for the woods as fast as their legs would carry them.

Mystified, Molly watched. An instant later, two strong arms grabbed her from behind, lifting her clean off her feet.

"Hey!"

"Enough is enough," came Marcus's voice. "Come with me."

He left her little choice. Since he carried her, his no-nonsense words were a mere formality. Of course she protested all the same, but in the next instant he twirled her in his arms to fling her over his shoulder. Molly had hardly any breath left when he'd finished, much less any choice in the matter.

She had never expected *this*.

"Put me down!"

His only reply was to flick her skirts away from his nose.

"You are a barbarian! A barbarian in a fine suit, but a barbarian nevertheless!"

He shrugged. As easily as she herself might have carried a sack of oats, Marcus balanced her between his shoulder and bent arm. Cradling her in this ignoble position, with one hand on her back for balance, he began to walk.

Decorum grew increasingly difficult to retain. Still she tried valiantly.

"I am a businesswoman. Stop this right now!"

He did not. Amidst all the commotion, her basket dropped. Delectables scattered to the pine-needle-strewn ground. Envisioning herself tumbling just as easily, Molly panicked. He *was* a tall man. Things looked more dangerous from up here. She clutched at Marcus's muscular back, her fingers encountering fine wool, strong male and unrelenting movement.

"Put me down," she ordered again.

"I won't." He shook his head, his hair brushing her cheek. "You are a danger to yourself. *And* my own sense of sanity."

Despite Molly's objections, Marcus grasped her tightly. His attitude held all the unyieldingness of a man who'd been pushed beyond his limits.

"Where has your sense of humor gone?" she asked, poking his back as though she might discover it tucked beneath his suit coat. "You used to possess a passing wit. Did you forget *it* inside your cookstove, too?"

His answer was a grunt of warning.

Molly persisted. "Perhaps I can help you find your good nature as easily as I found your lost boot jerky. Ouch! Did you *pinch* me?"

Marcus glowered and moved on across the yard.

Sagging in temporary resignation, Molly tried to make herself as burdensome as possible. She thought of stones, boulders, wagonloads of railway steel. *Heavy, heavy, heavy.* Thank goodness, most of the men had dispersed, because she wouldn't have wanted witnesses to this display. Or to the childishness Marcus seemed to bring out in her.

Church bells, iron stoves, two-ton oxen, she thought.

Her efforts affected Marcus not at all. Stopping beside her new sales stall, he gave it—and its pretty ribbons—an unaccountably black look. Then he threw some folded currency into the tin that doubled as the cash bin.

Intrigued, Molly twisted to see. She gawked at the quantity of money he'd just spent. With that, she could buy butter, baking molds, even the expensive candied flowers she typically denied herself. Perhaps, she mused prosaically, those things were worth being carried.

"I am purchasing all the rest of your baked goods for today." Marcus picked up the tin, which rattled with coins, and tucked it beneath his free arm. He turned, careful not to clonk Molly's noggin against her stall's twin beams, then addressed his foreman. "Smith, clean this up and stow Miss Crabtree's basket."

"You don't have to do that, Mr. Smith!" Molly disagreed, desperate to assert herself in some way—any way. "Remember your ingrown toenail. The plaster will dislodge itself if you exert yourself overmuch."

She sensed, rather than saw, Marcus's confusion.

"I gave Mr. Smith a medicinal plaster for his foot," she explained, trying to be sensitive to the foreman's sheepish expression. "You really oughtn't expect a man his age to do the kinds of work he does. As soon as he described his troubles to me, I knew something had to be done. If you'd only let Smith sit for part of the day, he'd feel much better."

"Now you presume to tell me how to run my business?"

"Well, 'presume' may be too strong a word—"

"I am escorting you to town," Marcus interrupted, saving her from disentangling herself from what was sure to become a subject as sticky as molasses. "Otherwise, who knows what sort of trouble you might find yourself in on the way. Smith, I'll return in an hour."

Approximately twenty minutes and seven entreaties to "put me down" later, Marcus deposited Molly at her bakeshop's threshold. He released her, then took a pace backward—the better to examine the exterior of her small shop. He'd never visited it before, but its peaked roof, lumber-sided exterior and gingerbread trim were about what he'd expected. Feminine and impractical, just like Molly herself.

"Thank you for letting me walk on my own once we arrived in town," she said stiffly, yanking her arm from his. "I thought you'd become deaf to my pleas."

"I hear everything you say. Some of it more than once."

"More than once?"

"Sometimes when I've left you, I keep hearing your voice in my head." Distracted, he thumbed flaking paint from the door trim. "I think it's a reaction to so much conversation, all at once."

He'd never in his life endured so much chatter as he had since becoming acquainted with Molly Crabtree.

"Humph," she disagreed. "It's only a conversation if *both* people join in."

Not dignifying that nonsense with a reply, he kicked her shop's corner beam. "This beam will crumble within two years. I'll fix it for you."

"You are proving my point nicely."

Marcus shrugged. Damnation, but she could

yammer on. He squinted. "I can see rotten shingles from here. Your roof probably leaks."

Her expression told him it did. Stubbornly she said, "You are still proving my point."

"I'll fix that, too."

"You'll repair my perceptions of you? Lovely! You can begin by being a little less observant—" she moved protectively in front of her building "—and a little more conversational."

"I mean," he said, favoring her with a smile, "I'll fix the faults in your shop."

"Thank you," she said loftily, still piqued over the way he'd handled things at the mill, "but I can manage quite well on my own. I don't need help from a barbarian like you."

His gaze swerved to meet hers. "Oh, yes. You do."

That much was obvious. Her shop had dry rot, peeling paint, sagging window frames and a poor foundation. It dearly needed a skilled hand. Marcus had, he reminded himself, *two* skilled hands.

Besides, Molly wasn't the only one who could invade a person's workplace and gussy it up to suit herself. He could do the same thing. Hell, she'd gotten her baked-goods stand turned into a functioning *part* of his lumber mill! With ribbons, no less. The two were conjoined so tightly now there may as well have been a dovetail joint snugging them fast. He might never get Molly and his lumber mill pried apart.

The notion was enough to send Marcus fully forward. He had to fight back somehow. It was only reasonable that he make his mark on Molly's business, as well.

"I'm doing the work," he told her. "You should be grateful."

"Grateful? Ha!" Molly stiffened, obviously put out. "My bakeshop is my concern. Your only part in it will be your help with my bookkeeping. And even there—" her expression took on a devilish cast "—your prowess remains to be proved."

"My 'prowess'?"

"Yes."

"'Remains to be proved'?"

"Yes." She raised an eyebrow.

Marcus did, too. Her provocative talk reminded him of all the nonsense she'd spouted at his mill about "servicing" his men and "satisfying their cravings." Had she no idea what words like that could do to a man?

She must. Marcus played along.

"I'll have to prove it to you, then," he said, grinning as he stepped nearer. His gaze passed over her, hot and daring. "My prowess, that is."

"Yes. See that you do."

Not for the first time, he wanted to. Wanted to show

her exactly what pleasures a man like him could accomplish with a spirited woman like her. Molly might seem innocent, but with bawdy talk like hers, surely she possessed a more…daring side. After all, she *did* come from a famously freethinking family.

Suddenly Marcus's matchmaker search seemed all the more interesting.

His grin widened. "You have a passing way with a turn of phrase, Miss Molly. I like it."

"You have a passing inability to converse properly," she returned. "Getting convivial conversation from you is like getting a game of pinochle out of my sister Grace. Or coaxing a bit of frivolity from Sarah."

"Your sisters are serious ladies, then?"

She nodded. "Mostly, yes."

"You wouldn't seem to fit in with your family."

"I don't. Not really." Molly waved her hand. "I possess neither Sarah's intellect nor Grace's lofty goals. I inherited only a fraction of my parents' liberalism. I am…not quite as I should be."

"Pshaw. You are."

"In a family of originals, I am not *nearly* outlandish enough to fit in," she insisted. "But that hasn't stopped me from trying."

She lifted her chin, as though armoring herself against his disapproval. Marcus could not give it. At her words, compassion for Molly and her struggles had crept inside him. Now it seemed to have taken up residence in his heart.

The sensation was completely unexpected, and not entirely welcome. If he couldn't see her as the tiresomely independent obstacle to uncovering the matchmaker he had been considering her all along, how could he go on? He certainly didn't want to feel *this* way toward her.

He tried to block the feelings. Surely if he ignored them, they would go away. But when next Molly turned her determined face to his, Marcus was nearly undone by an urge to protect her. He wanted to hold her in his arms, to make her dreams come true, to see a smile enliven her features.

What was the matter with him?

He cleared his throat. "That must be difficult."

Her grateful gaze made him a hero. Damnation, but he didn't want that. Didn't want her looking at him as though he might actually satisfy these sappy longings of his.

"You're being terribly kind," Molly said. "Did you injure your sense of grouchiness while toting me back to town?"

Choking back a laugh, Marcus relaxed. Things had returned to normal between them.

"I may have. Your skirts weigh a ton."

"So does your swelled head, if you think I'll not take offense at *that*."

"I'm sorry." Reaching for her, he took her gloved hand. It felt dainty in his grasp, and peculiarly at home there. Set akilter by the notion, Marcus hastily made a jest. "I'm too blinded by your beauty, light as a feather though it is, to listen properly. What did you say?"

Molly laughed. The brightness it brought to her face made her truly beautiful. Marcus didn't know why he hadn't fully appreciated it before.

Perhaps because she'd been too busy vexing him at every turn.

"I said, thank you for your escort," she told him. "I'll see you tonight for your next baking lesson. Shall we say, six o'clock? All right, then. Goodbye!"

Briskly she retrieved her hand, then whirled to step inside her shop. With typically businesslike gestures, she bustled away. Marcus was left to stare after her…befuddled by his own feelings, and by her hasty departure.

He glanced again at the rotting windowsill to his right. Then, through the clean but imperfect window glass, he looked at Molly. There were unfinished dealings between them. He would see them done, Marcus vowed.

They'd shared something just now. Something both light and strangely necessary. Something true. The unexpectedness of it wouldn't leave Marcus's head—nor would the realization he made in the next moment. Decisively, he followed Molly into her shop.

This was something that could not wait.

Chapter Seven

Molly opened her shop and whooshed inside. Relief swamped her. Free at last! Free to go on about her business without interference, free to walk without fear of being swooped upon and carried, free to lose herself in baking goodies to tempt the Chautauqua committee with.

It meant a great deal to her that she obtain the booth she wanted. Being granted permission to host a booth would mean that Molly had achieved respectable businesswoman status in town, and that she had carved a niche for herself within her family. No longer would she simply be the youngest, the baby, the least capable.

The most patronized.

Marcus patronized her. What else could his behavior be called, when he toted her over his shoulder at will? The man was a rogue. Despite his moments of gentlemanliness, he was at heart a skeptic when it came to the capability of women in business—and

Molly's capability in general. She knew that, and always had. That should have meant any alliance between them was doomed. And yet…

And yet. Standing on her shop's threshold with him, something had happened. Something entirely unlikely and completely perplexing. In one moment, Molly had been sparring with him, as usual. In the next, she'd caught him watching her with the utmost compassion in his gaze, a compassion that had nearly tempted her to unburden her troubles to him—the very man who'd forcibly carted her away from her bake-sale business this morning.

This change in him was outrageous. Unacceptable. Her liking it was foolhardy. What's more, the longing she'd experienced in Marcus's presence was dangerous. She was fortunate, Molly told herself now, that she'd escaped from him when she had. Otherwise, who knew what secrets Marcus might have prompted her to reveal? And yet….

And yet. All of a sudden he possessed a certain manner, a manner both caring and wonderfully protective. While with him, Molly had had the unmistakable impression that she could have confided anything in Marcus and he would have kept it safe.

Even more, she'd felt almost…watched over by him. Seeing him examine her shop with his practiced eye, hearing him promise to make things right, had almost tempted her to let him do exactly as he wished. To let him stomp his extralarge boots over the threshold of her shop and just take charge.

How could she, at one and the same time, want to be independent *and* want to be cared for? The contradiction had confounded her. It had sent her scurrying away, far from Marcus's commanding presence.

But not, as it turned out, for long.

"You don't lock your doors?" Marcus roared.

He entered right behind her, a scowl on his face. His boots thumped loudly across the floorboards as he advanced farther inside, looking incongruously masculine in so delicate a space. Beside her spindly wirework chairs and pastel paint, Marcus seemed rugged and ready even in his customary suit.

"Pardon me?" she asked.

"Your doors. You don't lock them," he accused.

He announced this fault as though it were truly grievous. As though it deserved the *leaky window* look on his face, the one Molly recognized from a few moments earlier. That was the same expression Marcus had worn while regarding the portion of the windowpane he'd traced with his skilled hand, the faulty portion that always let in the rain.

Well, no one gave Molly Crabtree a leaky window look and got away with it. She girded herself for battle.

"Of course, I don't lock my doors." She glanced

down at her gloved hands where a key would have been, had she possessed one. "Why should I?"

"To prevent theft."

"Pshaw! No one will steal my things. Everyone in Morrow Creek is trustworthy. Besides, anyone who would help themselves to my baking supplies undoubtedly needs them more than I do." Molly gave a careless gesture. "They're welcome to them."

"You can't possibly believe that."

She stood her ground.

Marcus stared at her. Shook his head. "I will send over a locksmith. Don't let him charge you twice. I'll pay his fee."

"You most certainly will not!"

"I'll be back later to start the other work I talked about," he went on, undeterred. He examined the floorboards with a critical eye. "I may need to take a few days away from the mill, but that can be—"

"No. No, no, no." Molly put her hands on her hips and regarded him with all the authority she could muster. Never mind her previous foolish yearning to have his help. She wanted none of it now. "You will not touch so much as a splinter here without my approval. I won't have it."

"Then give me your approval."

He waited, impatiently. She had the distinct impression Marcus thought his demand was reasonable.

Men. She would never understand what passed for logic with them.

Clearly, though, out-and-out refusals were not effective. The morning she'd passed thus far—largely flung over Marcus's shoulder—had proved that much. So did the fact that he was, even now, studiously examining the interior walls of her shop. Doubtlessly he was searching for additional flaws.

Worse, a part of her feared he'd find them. Drat the man.

Molly tried another tactic.

Crossing the room, she captured Marcus by the elbow and led him to her counter. "You've had such a difficult morning," she fussed, "arriving tardily at the lumber mill, swearing at your men, carrying me back to town. Why don't you come on over here and sit down for a spell?"

She pushed him onto one of her stools. Doing so required three tries before her determination overcame his greater strength. With a suspicious look, Marcus allowed himself to be settled. Molly's skirts brushed against him as she stepped backward. The rustle of their clothes parting sounded loud in the quiet shop.

"It didn't escape my notice that you didn't get your customary cinnamon bun this morning," Molly said, giving him a knowing smile. She would feed him, cheer him up, and make him forget he'd ever intended to meddle in her shop. Men were simple creatures, after all, easily led by their appetites. "You're probably cranky because it's been so long since you've tasted something sweet."

"It *has* been a while," he agreed, watching her.

She nodded briskly. His perusal gave her a peculiarly heated feeling, though, a feeling as though her ovens were all stoked full-bore with their fires burning brightly. Molly loosened her dress's collar a bit. That was better. She clasped her hands behind her back.

"See? Surely you can dally a while with me, then."

At least long enough to forget your intentions to meddle in my shop.

"A while," he agreed, nodding once.

He leaned lazily against the counter, for all purposes seeming enraptured by her suggestion. His easy surrender emboldened her. She'd been right. Marcus was just like every other man—made sweeter by sweets and grouchy by the denial of them.

"Good," she said brightly. "You can help me choose items for the Chautauqua committee, then. A taste testing, of sorts. You know what they say, don't you? The hungrier you are, the better *everything* tastes."

Molly reached for the plate of cold apple fritters she'd left nearby. Before she could grasp more than their cinnamon scent, Marcus's hand clamped atop her wrist.

"I *am* hungry," he admitted, his gaze searching hers. "I didn't realize exactly how hungry I was until this moment."

"Well," she said patiently, "if you'll let me go I can get you a fritter."

"I don't want fritters."

Frowning, Molly regarded him. "Tea cakes, then?"

"No. Something more." His grasp loosened, became more of a caress. His thumb stroked over the sensitive skin at the underside of her wrist. "Something... sweeter."

Molly trembled. Staunchly she made herself stop staring at the lovely contrast between Marcus's big, sun-browned hand and her lace-trimmed gloves. He'd magically found the one gap between those gloves and her long-sleeved dress, and he toyed with it even now. The sensation caused by his thumb against her bare skin made her want to close her eyes to savor it. Instead, she summoned all her will to address Marcus directly.

"Perhaps a dumpling, then? They're quite fresh."

So are you, Marcus's teasing expression said.

"No. Sweeter." He tugged her nearer.

It was true, then. He *did* have more in mind than mere delectables.

No sooner had this scandalous realization fully penetrated than Molly saw her skirts swish against his trouser legs. She stared at the mingling of her clothes and his, struck by the intimacy of their position. She gazed up at him. Their faces were nearly at the same height, thanks to his perch on the stool, but Marcus's expression held none of the caution Molly felt certain showed on hers.

This was proceeding much too quickly between them. First, a moment of camaraderie shared on her bakeshop's porch. Next, a daring flirtation. What next? A courtship? *A wedding?*

My, how the matchmaker would approve of *that!*

Molly reminded herself she was still making her own decisions in this matter. Not Marcus, nor anyone else. Thank goodness.

"Nothing's sweeter than tea cakes, save pure sugar," she debated, borrowing time to regain her composure. "I can hardly recommend that you eat it by the spoonful, though."

"You are sweeter." Not at all taken in by her delaying tactics, Marcus used his free hand to touch her face. He curled his fingers around the edge of her jaw. "I know it."

Oh, but his touch felt good! No man had ever caressed her this way. Molly couldn't have imagined how wonderful the sensation would be. She wavered beneath it.

"You can't know that," she argued, fighting to remain sensible. "You can't."

Marcus nodded. "Oh, *I can.*"

He was always so certain about things, she mused. His fingers never left her face. Neither did his steady regard. Molly found herself savoring both, however unwisely.

With a flex of his hand on her wrist, he urged her nearer. Like magic, Molly felt herself drawn fully into the V of his legs—a place nigh forbidden to a lady like her. This was dangerous. This was… magnificent.

"You're talking nonsense." She refused to let him see her nervousness. She could do nothing about her pounding heart, save hope he couldn't hear it. "I am not sweet."

"And I am not able to confirm that fact," Marcus agreed. "Not without…a taste."

"A taste?" She should have known there'd be a catch.

He nodded. There it was again, that certainty in him. How could it be that Marcus knew so firmly what he wanted? Molly still hadn't found the things she'd been searching for her entire life.

But here, now, she could not find the will to disagree with him. Not when Marcus bedeviled her senses the way he did. Not when he lured her nearer still and helped her put her hand on his chest. The gesture was both pure and tenderhearted. It bespoke thoughtfulness, betrayed Marcus's intent that she be as comfortable touching him as he so obviously was touching her.

It moved her, plainly as that.

The safeguards she'd placed around her heart crumbled, just a bit. Marcus squeezed his hand atop hers, then released her. Tentatively she spread her palm over his shirtfront, beneath his suit coat. His chest felt warm and solid. Exactly the way she'd always fancied it would feel, during the times she'd dared to sneak glances at him.

She simply couldn't resist the invitation in his face, the comfort in his touch, the seductiveness in his manner. In this moment, she and Marcus were not enemies. Instead, they were simply a man and a woman—two people brought together by something she couldn't explain.

"May I taste you, Molly?" he asked.

She hesitated. His question should have shocked her. Truth be told, it did not. She was a grown woman, a woman of more than twenty years' experience in living. She'd caught the direction of their banter early on, and had not stopped it.

Indeed, she'd encouraged it.

Their faces were only a forearm's length apart,

but that distance still separated them. Once it was breached, there was no telling how things might change.

Molly, however, had always been a woman ready for a risk.

"Yes," she told him, and felt her belly tighten at the enormity of what she was about to allow. Her skin tingled with excitement. Her breath quickened. This had gone beyond the distraction she'd meant to deliver Marcus, all the way to something deeper. "Yes, I'm ready."

But she wasn't ready. Not in the least. Molly discovered it the moment Marcus's warm breath feathered over her lips, the moment his mouth touched hers. Theirs was a union as unlikely as it was irresistible, and those qualities showed as well in Marcus's kiss. It was gentle but decisive, tender but expert. It was all the things she might have expected—had she possessed the wit to expect anything at all—and so very, very much more. Marcus cradled her cheek to hold her to him, murmured something in a hushed voice, kissed her again.

"What?" Molly asked, letting her eyelids flutter open.

"Very sweet," Marcus repeated. "Sweeter than I imagined."

She felt foolishly pleased. Then wickedly eager, as Marcus lowered his head again. His gaze was half-lidded, his attention fierce, his manner languid in a way that suggested to her now-experienced self that he intended to kiss her once more.

"You are sweet also," she said before he could. There was no reason, after all, not to deal with this politely. "Tender and delicious."

His grin flashed. "See if you find *this* sweet."

His mouth touched hers. Molly relaxed the merest amount, letting her fingers uncurl from the fine cotton of his shirt. This was familiar now. The brief hesitation before their lips met, the heated slide of Marcus's lower lip across hers, the tiny nip he gave the bow of her upper lip. All of those were delicacies she'd mastered, with Marcus's tutelage.

"Yes, very sweet," she announced when their next kiss had ended. With relief, Molly realized something more. "I feel quite proficient at this kissing, in fact. Perhaps I'm a prodigy! I had no idea."

"You look so pleased with yourself."

"You look pleased that I'm pleased."

"I am," Marcus said. "But there's more."

"I find myself quite eager," she said boldly, "to discover it."

She couldn't believe she'd blurted as much, but Marcus didn't appear to mind. With him, Molly realized, she felt curiously free to say anything. Perhaps that was because he so often disapproved of her.

Since she wasn't likely to please him, she was free to be herself.

It was an odd notion. One she didn't want to entertain just now. Instead, she remembered what he'd promised, and gave in to her curiosity. "How much more is there?"

"This much." Marcus lowered his head then paused long enough to warn, "And it won't be sweet."

"Not sweet? I doubt very much that you—*oh, my!*"

Deceptively this kiss began as the first, with careful touches and a gentle coming together. Quickly, though, it became something more. Marcus thumbed her chin, urging Molly to part her lips; trusting him, she did, and discovered a subtle invasion more passionate than anything she'd ever known. Marcus delved his tongue inside her mouth, stroking her from within, angling his head to deepen the contact between them. Shocked, Molly fluttered her hands against his shirtfront, beat gently on his chest, issued a startled cry.

Within seconds, that cry became a moan of enjoyment she hardly recognized as coming from her own throat. Marcus's kiss went on and on, and she discovered that it was, indeed, not sweet at all. Instead, this kiss was ardent and giving, demanding and needful, all at once. It made her mind whirl and her heart pound. When it was finally over with,

Molly could only look at him with what was surely a dazed expression.

"Still feeling proficient?" Marcus asked.

She shook her head to clear it. "I'm feeling," she said, "as though you ought not be grinning quite so cockily at a moment such as this."

"Why not?" He took both her hands in his and squeezed. "Right now, I feel stupid with happiness. Daft with enjoyment. You bring out those things in me, Molly."

"I don't know if I should be pleased—or consigned to Sheriff Caffey's jail for the sake of public safety. I can't very well go about making people daft."

Marcus laughed. "Be pleased. I'll have it no other way."

"Very well. I'm pleased."

She was, Molly realized. Deeply, joyfully, surprisingly pleased. Somehow, she and Marcus had wrought an accord today—more than that, even. They'd fashioned a new beginning between them. That fact made her feel more lighthearted than she could ever remember.

Perhaps, she thought giddily, Marcus *wasn't* in pursuit of the matchmaker's secret. Perhaps he was in pursuit of *her,* and all her caution had been wrongly directed.

She hugged herself. Watched him with a smile.

Felt her smile waver as Marcus took out his pocket watch and consulted it.

"Smith will be expecting me." He touched her shoulder, leaning forward for a quick kiss, one that had the feel of a goodbye. "I'll stop at the locksmith's on my way to the mill. I'll send over some men with lumber and supplies for those repairs I talked about, too. Just have them pile up everything someplace out of the way until I can get to it."

After one last smile and a brief caress of his fingers across her cheek, Marcus strode to her shop's front door. There he paused to regard her with a triumphant, masculine look.

"Don't worry about a thing, Miss Molly. I'll have everything here in perfect running order in no time flat. I promise you that."

He winked—the rascal—and nodded. Then he left. Stunned by his rapid departure, Molly stared after him. How could he kiss her like that, so passionately and so stirringly, only to—

The sound of the door slamming shut behind him brought her back to her senses.

Everything here in perfect running order, she recalled. Humph! Marcus meant he'd have *her* in perfect running order, Molly mused, she was sure of it. She'd been foolhardy enough to let down her guard. Now Marcus thought he could dictate what was best for her, just like everyone else in her life did.

Well. If Marcus thought she would knuckle under to tactics like those—however sweetened with a kiss!—then he had better think again, Molly vowed. She intended to establish her independence, her competence *and* her business ability, and she would do exactly that. No matter how Marcus tried to thwart her.

With that thought in mind, Molly packed up a basket of potential Chautauqua goodies. She arranged it nicely, put on her best hat and then headed out to pay her calls. By the time she was finished, Morrow Creek wouldn't know what had hit it. Today, for the sake of securing her Chautauqua booth, Molly meant to cause the biggest stir since…well, since the matchmaker's arrival!

Marcus realized there was trouble afoot at approximately half past five, during his walk home from the mill. He'd detoured apurpose past Molly's shop, planning to check on the lumber, bucket of nails, saws and hammers, and other supplies he'd had sent over earlier. But when he got there, the shop was deserted, and there was no sign of the materials he'd issued.

Scratching his head, he lingered outside the vacant shop. The quantity of lumber he'd sent couldn't have simply disappeared. It was expensive and fine-planed into perfect, straight boards, pieces Marcus had selected himself. Where could Molly have stowed it?

It would be just like her to gussy it up somehow, he decided. Perhaps she'd buried it beneath ribbons, or tied flowers to it. Perhaps she'd created a life-size sculpture of a Grecian goddess, with a nail bucket for a head and two hammers for arms. Cheered a bit by the whimsy of that notion, Marcus strode the outside perimeter of the shop, investigating. After today, Molly's eccentricities didn't strike him as quite so odd, or so aggravating. Instead, they seemed almost…endearing.

Imagine that.

Marcus found he didn't mind the search for his missing supplies, either. He had remembrances of Molly to fill his thoughts.

She kissed like a woman eager for him and his touch—exactly as he'd imagined she might, during all those times he'd dreamt of her. Being with Molly today, touching her, had spoiled his concentration for most of the afternoon, Marcus realized, feeling a carefree grin spread across his face. He didn't mind a damned bit.

That would abate, he felt certain, once he'd tasted her a bit more…thoroughly. There was no reason their dalliance had to affect either of their lives unduly. After all, Molly herself had suggested he "dally a while" with her. There had been no mention of courtship, a development he attributed to her unusual upbringing. Their togetherness could offer the best of all worlds.

With Molly, Marcus had found a woman both sunny and sensual. She was pleasant enough company *and* might eventually be helped into baking passable breadstuffs, too. Now if he could only get her to quit talking so much—and to quit hiding his building materials—things would be perfect.

He continued his search. Maybe around the back?

"Oh, Mr. Copeland!" someone hailed from nearby.

He glanced up to see Grace Crabtree heading toward him, perched on her monstrosity of a bicycling apparatus. She saw him looking and hailed him again. The gesture didn't even make her bicycle wobble. 'Twas impressive—there were grown men in town who didn't dare ride that newfangled invention.

Politely Marcus took off his hat. He waited for Miss Crabtree to pedal to him across the rutted dirt road, then come to a stop. She did, jauntily jumping down to stand beside her unconventional transportation.

"I'm so glad I've found you this way," she said, an uncharacteristic smile on her face. Unlike most women, she did not so much as straighten her bicycling costume, but allowed the garment to flutter in the breeze. "I've been meaning to thank you."

"Thank me?"

"For the lumber and supplies, of course," Grace said. "When Molly told me you'd donated them to the cause, I could hardly credit it. Frankly, I hadn't pictured you as part of the women's suffrage movement. You don't seem terribly liberal minded to me. But the proof is in the pudding, as they say. And Molly assured me—"

"Lumber and supplies?"

"Yes. The things you donated this afternoon? Brought over by four burly men from your mill?" She looked at him as though he were addled. But then, perhaps suffragettes like Grace Crabtree looked at all men that way. "They will be used, as you suggested, to construct a *wonderful* platform for use by our women's rights speakers at the Chautauqua next month."

"Your speakers? As *I* suggested?"

"Of course. Naturally, we'll feature your name prominently in the program." Again Grace examined him with that starchy, skeptical expression of hers. "All supporters of our cause receive the proper recognition."

"Supporters."

"Yes. That's what I said." She peered closer. "Are you quite all right, Mr. Copeland? You look unwell."

"I'm fine," he gritted out. So *that's* where his supplies had got off to. To benefit a bunch of radical social equality activists. Activists who doubtlessly didn't approve of men like him. When he got ahold of Molly—

"You seem to have a propensity toward repeating things." Grace peered at him. "I find myself rethinking my plans to have you make the opening remarks at our portion of the Chautauqua."

"I have plenty to say, Miss Crabtree," Marcus assured her. Jaw locked, he surveyed the bakeshop, home of the deceptively good-natured Molly the Meddler. "I merely require your sister's presence in which to say most of it."

"Most of it?"

"The most dastardly parts." He tugged on his hat and tipped it to Grace with a gentlemanly gesture. "If you will excuse me, I believe she and I have an overdue appointment."

Chapter Eight

After a brief but exceedingly aggravated stroll, Marcus arrived at his house on the outskirts of town. He stomped toward the porch steps, keeping his gaze alert for signs of his erstwhile baking tutor. She should be here. A glance at his pocket watch told him it was already past six o'clock.

There was no sign of her, though. In the deepening dusk of a September evening, the only movement came from the trees leaning in the wind. The only spot of brightness came not from Molly's characteristically vivid clothes, but from a lantern burning inside his house.

Puzzled, Marcus hurried onward. Dry leaves and browned pine needles crackled underfoot. He never left a lantern lit, and he always kept his doors locked. Growing up the way he had had taught him the foolhardiness of doing otherwise.

He slipped his key from his pocket as he thundered up the steps. His hand reached the doorknob.

Marcus worked the key, ready to hurl himself inside and discover the source of that disturbing lantern's glow. He *knew* he hadn't lit it. Doing so would have been unwise in the extreme, everything but a plea to have his hard-earned possessions taken by fire. Even if he had lit the lamp, he knew it would have consumed all its coal oil by now. That didn't explain why it still burned.

His key didn't work. Staring dumbfounded at it, Marcus tried again. Once more, the sturdy lock refused to budge.

He scowled at the door. He jiggled the knob. He peered at his key and double-checked to see that it was the correct one. It was. Confounded, Marcus put his hands on his hips and considered the situation.

There was nothing for it. His lock was not working.

Five minutes later, Marcus gritted his teeth and measured the weight of the rock in his hand. He surveyed the window glass in front of him. Destroying it on purpose made him feel sick at heart, but there was no help for it. He'd deliberately constructed his house with locks on all the doors and windows.

He set his jaw, checked to be sure his arm and hand were still protected by his wrapped suit coat, then angled his body away from the window. Finally, sighting one particular pane, he bashed the glass.

It shattered with an insignificant-sounding tinkle,

sending two pieces of expensive window glass falling. Grumbling, Marcus reached inside and released the lock, then slid the window sash upward. He unwrapped his suit coat and threw it inside.

"Having a bit of trouble?" someone asked from nearby.

With his hands poised to boost himself inside, Marcus paused. He glanced over his shoulder at the tanner, who was passing by on his way home from his shop. Marcus could not believe he'd just been spotted trying to invade his own home, like a burglar.

"I'll need to fix this window," he said with deliberate casualness, nodding toward the shattered glass as though that were the extent of the problem. "That's all."

The tanner grunted in understanding. "I'll give ya' a couple of rifle cozies to keep out the draft till the window glass comes in," he offered. "You could stuff 'em right there in the broken spot."

"I might do that."

A few minutes later, after some shared grumbling about the matchmaker, the tanner headed on his way. Marcus fixed his gaze on the window, spread his hands along its sill and boosted himself inside.

He landed near his suit coat—and at a woman's feet. Befuddled, he gazed past her buttoned shoes, up the length of her bright, flowery skirts, all the way to the leather-bound book in her hand and the aghast expression on her face.

Molly.

"Marcus! What are you doing?"

"Coming home. I live here. Remember?"

"And *what* have you done to your window?" She stared past him at the sprinkling of glass that remained on the floorboards. "When I heard the glass break, I thought for certain you were a burglar. You frightened me half to death! It's taken me this long just to find a suitable weapon."

Earnestly she gestured with it.

"You thought to defend yourself with a book? Did you plan to read a bedtime story and lull the thief to sleep?"

She shook her head. "It was either this or your bottle of hair pomade. I already had this in hand. I reasoned it would be less likely to do permanent damage to the robber."

He frowned at her. "Now you're casting aspersions upon my choice of grooming products?"

"Well…your pomade does smell very strongly of bay rum."

"I only apply it on special occasions," he said with dignity.

Preparing to get up, he grabbed his suit coat from the floor. He debated putting it on, then tossed it onto a nearby chair instead. Interloper that she was,

Molly deserved no special attire. She would just have to cope with seeing him in all his masculine glory, shirtsleeves included.

Marcus got to his feet. Molly shuffled out of the way with a small cry. She *had* looked fairly shaken when he'd fallen into the room. Oddly enough, a part of him regretted having frightened her. The rest of him wondered what the hell she'd been doing there in the first place.

Molly grabbed his arm as though to steady him. "Are you all right? That was quite a thud you made, you know."

Squinting, Marcus shook his head. This was beyond strange. Surely he was imagining this. Molly, here? In his home? Without him? She looked cozy and secure there, he noticed, now that the immediate danger had passed.

Molly behaved as though her presence there were utterly natural. Expected, even. Limned by the lamplight behind her, she bustled about his home, seeming altogether too comfortable for his peace of mind. Her air of contentment went far beyond what he would have expected of a tutor meeting him for a baking lesson—even a tutor whom he'd kissed.

"Have you taken up residence here?" he asked suspiciously. "Has your family finally gotten fed up and forced you out?"

"Of course not." Molly waved away his questions. "Why did you break your window?" she asked again.

"The lock on my front door was broken. I—" Something in her expression made him stop. Marcus examined her, growing increasingly certain she'd had a hand in his faulty door lock somehow. "I had to break the window to unlock it and get in."

"Why didn't you just knock?"

"Knock?"

"You were supposed to knock on the door!" she wailed. "That's why I lit the lamp!" Looking distressed, Molly set aside the book. She knelt and began picking up glass shards with careful gestures, bundling them in her apron. "So you would see it and know someone was here. So you would know to knock. You've ruined my surprise!"

"Locking a man out of his house is a passing strange way to surprise him."

"Well, it wasn't a surprise *exactly*." More glass fragments tinkled as they struck the small pile in her apron. "It was more of a…lesson. Yes, a lesson. When the locksmith came to my shop late this afternoon, I brought him out here—"

"And had *my* locks changed?"

"You deserved it! For being so high-handed, and for *carrying* me to town today. I won't be treated that way."

She lurched to her feet, cradling her glass-filled apron. She reached behind herself to untie the garment.

He watched her for a moment, flabbergasted. Molly had actually locked him out of his own home to teach him a lesson. Then she'd cleaned up the mess he'd made while breaking in, appearing fairly contrite all the while. Was there no end to the contradictions in her?

Molly twisted, struggling to remove her apron without dropping the glass she'd gathered.

Marcus relented. "You're going to hurt yourself with that," he said gruffly.

It appeared there were contradictions within him, too. With efficient movements, he bundled the glass-filled fabric in his hands. He waited as Molly finished untying her apron strings. Then he set the whole mess on a side table.

"Thank you," she said, head held high.

Her expression mulish, Molly picked up her book and flounced to a neighboring chair. She buried her nose in the leather-bound volume, for all appearances devoutly interested in it.

"Is that all? A mere 'thank you'?" he asked, following. He stopped near her chair and glowered. "What about *I'm sorry?* What about *It's a shame about your window?* What about *Here is your new key?*"

She turned a page, not looking up. "I haven't decided whether or not I'm giving you the key. It may suit my fancy to let you in and out at my leisure."

Marcus gaped. He could hardly believe this. First, Molly had had the audacity to send his building supplies to the aid of several militant suffragettes. Next she'd waylaid his locksmith and influenced the man to change Marcus's locks—a hindrance Marcus himself had paid for in advance. Now she dared to flaunt her trespassing presence in his home as though she belonged there *and* make threats to him?

Polite threats, to be sure. But still…

"You will give me my key."

Molly shrugged, absorbed in her book.

"Don't make me search your person for it."

Her fingers clenched on the corners of the page, betraying a bit of nervousness. But all she said was, "I would very much like to see you try. My corset is quite as impenetrable as a bank safe, and comes equipped with much wilier personnel."

"Meaning you."

"Naturally."

Marcus shook his head. She was deluded, of course. She could not keep a thing from him. On the verge of revealing his experience in dealing with ladies' undergarments—and their willing removal—though, he squinted.

"Is that my ledger in your hand?"

Airily Molly nodded. "I thought I might teach myself proper bookkeeping practices, with your accounts as an example. I must say, it's been quite enlightening so far."

"Has it?" He snatched the ledger from her overly studious grasp, then slammed it down on a table. "You, Miss Crabtree, need to learn that you cannot accomplish everything."

"I fail to see why not. If I try hard enough."

"Nor can you *do* everything you wish to."

"I can, and I will."

"Not with me, you won't," Marcus said. "I'd begun to think you actually had reasons for the things you do. But now I'm not so sure."

"You carried me to town. It was humiliating."

Beset with aggravation, Marcus looked away. Molly had lit a blaze in the fireplace, too, he noticed. The crackling warmth gave the place a coziness it typically lacked when he arrived. What would it be like, some perverse part of him wondered, to come home to such warmth every day?

"Very well." He clenched his jaw. "I'm sorry."

"Oh, Marcus!" To his shock, Molly leapt up from her chair and flung her arms around his neck, hugging him. "That was all I wanted to hear. Thank you."

He would rather have pretended never to have uttered the phrase. Especially if she meant to fuss over it so much.

He shrugged. "That fire needs a bigger log. It will burn too quickly."

She didn't so much as glance at the fireplace. "I'm sorry, too. About your window. To make up for it, I've decided to agree to your plan."

For a moment, Marcus thought she meant his plan to uncover the matchmaker. He went rigid with expectation.

She stepped away from him, with the air of someone about to say something very important.

"You may," she announced magnanimously, "do whatever work you wish on my bakeshop." Spreading her arms wide, she beamed up at him. "You have my permission."

Disappointment pricked him. He'd have to wait longer for his next inquiry into the matchmaker's identity, unless he could lead her to that conversation this evening.

"Your permission? You sound as though I should be grateful to have it," Marcus said, feeling a helpless grin rise to his face. She was simply too audacious to be borne. Her vigor must have worn him down. "That's quite a remarkable trick, to make a man feel lucky for the privilege of laboring on your behalf."

Molly shifted one shoulder dismissively, then

hugged him again. "Let's carry on with your cooking lessons, shall we? Tonight we will be improvising a dinner. Come along!"

Marcus did. Nothing good could come of this 'improvising.' Not while Molly Crabtree headed the task. But if he was lucky—and very skilled—perhaps he could trade her homey intrusion for a matchmaker interrogation, and have something productive to show for this night after all.

Followed by Marcus, Molly hurried into her unwilling pupil's kitchen, her mind on the task at hand. Now that she'd finished with her other business of the day—showing Marcus that Molly Crabtree was *not* a woman to be trifled with—she was ready to settle into some peaceful cooking and baking.

"Today I intend to teach you how to avoid that slop they serve at Murphy's saloon—" she began.

"Hey!"

"—and prepare something delicious for yourself with whatever you have on hand. Even something so simple as griddle cakes or fried eggs can make a passable dinner, so long as they're prepared with care." Molly surveyed the supplies she'd brought, then faced the pantry at the kitchen's far corner. "First, let's see what you have available."

"I'd think you would already know that," Marcus

remarked, "since you've investigated my hair pomade and scoured my ledgers. Who knows what else you've uncovered?"

"I am not a snoop."

"Hmm. Merely curious?"

"No. Merely dedicated to proving my point." At the pantry, Molly glanced over her shoulder. She delivered her best smile. "Since I've already done that, we can move on."

Marcus grumbled, then leaned his shoulder against the wall. He watched her with lazy fortitude.

Cheerfully Molly opened the pantry doors. Then she stopped in surprise.

Row upon row of store-bought goods stared back at her. Tinned peaches, beans, Arbuckle's coffee. Cones of sugar, packages of jerky, crackers and apples. Goods were stacked upon one another on foot-and-a-half deep shelves, and below them three unopened barrels of additional foodstuffs waited.

This was not a pantry, Molly thought in astonishment. This was a storehouse—a storehouse befitting the most organized grocer or well-equipped military fort. Marcus's food stores rivaled those of Camp Verde, she was sure. They were that comprehensive.

Mystified, she asked, "Are you…expecting company soon?"

"No."

"Did you strike a special bargain with the mercantile?"

"No." He leaned away from the wall, gazing into the pantry along with her. "Why do you ask?"

Molly couldn't believe he could not see the reason for himself. Again she scanned the overflowing shelves. "This is a great deal of food for one person."

He seemed unconcerned. "It will keep. I only stock items the grocer told me will last in storage for a long time."

"But...it would take you a year to go through this." She looked at him. "At the very least."

Beside her, Marcus examined the pantry's contents. A shadow passed over his face—the remembrance of...something Molly couldn't decipher. Whatever it was, the memory troubled him, though. She could tell, and found herself concerned for him.

How that could be, she didn't know. A mere few kisses hadn't knit them together so closely as that, that she should feel a bit of his pain for her own. All the same, Molly's heart stirred with sympathy, and a deeper form of affection, too.

Before she could speak, he snatched two tins.

"Beans for tonight, I'd say."

After kicking the door closed, Marcus carried the beans to the worktable. By the time Molly overcame her surprise at his rough manner, he'd already set to opening them.

"I expected you to have coffee on hand in your bachelor's kitchen," she said as she followed, trying to lighten things between them. "Or maybe some crackers. Otherwise, I thought your shelves might be empty. After all, you do dine at the saloon fairly often."

He worked at the second tin. "I like keeping the pantry stocked."

Molly examined his broad back, his shoulders, his hands working at the task of opening the beans. She studied his profile. Although a hank of hair had fallen over his forehead, she could still see quite clearly the frown on his face. She didn't think it owed itself to the difficulty of his task.

She moved nearer. "Why?"

"Why what?"

"Why do you like keeping your pantry stocked?"

His hands stilled for the barest instant.

"You can tell me," Molly prompted. "Things are different between us now. We've shared a kiss. More than one." At that, she felt her cheeks heat but made herself forge onward. "And before that, we were fast becoming friends. Tell me, Marcus. What is this about?"

He put down the can opener, with its straight blade

and fixed handle. "I am not a man who confides in other people," he said.

"Neither am I."

A faint smile. "No, you seem all woman to me."

"I mean, I don't share confidences easily. Just like you. Who better, then, to keep your secret?"

"Now you've decided to make sense? Ah, Molly. I can't keep up."

"You are teasing me again. Fine." Hurt, Molly picked up the can opener herself, intending to go to work. "Just remember that I was only trying to help."

"I'm not teasing you." Marcus lay a hand on his heart and faced her. "I'm not. It's only...Lord, Molly! Why do you demand so much of me?"

She blinked. "Demand?"

"Conversation. Confidences. Admission to my house, my ledgers *and* my business." He flung his hands about as he spoke, then raked a hand through his hair, looking frustrated. He glanced away. "This is *not* what I agreed to."

She'd understood him, all the way to... "Agreed to?"

Marcus froze. Something shifted in his expression, some realization he clearly didn't want to share. He cocked his head. "When...I agreed to this bargain between us."

Molly peered at him.

"This is difficult for me," he confessed. He took the opener from her hand and cut off the second tin's lid with a few savage motions. "Being with you…is not what I expected."

"You are not what I expected either. Until we'd been together, I'd thought you were an autocratic, penny-pinching businessman with no regard for entrepreneurial women."

"And now?"

"Now I think you're an autocratic, *secretive,* penny-pinching businessman with no regard for entrepreneurial women."

She delivered her pronouncement cheerfully, with all the matter-of-fact acceptance it deserved. "I've no illusions about you, Marcus. Not even your kiss has changed that."

He gazed at her thoughtfully. "I'll have to try it again. The first one didn't take."

"The first few, you mean."

"As you wish. You clearly need more." Pretending determination, he stepped closer. "Let's start now."

Molly held her ground and smiled up at him. He was trying to divert her from the answer she sought. For the moment, she'd let him think he had.

"I'm forced to amend my opinion," she said lightly. "For I'll admit, you *are* generous with one thing— your kisses."

"With you?" Marcus smoothed an errant strand of

hair from her forehead. He tucked it behind her ear, where it could join her chignon. "I could be nothing but generous."

Molly almost sighed. His words touched her, nearly as much as the fond look he paired with them. If she weren't careful, Marcus would send her off course altogether. Reminding herself where her curiosity lay, she glanced at the pantry. *Ask him again,* she ordered herself.

What emerged was, "Oh, are you different with other women, then?"

No, no, no. Where had her single-mindedness gone? When Marcus was around, Molly seemed to lose her ability to concentrate altogether. All she wanted was him, studying her as though she were special. Touching her as though she were rare. Smiling at her as though…*oh, dear.* As though she were quite obvious in her curiosity about how she compared with the other ladies he'd known.

Marcus shook his head. "There have been no other women. Not for some time."

Perhaps she could still salvage her pride. Molly waved her hand. "Not that it really matters to me—"

"There could be no other women for me," he went on doggedly, a knowing gleam in his eye. "Not so long as you are here. Not so long as you go on looking at me that way."

What way? She didn't know. But judging by the warm, faintly glowing sensation she felt in her heart, it was probably quite lovelorn and pathetic and needy.

Hastily Molly directed her gaze elsewhere. She didn't want to need anyone, least of all Marcus. She pressed her fingers to her cheeks, embarrassed to have been so open to him, especially while he remained so closed to her.

"What about your pantry?" she asked.

"Give in, Molly. I don't want to talk about it."

"You must," she demanded.

"Eat your dinner." He pushed something in her hand.

"But we haven't—" She realized what it was. A cold tin of beans, with a fork speared in the center like a candle in a birthday cake. Molly held it at arm's length. "I'm not eating this."

"It's good." He took a gigantic bite, chewing happily.

"It's cold. It's still in the *tin*. It lacks presentation, finesse and wholesomeness. It's the very opposite of all I'm trying to teach you."

"It's good," he repeated. "And it's quick. While you've been nattering on, I've been starving. All we need is some bread, and we'll be—"

As though something occurred to him, Marcus

broke off, abruptly setting down his beans. He crossed the room, rummaged through the pockets of the suit coat he'd flung over a chair and returned. When next he offered something to her, it was a napkin-wrapped bundle.

"Here you are, madam," he said, giving a teasing bow.

Curious, Molly plucked open the napkin with her fingertips. Inside it lay a piece of soft brown bread. Raising her eyebrows at him, she asked, "You carry bread in your pockets?"

"It's fresh," he assured her. "Baked in the kitchens of the Lorndorff Hotel just this morning."

That was beside the point. Couldn't he see how odd this was? It rivaled his pantry for sheer unexpectedness.

"We can share it," Marcus told her. He broke the bread in half and offered her the larger portion. As he did, he noticed that she'd put down her beans.

He seemed disappointed. "Try it. This meal is better hot, but it's passable when cold."

"If I do, will you tell me what I want to know?"

"Molly—"

"It's a fair trade. One reluctant deed for another."

"Eat first."

She regarded the tin of beans. "I don't think I can."

Marcus shrugged. He nudged his half of the bread closer to her. "You can have all of the bread, then. Never let it be said I'm not generous. In *all* things."

He waggled his eyebrows roguishly. His playfulness brought a smile to her face, despite her best intentions. Shaking her head, Molly picked up the bread with resignation. She began to eat. Marcus may have thwarted her for now, but soon she'd uncover the story behind his pantry, and then she'd do whatever she could to help him overcome it.

No matter what.

Chapter Nine

Marcus stood inside Daniel McCabe's blacksmith shop, where the fires burned hot and the smell of steel hung sharp in the air. He took off his shirt coat, then loosened his collar.

In rolled-up shirtsleeves, Daniel hefted his hammer. He'd been fashioning sleigh runners for the coming winter when Marcus had arrived. One of the graceful implements waited on the workbench before him. Outside the shop, wagons and riders passed by, adding to the bustle of town.

"How do you fare with Sarah Crabtree?" Marcus asked. "Has she let slip anything about the matchmaker?"

"No. And Jack Murphy says the same about her sister, Grace." Daniel abandoned his hammer to wipe the sweat from his face, then tossed down the cloth he'd used. "I'd thought for sure we'd have something by now."

"The men's club is getting impatient," Marcus

agreed, disappointed not to hear more encouraging news. Still he couldn't blame Daniel and Jack for making as little progress as he himself had. "But those Crabtree women are damnably closemouthed."

"That's for certain. Except for Molly." Daniel shook his head. "Does she ever stop yapping?"

When I kiss her, she does, Marcus thought. Kissing, long and often, was the secret to a peaceable existence with Molly, he'd decided. If he'd been kissing her, she'd never have been able to give away his supplies and change his locks yesterday.

Clearly he needed to be more diligent about kissing Molly. It was for the common good, after all.

He stifled a smile. "Occasionally she's quiet."

Daniel grunted. "Thank God. You drew the shortest straw of all of us, that's for certain."

"Sarah's no challenge for you, then?"

"Sarah?" For a moment, Daniel's gaze turned faraway. Something akin to befuddlement passed over his face, then vanished. He grasped his hammer again. "Hell, I've known Sarah since we were this high." Daniel held his hammer at waist height. "Since we were in the schoolhouse together. There never was a better girl for copying answers from. She used to tilt her slate toward me so I could see."

"Cordial of her."

Without a trace of irony, Daniel agreed. "Other girls did the same thing. But Sarah was always smart enough to have the *right* answers. She's no trouble for me. No woman is."

Despite his boast, something Marcus had glimpsed in Daniel's expression niggled at him. He didn't believe the blacksmith. Had Sarah Crabtree knocked Daniel as far off the mark as Molly had Marcus? If so, that wouldn't bode well for their matchmaker search.

"She's been a help with my nephew," Daniel went on, absently squinting at the work arrayed before him. "He's been in my care since my sister sent him to me."

Marcus nodded. He remembered the child's arrival on the train, recalled there being a measure of gossip in town about the blacksmith's responsibility for him.

Some said Daniel was not the boy's uncle, but his father in secret. They said that Daniel had gotten a woman with child, a woman his sister had taken pity on and sheltered at her home in the East to avoid a scandal. Since Marcus didn't have much use for idle chitchat, he didn't know any more than that.

He returned to the matter at hand. "Then all we know," Marcus mused, "is that the matchmaker's personal advertisements are delivered to the *Pioneer Press* via courier. Nothing else."

"Right. And nobody knows who the courier is."

"Nobody's ever seen him."

"Or her."

Marcus made a thoughtful sound. "Perhaps chasing the daughters is the wrong tactic, here. Perhaps Adam Crabtree holds the key to who is placing those advertisements."

Daniel snorted. "Good luck cozying up to him. He's a mite bonier and uglier than his daughters. His wife might have a say in your plans, too."

The blacksmith's overly innocent expression stared blandly back at Marcus. Rolling his eyes, Marcus made to smack the smirk from his face. Quick for a man of his size, Daniel sidestepped the movement. He chose a few more lengths of steel, chuckling with amusement.

"But if you truly want to find the matchmaker," he said as he tromped across the shop with the steel in his arms, "then I'll not stop you. Even if it is with Adam Crabtree."

Daniel shuddered with mock horror. Always a prankster, he was. Marcus had learned that much during his time in Morrow Creek. It was one of the reasons he liked the muscle-bound, plainspoken blacksmith.

"There are other ways to extract a secret, McCabe," Marcus told him, playing along, "aside from seduction."

"Truly?" Daniel pretended astonishment. "You should have told me that from the first. If not for the seduction involved, I'd never have taken on this task of finding the matchmaker."

He shook his head, pretending chagrin. Marcus didn't believe it. McCabe might be burly, bull headed and a little too quick to smile at a pretty lady—or a passel of them—but he was a good man at heart. He'd taken on the matchmaker search, Marcus didn't doubt, for reasons aside from seduction.

"After Sarah, I intend to work my way through a few more likely ladies," Daniel offered with a wolfish grin. "Just in case the matchmaker proves hard to pin down."

"With you on the search? Hardly."

They both grinned, co-conspirators on the hunt for the meddlesome woman who'd bedeviled the bachelors for months. Had Jack Murphy been there, they'd have been a trio of dedicated males, determined to reclaim the peace they deserved.

A few minutes passed, during which Marcus contemplated the matchmaker search and Daniel finished forming the sleigh runner he'd been fashioning. The blacksmith started in on a smaller piece of steel, holding it in the fire with long-handled tongs until it glowed sunset-red. He transferred it to his work area, then pounded it with his hammer.

Between clangs of metal on metal, Marcus announced, "It will have to be you or Jack Murphy to find the matchmaker. Molly Crabtree is not her. I'm sure of it."

He was even more sure he wanted no more of questioning her. No more of deceiving her. If he were wise, Marcus knew, he'd want away from her altogether. But since that wasn't quite true...

Daniel quit hammering. Stared at him. "Aw, Lord. Not you, too, Copeland!"

"What?"

"Another damned victim of the matchmaker." Shaking his head in obvious disgust, Daniel thrust the piece he'd pounded into a water barrel to cool it. "She's snared herself another bachelor. I can hardly believe it. You'll be fitted for a wedding suit by the end of next week. Mark my words."

"Not me," Marcus disagreed. He had no intention of letting things between Molly and him proceed beyond the dalliance she'd mentioned. It didn't seem right to tell Daniel as much, though. "Especially not with Molly Crabtree. I want a woman who's sweet. Biddable. *At home*. Molly is none of those things."

"Oh, Molly's sweet, all right." Grinning, Daniel pantomimed cradling a pair of enormous bosoms in front of his chest. "Or haven't you noticed?"

Hot with fury, Marcus had him by the throat in an instant. "I ought to flatten you for that," he growled. "If you weren't my friend—"

"Easy, Copeland." Daniel spread both big arms

wide in surrender, watching Marcus closely. "It was only a jest."

Marcus jerked the blacksmith's collar in a final, warning tug. He released him. Stepping away, Marcus gave a dismissive wave. "It was a bad jest. I'm off to Murphy's saloon."

"Need a drink already?" Daniel asked, laughter in his voice. "Being hog-tied and turned sappy-headed with *love* bringing you low?"

"You're wrong." Daniel could see nothing in him, Marcus was sure. There *was* nothing in him, nothing changed because of the matchmaker *or* Molly. The blacksmith was guessing. Marcus held up a hand in farewell. "Good luck with Sarah."

"Good luck yourself, with Molly!" Daniel's chuckle followed him out the doors. So did his parting words. "Not sweet on her, eh? For a man who doesn't care, you're damned quick to defend her!"

At half past noon, Jack Murphy's saloon was dim, quiet and mostly bereft of patrons, save those few determined drinkers who downed whiskey at sunrise and sunset alike. Marcus walked inside with purpose, pausing only long enough to let his eyes adjust to the gloom.

Behind the long, intricately carved bar, Jack greeted him with a nod. He slapped a dry cleaning cloth atop something lying opened before him—a book, Marcus realized in surprise—and angled his head expectantly.

"What can I get you, Copeland?"

Delivered in the man's faint Irish brogue, Marcus's name sounded foreign to his ears. As he stepped up to the bar, Marcus took a minute to size up Jack Murphy. He didn't know the man well. No one did. A stranger to Morrow Creek come even later than Marcus had, Jack was both jovial and solitary. He refused to speak of himself. Under ordinary circumstances, he didn't speak of much at all.

Marcus reasoned that fact in itself made them of like mind. He decided he respected the man.

"Whiskey." Marcus tossed some currency onto the bar. He watched as Jack filled a glass partway, then set it in front of him. Their gazes met.

"I never see you here, Copeland, except for the men's club meetings," Jack said, spreading his palms along the bar. "I guess you're here about the matchmaker."

Marcus nodded. "Any luck with Grace Crabtree?"

Jack shot a disgruntled look at the ceiling of his saloon. "That hellion on a bicycle? Hell, no. Not unless you're wondering if I've had any luck with hosting a dozen ladies' clubs in my upstairs rooms every week. Did you know Grace Crabtree had a half lease on this building?"

"The upstairs portion?" Marcus guessed.

"The part I don't live in," Jack agreed. A noise sounded overhead. He shook his head. "The part I'd as soon put to use for boardinghouse rooms, if only the bullheaded Miss Crabtree would give over her portion. I've offered to buy it from her. So far, no amount of coin has been enough."

"She must have another reason for keeping it."

Jack grunted an affirmative. "Course. She wants to use it to drive me mad. That much is plain."

A hymn, sung by several female voices and accompanied by the sound of a piano, drifted downstairs. Grabbing the whiskey he'd poured for Marcus, Jack Murphy took a slug. He winced at the liquor's tang, or at the banged-out rendition of "Amazing Grace" filling his saloon. Marcus couldn't tell which.

He grinned. "There's something downright aggravating about those Crabtree women. But the minute you realize it—"

"—they go and do something nice," Jack finished, nodding in recognition. "Ah, I know it. I can't puzzle it out."

They shook their heads at each other, mystified at the vagaries of women—Crabtree women, in particular.

"Daniel McCabe says Sarah is no trouble at all to him."

"He's lying."

"That, or deluded," Marcus agreed, holding his

whiskey to the light. He took a sip. "Although he does seem to have uncommon luck with women. There's no denying it."

Jack scoffed. "There's no challenge to having luck with women. The challenge is getting rid of them."

He shot another disgruntled look at his saloon's ceiling. Now, stomping feet could be heard treading across the second story's floorboards.

"I'd say Grace Crabtree would be a mite less popular for hosting those meetings of hers if she were revealed as the matchmaker," Marcus mused. "Uncovering her secret could be the key to those boardinghouse rooms you want."

"What makes you think it's not Molly who's the matchmaker?"

"I know she's not. Plain as that."

Jack peered at him. Whatever he saw made him shake his head. "Aw, hell and brimstone, Copeland. The matchmaker's got you, too. McCabe warned me this would happen."

"I haven't—"

"You were the weakest, Daniel said. The one most likely to throw over the search for the sake of *true love*." Jack made a face. "Couldn't you have held out a little longer?"

"I have not succumbed."

"You have, if you're ready to abandon the search."

Faced with Jack's obvious disgust—and Daniel's cockamamie opinions on the subject of his susceptibility to the matchmaker—Marcus knew he wouldn't be able to give up the search yet. No matter that he thought Molly could not be the meddler they sought. He refused to give the other men in town the satisfaction of believing Marcus Copeland was a quitter.

Or worse, a lovesick fool.

Marcus pounded back the remainder of his whiskey in one swallow. "I'll find her," he grumbled. "Don't think twice about that."

"You might want to see this, then." Looking to the sides as though searching out eavesdroppers, Jack slipped something from his vest. "I found it in Grace's skirt pocket."

Eyebrows raised, Marcus examined the piece of paper Jack handed over. "What were you doing rifling through the lady's skirts?"

"Not what you think. And I nearly earned a black eye in the process. Ah, hell. Just read the damned thing."

Marcus did. He could scarce believe what he read. "This sounds like one of the matchmaker's personal advertisements."

"Written in the matchmaker's own hand, too, I'd

say," Jack pointed out. "If we can match up this writing, we'll have her."

They shared an eager glance. Finally, a break-
through!

Marcus turned over the scrap of paper. On the back
side was scribed the name of Adam Crabtree's newspaper, the *Pioneer Press*. "What was Grace doing
with this? Is she the courier? Or the matchmaker
herself?"

"I don't know," Jack confessed. "I've never seen
her handwriting. And who can keep up with her, to
ken exactly where she goes in a day? But it's the best
clue we've had so far."

Marcus examined it, the better to imprint the
memory of that distinctive curved script in his mind.
If he saw it again—say, in Molly's bakeshop ledgers—he intended to recognize it.

"Keep that safe," he instructed Jack. The saloon
keeper folded the matchmaker's note and tucked it
inside his vest again. "We'll need it for proof, when
we uncover the matchmaker once and for all."

Molly strolled alongside Sarah in the Morrow
Creek mercantile, watching as her sister fingered
fabrics, then oohed and aahed over tin soldiers. She
stopped at the row of jarred candies. They both
waited for the owner, Jedediah Hofer, to finish with
another customer.

"Candy, Sarah?" Molly asked, eyebrows raised. "I have to say, I'd like not to feel offended by this, but with my bakeshop only steps away, waiting to assuage your sweet tooth—"

"It's not for me." A secret smile lit Sarah's face. She instantly stifled it and assumed a blithe demeanor instead, raising her chin. "It's for Daniel's nephew."

Molly gawped. "You mean his illegitimate son? Sarah, how could you?"

Her sister gave a *pish-posh*. "Those ugly rumors aren't true. They're simply the meanderings of small minds and underutilized intellects."

"Oh, Sarah. You're usually so sensible, but this—"

"Is sensible as well. The boy needs a little kindness."

"Then let his 'uncle' be the one to give it," Molly urged in a hoarse whisper, leaning close to keep their conversation private. She touched her sister's sleeve, worried for Sarah's well-being. "You're being far too thoughtful. Are *always* far too thoughtful. Daniel will take advantage of you."

"Nonsense. You sound as hard-hearted as Grace."

For once, Molly didn't mind being compared with her straitlaced older sister. If it kept soft-as-goose-down Sarah safe and happy, then she would be as hard-hearted as necessary.

Another thought occurred to her. "This is why you've been examining playthings today!" she said, remembering the tin soldiers. "Have you already bought some of them as gifts for this boy?"

Sarah flushed guiltily. "He hadn't many when he arrived on the train…" she began, her voice quiet with sympathy.

Molly wanted to shake her. Her own weakness might be a tendency toward flights of fancy, but Sarah's was a propensity for performing unreasonable acts of kindness, sometimes to her own detriment. In the hands of a rogue like the burly blacksmith, who knew what she might be persuaded to do?

Before Molly could begin to find out, the shopkeeper arrived. Sarah turned her back to her sister—not without a small measure of relief, Molly thought. After purchasing several pieces of striped hard candy, Sarah carried her sack of sweets to the street.

Molly pursued her. "Don't let Daniel McCabe do this to you!" she implored. "I know he has a reputation for being charming, but to ask you to take care of this boy is—"

"I am managing this perfectly well, Molly."

"But—"

"Enough."

"Sarah—"

Her sister stopped on the boardwalk, paying no mind to the townsfolk strolling alongside her and the wagons and riders passing on the street. Molly nearly collided with her.

"I am your older sister!" Sarah folded her arms, crumpling her paper sack. Her heated gaze could have melted the goodies then and there, had she directed it toward them. "Have you no respect for my judgment at all?"

Taken aback, Molly blinked. Good-natured Sarah *never* gave in to outbursts like this. What had possessed her, that she would now?

"Of—of course I respect you," Molly said. She reached out to uncrumple the candy sack—a peace offering, of sorts. "In fact, that's why I sought you out today. I need some advice."

"Well, you shouldn't have come to me for it, now should you? I might not have enough backbone to voice my own opinion."

"Sarah, I'm sorry. Truly. I didn't mean to hurt your feelings."

Suspiciously her sister examined her. Then she relented. "Very well. You're forgiven. What is your dilemma?"

"It's Marcus." Molly blew out a gusty sigh as they began strolling again. She shook her head, remembering the moment she'd opened his pantry door to discover the foodstuffs inside. She worried about him. "He has a secret. Something that deeply bothers him. Yet he won't tell me what it is so I can help him with it."

"Perhaps it's something you can't help him with."

"Of course I could help him! If only I knew what it was."

Sarah shrugged. "When I need to uncover a secret in my schoolroom, I practice repetition. Gentle inquiries, made again and again, tend to unravel even the most tightly held secrets."

"Truly?"

"Distraction can be useful, too. If I induce my students to sing a lesson, for instance, they're sometimes unaware that they're also learning."

"Let me guess. They're too engrossed in singing as loudly as possible?"

"The boys are," Sarah agreed. "The girls are quieter. Also, the promise of a reward helps. My students will do almost anything for a sweet, a scrap of ribbon, the privilege of sitting near the woodstove."

"But they're children," Molly protested. "Marcus is a *man*."

"In my experience, men are simply larger boys."

"Hmm. Interesting notion."

Molly considered what Sarah had advised. Certainly she could keep after Marcus for the answer she sought—she'd intended to do that anyway. Distracting him was possible, and might even prove entertaining. She could probably devise some sort of reward, as well.

Perhaps…a kiss? That would reward *her,* also.

Her belly fluttered at the thought. No matter how

high-handed he was at times, Marcus was surely a magnificent kisser. She probably oughtn't to like that quality in him so well, but she did. His sure touch, his gentle words, his heated looks…

Sarah interrupted her reverie. "Is Marcus still pestering you for the matchmaker's secret? Have you revealed it yet?"

"'Yet?' You say that as though my downfall is inevitable."

Her sister eyed her meaningfully.

"No! Of course I haven't revealed it yet. I don't mean to, either." Disgruntled, Molly picked up the pace. She lifted her skirts above the dusty boardwalk, shaking her head. "If all three of us hadn't agreed *not* to reveal the matchmaker's identity, this scheme could never have worked. I know that as well as you do."

"Well, be sure that you remember it," Sarah cautioned. "Sometimes, a man can have persuasive powers. Powers we're not even prepared to be on guard against."

"That sounds like the voice of experience." Molly gave her sister an inquiring look. "Has Daniel persuaded you to do more than look after his 'nephew'?"

Sarah's expression turned guarded. An instant later, she pointed to a nearby shop sign that swung in the breeze. "Look! I believe the book depot has changed its hours of business. We'd better stop by before they close."

Molly looked. "Sarah, it's four hours till they close."

"But first, some sweets!"

Sarah opened her sack and extracted a striped candy. She shoved it into Molly's hand then hurried toward the book depot...leaving Molly to suspect that schoolchildren and men weren't the only ones her sister applied her *philosophies* to.

She was certain she'd just been distracted and rewarded, whether she wanted to be, or not.

"I have something for you," Molly told Marcus when next they met. She opened her reticule and pulled out the item she'd brought, then pressed it into his hand. "Go ahead. Open it."

"A letter?" Looking mystified, Marcus lifted his gaze from the folded paper she'd given him. His expressive brown eyes met hers. "Surely you can just talk to me, Molly. There's no need for formality between us."

She tilted her head. "Despite my unconventional upbringing, I do retain some vestiges of proper behavior. This bit of correspondence, for instance. And other things, as well. You'll just have to get used to them."

"With you, I'll need to get used to many things," he mused, turning over the paper. "I don't know why it didn't occur to me before."

"You don't?"

"No."

He smiled down at her. The warmth in his expression, the deep rumble of his voice, both made her tingle with excitement.

"I think you delight in confounding me," he told her. "In keeping me on my toes, unsure of what to expect."

Molly shrugged, secretly pleased. She gave a brief, careless wave. "The matchmaker says a little mystery in a woman is a good thing. So is a little propriety."

"The matchmaker says that, does she?"

"Indeed."

Breath held, Molly waited for Marcus to pounce upon her mention of the matchmaker, the way he always had before. She braced herself to deflect his inevitable questions.

Instead, Marcus examined her with clear suspicion and a goodly measure of trepidation, too, if she wasn't mistaken.

"Exactly how much proper behavior are you in favor of?" he asked. "How far does this hidden decorous streak of yours run?"

She smiled. "If you're asking whether or not I'll boot you out of my shop for being here alone with me after hours, the answer is not that far. I'm afraid my sense of ambition happens to outweigh my sense of correctness."

He looked relieved. Probably that meant he intended to kiss her again soon. Molly could scarcely wait. Filled with anticipation, she fluttered her hands over the stack of ledgers she and Marcus had agreed to work on together. Then she saw him watching her fidgety movements. She made herself clasp her hands serenely instead.

"Just open it," she prodded. "Go ahead."

He did. As he read, Molly had a perfect opportunity to watch him. Unobserved by Marcus, she savored the masculine angles of his face, the healthy, sun-warmed color of his skin, the jagged patterns his dark hair made as it fell over his forehead. Marcus truly was a wonderful-looking man. More and more, Molly suspected he had a fine heart to go along with his fine countenance, too.

"This is an invitation to dinner. At your parents' home."

"It's my home, too," Molly pointed out. She touched the hand he'd splayed across her bakeshop desk, daringly giving it a squeeze. "Say you'll come?"

"But...*dinner?*" He shook his head.

"What is the problem? This invitation is as correct as it could possibly be. People share meals every day."

"Families," Marcus agreed. "*Families* share meals."

His inexplicable reluctance confused her. "If you agree to join us, *you* will share a meal, also."

She'd reasoned that inviting Marcus to dinner at the Crabtree residence would serve several purposes. First, it would doubtlessly provide the distraction Sarah had recommended—hardly anything was more chaotic than an evening with her family. Second, it would offer rewards—Cook's good food and her own good sweets. Third, it would…

Well, it would give Molly an opportunity to see Marcus with her family. It was as simple as that. She was eager to discover how he would fit in, what her mother and father would think of him.

As their time together had lengthened and their camaraderie had grown, Molly had found herself envisioning a future with Marcus. A courtship, a togetherness and—dare she imagine it?—perhaps even a proposal of marriage. She didn't dare tell him as much yet. But if all went well with her family…

"Will your father be there?" he asked suddenly.

Her father? Perhaps Marcus felt as she did! Perhaps he meant to seize this opportunity as a means to discuss a potential future between them with her father! Buoyed by the notion, Molly nodded.

Was this, what she had with Marcus, the beginning of the "true love" her mama had encouraged all her daughters to wait for? In that moment, Molly believed it was. Even better, it had nothing at all to do with her bosoms.

Marcus truly was a prince among men.

"Yes, of course," she said, as coolly as she could. "My father will be there. So will my mother and my two sisters, Grace and Sarah."

"Grace and Sarah." Marcus's expression brightened still further. He smiled and lay his palm atop her hand, effectively sandwiching her hand between both of his. The resulting sensation was both cozy and intimate. "Yes, I'll come. I'd be delighted."

He squeezed her fingers fondly, then folded her invitation and tucked it away in his suit coat. As he did, Molly couldn't help beaming. Things were proceeding exactly as she'd hoped! A few evenings hence, she'd test Marcus's compatibility with her family *and* uncover his pantry secrets, both at the same time. Her plan couldn't have been more perfect.

At least it couldn't have been…until Marcus revealed what the rest of the night held in store for them.

"But first," he said, drawing forward the first of her ledgers, "we have bookkeeping to do!"

Ugh, Molly thought, frowning as she surveyed the job at hand. Bookkeeping most definitely *wasn't* perfect at all.

Chapter Ten

Marcus hadn't expected much when he'd first cracked open Molly's ledgers. In his experience, most people paid poor attention to detail, something strictly required for proper bookkeeping. Further, they added and subtracted carelessly, wrote in figures sloppily, and usually neglected to double-check their reckonings.

In Molly's case, though, Marcus simply didn't find those faults.

He found those faults—*and* many, many more.

It was beyond him how she'd managed to stay in business as long as she had. Her ledgers were haphazard, her inventories were nonexistent, and her business practices were nonsensical at best. For nigh on two hours, wreathed in the glow of a lantern in her bakeshop's back office and with Molly herself by his side, Marcus examined her accounts. In the end, he knew there was only one thing to do.

"We'll have to burn these," he said.

"What? No!"

"I'm afraid there's no other solution." He shook his head. "These accounts are hopelessly convoluted. Your best chance is to start anew."

"No!" Molly flung herself protectively across the opened ledgers. "I won't do it!"

She looked at him askance, as though he'd suggested they strip themselves naked and dance on the bakeshop's tables—an idea that held more merit, Marcus thought, than pointlessly examining her convoluted accounts. At least while dancing they would enjoy themselves. And while naked…well, he *knew* they would enjoy themselves.

Molly spoiled his reverie by shaking her head. "You simply haven't grasped my system yet, that's all. Be patient. You'll understand it eventually."

She patted his hand encouragingly, as though he were a simpleton. Marcus shook off her touch. He glared at her.

"I have never seen the like of this," he said, waving a hand to indicate her morass of ledgers. "Never in all my years in business."

She brightened. "My methods *are* unique," Molly agreed.

"That was not a compliment. Your 'system' consists of partial ledger entries and a few hasty attempts at inventory. Oh, and *these*. A few scraps of ribbon."

Marcus snatched a handful from the twin boxes

Molly had set out along with the ledgers. Scornfully, he let the colorful strips waft from his fingers to the desk, where they adorned the opened pages like lacy, satiny and polka-dotted snowflakes.

"Stop!" Molly shrieked. "Those are my profit-and-loss markers!"

She scrabbled among the scraps, hastily sorting them back into their boxes. Marcus watched, puzzled.

"They're your what?"

"My profit-and-loss markers." Molly stuffed the last few ribbon pieces into the right-hand box. "One box is for profitable days, days when paying customers come into the shop and purchase things. One box is for loss days, days when I have to give away baked goods to the railway workers before they go stale. This way, I can see at a glance how well I'm doing."

"Which box is which?"

"You can't tell?"

Marcus shook his head. This whole thing befuddled him.

"You really can't tell? It's so simple!"

He refrained from an unmanly urge to wipe the gloat from her face. "I—can't—tell."

"The one with the *pretty* ribbons is the profit box. See?"

He squinted at the boxes. Shook his head. "No."

"This one." As though he were kidding, Molly grinned and gave one box a little thump. The polka-dotted-and-green grosgrain ribbons inside fluttered. "This is the profit box."

"I see."

"I'm not sure you do." Thoughtfully she peered at him, chin in hand. "You're an intelligent man. I thought you'd be able to grasp my accounting system straightaway. I can see now that I've been remiss. I'll have to explain it to you."

He gritted his teeth. "I do not need accounting principles explained to me."

"Obviously, you do. Don't feel bad about it, though. My papa couldn't understand my methods, either. He was so embarrassed about it, he completely washed his hands of my business."

Marcus figured the man had simply gotten out while his sanity was still intact. But he only nodded.

"All right, then. First…"

Molly launched into a long-winded explanation of how she'd come to devise her system. It included several tangential musings about her reputation in Morrow Creek, her family's lack of faith in her business acumen, treatises she'd read on the world of commerce…and a digression he could have sworn dealt with her thwarted attempts at the age of sixteen to become a prize-winning glassblower. Marcus

listened, nodded occasionally and tried hard to com-
prehend it all.

"For instance," she said, sunny in her enthusiasm,
"most stores in town carry accounts for people. The
shopkeepers tally a record of purchases, and folks
pay for them when they can. But I figured, why do
all that extra bookkeeping? I simply issue my own
currency instead, and let people pay for their baked
goods with Molly Money."

Proudly, she snatched up a demonstrative handful of the stuff. Cut into rectangular pieces slightly
larger than typical currency, "Molly Money" was
inked with curlicue script, flowers, and its value,
then signed with a flourish by its namesake.

Lord help him. Marcus had been afraid of this ever
since encountering the stuff, shoved haphazardly into
a hatbox. "You do realize that's not *real* money…
don't you?"

She snorted, still explaining. "Townsfolk who need
it receive a Molly Money allowance each quarter.
Then, for all the months that follow, they can come
into my shop and buy as many of my special-recipe
cinnamon buns or whatever else they fancy as they
want. And *I* can avoid unnecessary bookkeeping."

Marcus canted his head toward the stack. "You do
realize you can't take that to the bank, don't you?"

"Don't be silly. Of course I don't take it to the bank."

"You merely allow your customers to buy baked

goods with pretend money. I see. That's *quite* an improvement." He covered his face with his hands, shaking his head.

She stopped him. Lowered both of his hands in her own. Gazed deeply into his eyes until she—apparently—felt certain she had his full attention.

"I'm not daft, Marcus. I'm inventive. It's not the same thing. Besides—" she paused, releasing him to examine a Molly Money note with tulips at its borders "—don't you think it's pretty?"

Marcus took in her cheery expression, her bright eyes, and knew he couldn't let her go on this way. "Tell that to your mortgage holder, when you try to make a payment with that stuff. He won't care how pretty it is. Molly—" He raised his hands to her delicate shoulders, resisting an urge to shake some sense into her. "You've got to listen to me. You need better accounting." *And a business sense to go with it.*

She gritted her teeth. "You don't understand. *I* don't use Molly Money. Only my customers do. They purchase it in advance, then spend it over the course of the next several months."

"Then you receive actual cash from them?"

Molly folded her arms. Gave him an exasperated look. "Didn't you so much as crack the lid of the cookie jar?"

"What?"

"The cookie jar. You didn't even open it, did you?"

She shook her head in dismay, reaching to drag the ceramic jar across the desk. The movement required her to stand partway. Leaning into the desk's edge squeezed her breath slightly, but she went on doggedly: "I have given you far too much credit. I can see that now. By any chance does Mr. Smith do your accounting at the lumber mill? Because with your lack of attention to detail—"

"I have plenty of attention to detail."

For instance, Marcus had noticed every intriguing detail of her feminine figure as she'd leaned next to him. But he'd also noticed how nonsensical her business methods were. It was those that he needed to concern himself with now. After seeing Molly's notions of business, he worried about her welfare.

"You realize, don't you, that your father won't be able to support you forever. To prepare for that day when—"

"If you pay attention to details as you say you do," Molly interrupted, "then I fail to see how you missed this." She removed the cookie jar's lid, then reached inside and withdrew something. Cash. Wads of it. Which she promptly waved in his face. "This is the result of my system, the same system *you* find so amusing."

He stared at it. "That is a great deal of money."

"That's because I haven't had to spend much of it on supplies yet. My regular customers buy their

Molly Money allowances in advance, remember?"
She gave him an exceedingly patient look as she returned the currency to its jar. "In effect, they are pre-
purchasing my baked goods, before I've so much as
beaten an egg or iced a cake. Do you understand?"

Marcus nodded. "You've devised a method of
removing most of your bakeshop's inventory risk."

"Is that what it's called? My, that sounds *much* more
impressive than anything I've come up with!"

She looked delighted. Marcus felt flummoxed.
Somehow, flighty Molly Crabtree had come up with
an original business plan that worked. He didn't understand how she'd done it, but she had.

Taken aback by the realization, he examined the
items on the desktop with new perspective. Perhaps
he'd been too hasty in dismissing Molly's methods.
Perhaps he *didn't* need to worry about her.

He chose a fancy pen and set of stationery. "What's
this?"

"I use that to write lists of supplies."

"Inventory maintenance materials. I see." Marcus
tapped a pretty volume of botanical prints. "This?"

"I store my recipes in it. I slip them between the
pages. It's nice to look at the illustrations when
I'm searching for a particular cake or sweet roll to
make."

"Why not just keep your recipes in their own
volume? Or in one of those little file boxes?"

"I told you," she said patiently, "it's nice to look at the illustrations."

"Fine." He couldn't help but grin. As filing systems went, hers was…unconventional. Still it appeared to work for her. Marcus reached next for a pair of glass jelly jars. One stood filled two-thirds to the brim with marbles; the other, larger jar jangled with a quantity rising about halfway. "What are these?"

Molly flushed. "They're my method for keeping track of how many folks in town have visited my bakeshop. I know it's silly of me, but I wanted to know. I found out from the courthouse clerk approximately how many people live in Morrow Creek— that's all the marbles put together. As each person stops by here or buys my goodies, I move them to that jar."

She nodded toward the one near his right hand. "The big jar," Marcus observed. "Optimistic of you."

With a shrug, Molly agreed. Despite her nonchalant pose, though, a bit of her customary determination showed through.

"I mean to fill it all the way to the top before I'm done," she said. "Your allowing me to sell my goodies at your lumber mill moved most of those marbles, that's for certain. I'll always be grateful to you for that."

Appreciation softened her face. She smiled and

squeezed his arm. "You don't know how much your help meant to me."

He hadn't at the time, Marcus agreed silently. But now he did. At the realization, he felt like the worst kind of cad for deceiving her. If Molly ever found out he'd been paying his workers to buy her baked goods, that they'd actually used them for shoe repairs and juggling practice and propping open doors with—well, Marcus just hoped like hell she never found out. It would hurt her too much.

He selected a basket of what looked like cigar-size strips of rolled tree bark. "I suppose you use this to account for receipts or some such?" Marcus asked. "Let me guess, the big pieces of bark represent large bills, and the small pieces stand in for small bills."

Molly rolled her eyes. *Don't be ridiculous,* her expression said.

He reconsidered. "These are your receivable accounts?"

"It's cinnamon." Her smile enlivened the whole room. "I rub it over a grater and use it in my cinnamon buns."

"Oh." Feeling foolish, Marcus pushed away the fragrant basket. At least he'd diverted her attention from the subject of the supposed help he'd given her business. "Is that all, then?"

"Not quite."

Molly went on explaining the various items she

used in her business. As she did, gradually Marcus began to see that her methods might not have been the methods he'd have chosen, but they were valid. They served the same purposes as his ledgers and receipts and inventories did, only in an intuitive, tactile way.

"I never thought I'd say this," he told her when she'd finished, "but…you don't need my help. You have something here that works for you. It's plain that marbles and cookie jars and illustrated books suit your needs even better than writing in ledgers would."

"I do like these things," Molly mused. With apparent pleasure, she rubbed her fingers over the jelly jars, stirred the marbles within. "They make sense to me. Seeing them, touching them, seems so much more real than writing numbers down."

He believed it. More and more, he'd come to realize that Molly Crabtree had a sensualist's heart. She appreciated the textures and temperatures and tactile qualities of everything around her, and couldn't help but reach out to experience them. Molly worked at business the same way she worked at everyday life— by filling herself with every part of it. By leaving no stone or marble or scrap of ribbon untouched.

She bit her lip, gazing thoughtfully at him. "But until you came here, no one else…understood that.

Are you certain it wouldn't be better to account for things properly?"

"I would have thought so."

Her gaze turned downcast. Gloomily she surveyed the ledgers. Her expression held all the eagerness of a man assigned to fell a mighty oak with a penknife.

She'd misunderstood, Marcus knew. Driven by a need to reassure her, he cupped her chin in his hand. He raised her face to his. "I would have thought so," he repeated. "Until I met you."

"Oh, Marcus." Her tremulous gaze lifted. "You *do* understand!"

"If you tell anyone, I'll deny it. These ledgers are an atrocity. Nothing like the ones at my mill."

Molly *pish-poshed* his warnings. That was when Marcus knew he truly was doomed. This woman did not fear him. Not even when he used his most fearsome voice, the one that worked wonders on burly lumbermen everywhere.

Instead, she beamed. "That's wonderful! I'm so glad."

He made a face, grumbling now. "You are changing me, Molly. And it's for the better, I fear."

It *was* for the better, if this sudden lightness he felt meant anything. For the first time, Marcus realized, he was beginning to see the world as a place filled not with tasks to be conquered, but with possibilities to be enjoyed. With Molly's example, he understood that wrenching things into their proper places wasn't always necessary.

Next thing he knew, Marcus thought sourly, he'd be leaving his doors unlocked, with Molly's open-to-the-public bakery to blame as inspiration. He'd be chattering for the fun of it. He'd be…losing his heart to the very woman who'd turned his life and his views upside down.

"Change is nothing to fear," she assured him with a wave of her hand. "It's the natural course of things. The matchmaker says so. A fine woman enlightens her man. She shows him the better sides of things."

The matchmaker. Her mention of the meddlesome creature should have prompted Marcus to question her. It should have stirred an interest in seeing the matchmaker's shenanigans put to rest. But for the second time that night, Marcus didn't care to delve into the secret he'd promised to uncover.

Let the men's club be damned, he thought. Now he was here with Molly, a beautiful and kindhearted woman. It would be a greater crime to forget that than it would be to neglect his fact-finding duties.

At least it would be…for now.

In that moment, Marcus gave in.

"Then show me a few of those better things," he said. He stroked his thumb over the curve of her cheek, marveling at her softness. "For I need them, Molly. More sorely than I knew."

I need you, he thought, and felt himself drawn still further into the warmth of being with her. All he could feel was the want of her; all he could know was that she held some secret, some *thing* that would make him feel whole.

At first, Molly's answer was silent. He held his breath to receive it, then in the subtle lamplight she gently touched his face. She dragged her fingers across his jaw—clean shaven for her, just before he'd come here—then caressed his cheek. Something akin to amazement passed over her expression, then was chased away by the smile that tilted her lips.

"Everything of mine is yours," she said. "Didn't you know that? After all, it isn't every man I allow to see my ledgers."

Her sassy smile lightened his heart.

"It isn't every woman I invite to improve me."

Marcus flattened her hand against his face, savoring her touch. He rumbled with pleasure beneath it, feeling like a lion gentled by the most unlikely of tamers. He captured her hand and pressed a kiss to her palm, then curled her fingers around it to keep that bit of his feelings safe within her grasp.

"But at this moment, I'm putty in your hands. You should take this opportunity and go wild. You should turn me into the kind of man you've dreamed of. Now, while I won't stop you."

"No." Molly shook her head. "I cannot."

"Am I so hopeless as that, then?" Despite everything, Marcus felt wounded. 'Twas his first inkling that these better things of hers might come with a cost to bear. A cost to his heart.

"I won't believe it," he scoffed in his most manly tone. "With the effort you exert toward all your projects, I could easily become the man you've dreamed of."

"No! I cannot…because you already *are* that man. Marcus, don't you realize how much you've given me? You've bolstered my business. You've kept me company in the most charming of ways. You've introduced me to kissing. Soon you'll even be embarking upon repairing my shop."

"Introduced you to kissing?" Stopping her on that point, he raised his brows, his curiosity piqued. "Surely you'd been kissed before."

"Not so it counted."

Unreasonable pride filled him. Wasn't that what every man secretly suspected? That *he* was the ultimate lover, the only one his chosen woman wanted?

Marcus cocked his head at a rakish angle. "Of course. This town is filled with loutish oafs who'd as soon slobber on you as kiss you. With clumsy buffoons who step on your toes. With long-nosed cretins who can't decide which way to tilt their heads so as not to jab your eye out."

"No. That's not it. The men aren't so inept as all that, I can assure you."

Was she laughing at him? Marcus thought so. Her eyes looked far too bright, her cheeks far too pink, for anything other than politely stifled amusement. Damnable woman.

"What, then?" he demanded.

"It's never counted before," Molly said softly, "because none of those men who tried to kiss me...were men I cared for. Marcus, I care for you. More deeply than I expected."

Shocked, Marcus could only stare at her for a moment.

Then...*what the hell,* he decided, and threw caution to the wind. It was what any marble-collecting, ribbon-sorting, pretend-money-creating person would have done.

"Then we are even." His heart hammered. He felt as though he'd run clear to his mill, out to the logging camp and all the way back here without stopping. Placing his hand protectively over his chest, Marcus swallowed hard and went on. "Because I never expected these feelings I have for you."

There. He'd said it. He'd revealed a piece of himself for her, to either accept or refuse. Not that she would refuse, he assured himself. Not when he gave the finest kisses she'd ever—

No. On the heels of his mush-hearted declaration, something changed. Marcus watched in alarm as Molly's expression faltered. Her nose crinkled. The magical warmth between them began seeping away, sometime between his first declaration and the next.

"You make me sound like a rash," she accused. "A rash you never wanted and can't wait to be rid of."

"No! Molly, you're not a rash at all." Befuddled but determined, Marcus lunged to hold her in her chair beside him before she could slip away. How could he explain? "At most, you're…a temporary lunacy. A lunacy I love."

There. That ought to smooth things over.

Her eyebrow rose. "Temporary? Temporary! When do you plan to cure yourself of me, Marcus? After you've wormed the matchmaker's name from me, I suppose?"

Marcus shook his head. "Given both 'temporary' and 'lunacy,' you choose 'temporary' to object to? I will never understand you."

"Very tidy avoidance of the real issue, Mr. Copeland."

"Now we're back to that? Marcus," he reminded her. "Marcus, Marcus—"

"I'll never give you the secret, you know," she

informed him. "I've sworn not to. My very image of responsibility and steadfastness depends on keeping that promise."

How had they come to this? One moment, they'd both been proclaiming their growing affections or so he'd thought. The next, they were adversaries again? Marcus raked his hand through his hair, confused.

"I don't care about the matchmaker! Do you think I would be here with this *mess*—" exasperated, he gestured toward her bookkeeping accoutrements. "—if I were only after that damnable woman's name?"

Molly gasped. "You said you *understood* my system!"

"I do. Listen to me." He grasped her chair, dragged it toward him, then kept both hands fixed on its seat on either side of her bustled behind in order to keep her with him. "Beyond all reason, I like spending time with you. I like learning your outlandish ways of looking at things. I even like being made to keep up with you, as senseless as it seems—"

"If this is your notion of sweet talk, you may as well quit while you're ahead," Molly said, crossing her arms over her chest. "Before you tell me that as well as being crazy and childish, I'm also unattractive and…and—" she churned her arm, seeking more "—and smell funny!"

"You smell delightful." He smiled fondly. "Good enough to taste."

"Ooh! How dare you remind me of that!"

Ah, their first kisses. "I dare much more than that. Care to test me?"

"I'm leaving."

She tried to rise. His arms on her chair prevented it.

"Let me go."

"Not until you hear me." Marcus nodded toward the chair.

Warily Molly settled fully into it again. Her arched brows bade him continue.

"When I said before that I never expected the feelings I have for you, it was true. I did not expect them. But I do believe in them. I will not be baited into denying them."

"I don't know what you mean."

"Yes, you do. You don't trust me because you believe it's the matchmaker I seek. Not you. But Molly—"

Marcus paused, caught between the old and the new, between what he'd promised and what he needed. He could not have both the matchmaker's identity and the woman he cared for, and he knew it. He chose Molly.

"From the moment I touched you, something in me changed. When I see you, the sun comes out. When I hear you laugh, my spirits lift. I might not be skilled at romantic talk—and that's probably why you were mad at me before—but I mean what I say. I want you, Molly. I can't promise—"

"Oh, Marcus!" She lurched forward, flinging her arms around him. With happy little movements, she hugged him close. "You *excel* at romantic talk! I don't know why I didn't see it before."

Molly slapped both palms gently on his cheeks, holding his face steady. She pressed rewarding, tiny kisses all over his jaw, his cheekbone, his neck and eventually, his lips. Her fervor was endearing, if a little lacking in finesse. Marcus didn't mind a damned bit. Not so long as she forgave him, and went on trying to perfect her technique.

Her lips met his. It was all he could stand. Grasping the nape of her neck in his hand, Marcus took control of her chaste kiss, turning it to something far deeper, far hotter, far more passionate. He could not get enough of Molly's mouth, of her breathy whispers, of her lush curviness as, after long moments, he finally let his hands wander lower, lower, to cup her breasts in both palms.

At his touch, she moaned into his mouth, arching toward him. Lace and satin met his callused hands…and beneath the fabrics, warm, willing woman awaited. Molly felt every bit as wondrous as he'd ever dreamed. Marcus knew he would never get enough of her.

Especially not tonight.

She held his shoulders, pulling him to her. Then, abruptly, Molly lurched away. She broke off their kiss and stood, her hands visibly trembling. "We mustn't do this."

Not do this? How else could he show her his feelings, save touching her? Meaning to do so, Marcus reached for her.

She sidestepped his grasp. "I'm sorry. I must leave, and that means you should, too."

"Is something wrong?"

"No. You were remarkable." She touched her lips, let her gaze turn faraway, shook her head to clear it. "But I fear I don't have the ability to resist you further, and I won't have my first time abed with the man I love be...*not* in a bed."

Flustered, Molly grabbed his discarded suit coat and flung it toward him. Just as Marcus caught it, something fluttered from within its folds to the ground. He bent, quite carefully due to his state of thwarted arousal, to pick it up.

By the time he straightened, again carefully, Molly had quit the office. "Just let yourself out!" she called from the front of the bakeshop. "Goodbye!"

The front door thudded closed. Left alone, Marcus shook his head. Just when he thought he had Molly reckoned out, she surprised him. His mind whirled with thoughts of Molly "lying abed" with him. Had she meant that? Given her unconventional family, she might. He no longer found it shocking that she never locked her doors, but he did find it startling that…

His gaze caught on the thing in his hand. Held. It was the note Molly had given him, inviting him to dinner. For the first time, Marcus recalled his determination to match Molly's handwriting with that bold script he'd studied on the matchmaker's note kept by Jack Murphy. With an uneasy feeling roiling in his gut, he made himself unfold the note.

He looked. Molly's note was printed, in a hand unlike the one he'd seen at Murphy's saloon.

With relief, Marcus shrugged into his suit coat. Although it wasn't quite as telling to match printed letters with cursive ones, this all but proved Molly wasn't the matchmaker. He tucked away the invitation, then reached for Molly's ledgers, left open on the desk. It was time to put them away and, along with them, some of his misguided notions about Molly.

Bemused, he flipped through her accounts one final time. It seemed Molly had made an attempt at proper bookkeeping some time ago, he saw as he examined an old ledger he hadn't looked at closely before. Because this journal held several inventory notations, each entered on its own line…in a distinctive curved script he recognized.

It was the matchmaker's handwriting.

Here, in Molly's ledger. Marcus would need Jack Murphy's note to prove it true, but logic told him there was no doubt.

His hand clenched above the page. Stunned, Marcus took out Molly's note again and lay it on the desk. He examined both, side by side. The truth struck him all at once, leaving him sick at heart. Likely Molly had deliberately scribed her invitation to him in a false hand, he realized, to try and lead him astray.

Her deceit had worked—until now.

Slamming shut the ledger, Marcus tucked it beneath his arm. He made to leave. This would change things, to be certain. But exactly how they would change remained to be seen.

Chapter Eleven

The next several days passed uneventfully for Molly. She continued making daily visits to Marcus's lumber mill, spending time behind the new baked goods stall the men had built for her. She met with her mother and the family's cook, planning an elaborate meal for Friday evening, when Marcus would join them for dinner. She collected petition signatures with Grace, filled paper cornucopias with Sarah for her students' autumn celebration, and called on several more townspeople in charge of assigning Chautauqua booths.

Her efforts on that matter still hadn't come to fruition. Not even specially baked miniature dried apple pies had been enough to tip the scales in her favor. But that didn't mean Molly intended to give up. Instead, she set her sights on baking a magnificent Lady Baltimore cake filled with fruit and nuts, telling herself that when the Chautauqua committee tasted it, they'd grant her *two* booths and a fanfare from the Morrow Creek municipal band, too.

As he'd promised, Marcus came by her bakeshop every day. He arrived after the noon meal, after seeing his mill off to a good start each day, and stayed till late, hammering and sawing and making repairs. His diligence was inspiring. Never had she seen a man work so hard.

Never had she seen a man appear more attractive to a woman's eye as he did so.

Each time Marcus wielded his hammer, she sneaked peeks from her worktable. Each time he strode along a length of wood—the better to measure it—she abandoned her bread dough to surreptitiously admire the strength of his legs, the width of his shoulders, the muscled curve of his backside. Each time he sawed, Molly watched his forearms flex; each time he plucked a nail from the cache held between his pursed lips, she sighed.

Like one of Sarah's impressionable schoolgirls, she followed his movements with her chin in her hand. Like those silly gigglers, she blushed when Marcus caught her looking. Twice she knocked over bowls of cake batter in her efforts to seem nonchalant. Three times she iced her hand instead of a cinnamon bun. Finally Molly just gave up.

"Thirsty?" she asked, stopping by Marcus's side

at the faulty window. She knew she looked at him with worshipful eyes, but she simply couldn't help it. He was doing all this work for her sake. It was powerfully kind of him, now that she'd decided to allow it. "I brought you a glass of water."

He glanced up distractedly, hammer poised in midair. Three nails dangled between his lips. "Mmm?"

"Water." Molly held up the slippery glass. "For you."

His faint smile made those nails wobble. Marcus plucked them away, then set them, along with his hammer, aside on his sawhorse. Sunshine streamed through the window to bathe his face as he wiped his forearm over his damp forehead. At the play of light over his features, she nearly sighed again. That golden glow made his eyes more amber, his dark hair shinier…his perplexed look truer.

He glanced at the water glass. "It has leaves in it."

"Oh, those are—"

With a decisive gesture, Marcus took the glass. He fished out the greenery with two fingers, then flung it aside. Molly started as the garnish she'd offered landed amidst broken glass, bent nails and sawdust.

"Those are wild mint leaves!" she protested.

"Mmm?"

"They're meant to make the water more refreshing."

"Mmm."

Marcus drank deeply, his Adam's apple moving with each long swallow. He tipped his head back to drain the glass, then returned it to Molly. A grin lit his face as he wiped his palm dry on his wool pants.

"Thank you. Most refreshing."

"It's *more* refreshing with the mint."

"Not possible."

Molly dragged over a chair from the several Marcus had shoved in a corner to make room for his repairs. She settled into it. "Definitely possible. You simply haven't learned to appreciate the finer things in life, that's all."

"Finer things? If they include floating weeds in my water, I'm happy without them."

"You should at least give them a try."

He shook his head. "I'm fine as I am. I've never had much, and I don't need much."

Molly gawped at him. Oblivious, Marcus grabbed his hammer, flipped it end over end in a move doubtless designed to impress her, then straddled the sawhorse over which he'd arrayed the new window frame pieces. He surveyed them.

"Never had much? You have a great deal!" she argued. "Your house is fine, your lumber mill is prosperous—"

"Either of them could vanish in an instant," he disagreed.

"Not with you in charge of them, they couldn't. Why, you've already measured that new window more carefully than any carpenter would have. I counted three separate measurements, at least." She should have been stoning raisins for pies, not ogling Marcus as he worked, but…that was neither here nor there. "Don't you realize how extraordinary you are?"

He paused with his measuring instruments in hand, squinted at the cut lumber before him. "There's no harm in being certain."

"You go beyond certain," Molly disagreed. "All the way to perfect. I've been watching you, you know—"

"You have?" Rakishly he angled his head toward her. "Do you like what you see?"

"Very much. But I—" She clapped a hand over her mouth. "Oh, dear. I mean—"

He winked. "Go on looking, then. I don't mind."

"I have work to do." With dignity, Molly stood, clutching the empty water glass. She flounced away, skirts swishing. "You can get your own water from here on out. I won't be watching to see if you need it."

"Oh, yes. You will."

"I won't, because I'll be too busy with my own work."

But she wasn't. Despite her best intentions, Molly found herself pausing amidst grating nutmeg to admire Marcus's deft handling of the windowpane replacements he'd bought. Sunshine sparked off the glass as he set it into the proper grooves in the new frame. Naturally the fit was perfect.

Intrigued, Molly continued watching. Eventually Marcus had mounted the whole assembly in the window opening. He stepped back to examine the finished job with a satisfied nod.

Of course, it had taken the better part of an afternoon to accomplish that task. Marcus never hurried, never seemed to take shortcuts, never diverted his attention from the matter at hand. The way he worked, it occurred to her, was very akin to the way he lived. He gave every task his every effort.

He brought the same sense of concentration to measuring lumber as he did to running his mill… as he did to kissing her. 'Twas heady stuff, to be the object of such attentiveness, such intensity. Perhaps that was why Marcus appealed to her so strongly, Molly thought. He was exactly as driven to succeed as she was.

But then, Marcus had accomplished a business of his own and a household of his own. Both were thriving enterprises, even if one was given to boot jerky accoutrements. She had a business, too, but it thrived only with Marcus's help.

Only with Marcus's help. Why should that be? Absently shelling walnut meats for later, Molly pondered the question. She knew she was just as determined to succeed as Marcus. She knew she worked every bit as hard as he did. So why were his efforts fruitful...and hers so often disappointing?

Distractedly dusting her hands with flour, she began rolling out piecrusts. She transferred the jagged circles she formed to the waiting tins, her gaze mostly on Marcus as he tested her wallboards for rot. Several needed replacing, Molly knew. There was a leak near the ceiling. The occasional rainfall brought water down the length of her wallpaper and wainscoting all the way to the floorboards.

Marcus crouched, running his hand along the top edge of the chair rail. He angled his head and closed one eye, peering at the wallpaper. He slowly crept along the wall, occasionally thumping it with his knuckles.

"If you were any other man, I'd think you were doing this job slowly in order to spend more time with me."

His grin flashed. "What makes you think I'm not?"

"The fact that your molasses-slow methods seem to work, however leisurely. Also the fact that you haven't taken the liberty of kissing me once today."

"Not once?"

"Not once." She raised her chin, pretending indifference.

"Are your workmen usually so forward as all that?" He paused, pretending to consider it. "In that case, I'm surprised you were so reluctant to have me make these repairs."

The rogue gave her a scandalous look. In response, Molly's fingers fluttered unsteadily over her piecrust crimping. A delicious sense of flirtatiousness sprang to life inside her, engendered by Marcus's teasing. She quite deliberately finished the tin she'd begun.

"Well, that's easily explained. I was reluctant to have you here because…"

Because you're so very overwhelming. Because you make me long for things I thought I wouldn't. Because…because you came to me with notions other than helpfulness in mind.

The statement he'd made while examining her ledgers returned to her. *You don't trust me because you believe it's the matchmaker I seek. Not you.*

"…because I was being silly." Sooner or later, she would have to trust him, Molly told herself. It may as well be now. With that decision, a sense of lightheartedness filled her. "It was foolish of me not to… accept your help."

And trust you, her heart finished for her. *It was foolish of me not to trust you.* After all, even if Marcus had believed her the matchmaker at first, what were the odds he still did? Surely the time they'd spent together had changed his mind. It wasn't for nothing that Molly had strived to keep her secrets close.

"I'm glad you see the sense in it." Marcus strode to her worktable, his clothes streaked with sawdust. He reached one muscled forearm toward the stack of date cookies she'd piled there on a plate. "Most women would have done so long ago."

She watched two cookies disappear beneath his gargantuan bites. Marcus chewed—then chewed and chewed and…perhaps his teeth weren't as strong as they should be. Molly frowned.

"Most women aren't as capable as I am," she said.

He coughed. "As you say." One meaty fist pounded his chest. "But a man likes to feel needed, Molly. He likes to help. He likes to know he's done all he can for his womenfolk. Doesn't your matchmaker have something to say to that?"

"The matchmaker believes in equality between the sexes."

"Equality is impossible."

"It is not!" Molly was glad Grace wasn't present

to hear such heresy come from his lips. "My sister would trounce you with her bronze Suffragette Of The Year cup to hear you say such a thing."

"Men are stronger. We're meant to care for women. It's as plain as that. If we can't do that much at least, then what good are we?"

"Some women don't need to be cared for."

Marcus shook his head. "I'd like to change your mind."

The notion shook her. Molly didn't want to consider it, nor dwell on wondering why Marcus might feel that way. In this, they were incompatible to the extreme. There were no two ways about it.

"Babies should be cared for. Competent women should not."

With a clumsy jerk of her rolling pin, she transferred the next bit of pastry to its tin. Before she could begin crimping it, Marcus was there.

He raised her chin in his fingers, forcing her to look at him. "I need a woman I can care for. I need a woman who needs me," he said bluntly. "I want that woman to be you."

Molly felt her eyes widen. *He wanted her.* Jubilation swept through her, followed by an answering need for him. Marcus was the only man she'd ever considered wanting for her own. To know that he wanted her, too, now—

But only on his own terms.

Only as a needful person Molly could never allow herself to be. Otherwise, what was the sense in proving herself now…only to surrender herself to someone later? To Marcus, later? Her family already believed her incompetent, treated her like the child she no longer was. Today Marcus claimed to want those same belittling rights for himself.

Didn't he?

Caught within his grasp, Molly hesitated. She sensed powdery sawdust against her jaw, smelled the faint, honest sweat and no-nonsense determination that clung to him. A part of her *did* want to give over to him. But the rest of her knew that doing so would prove too dangerous by far.

"Why do you think I've done this work on your shop?" he prompted fiercely, his gaze never leaving hers as he nodded toward the lumber and equipment spread everywhere. "Why do you think I've called on you, and kissed you, and let you turn me inside out with your locksmith pranks and your Chautauqua donations and your baking lessons? Lord, Molly! Do you think I *wanted* this?"

"I don't want to hear this."

She jerked her head to break free. Marcus didn't let her. His grip remained fast.

"I can do things for you. I can help you. You don't have to shoulder your burdens alone."

"I do. I must." Didn't she?

"Let me help." He tipped her chin higher, brushed his lips against hers. "Let me, Molly."

His mouth touched hers again persuasively. His free hand cupped her shoulder, holding her steady as he deepened his kiss. Wavering beneath it, Molly found herself unable to resist. Her palms rose to the broad wall of his chest before she'd so much as willed it; her body softened into his before she'd even realized she wanted the welcoming connection of their hips and bellies and thighs coming together. She moaned beneath his kiss and gave herself to Marcus, if only for this one perfect moment because later, when she'd refused him, wouldn't she need the remembrance of this to sustain her?

She would, because refusing his help was what she fully intended to do. Later. Now, right now, all Molly wanted was to feel protected in his arms. To feel beautiful and beloved. To feel all the things Marcus made her feel…and to pretend that he didn't want so much from her that she couldn't give.

"See?" he said when they broke apart at last. "There *are* things you need from me. Things only I can give you."

Dazed, Molly opened her eyes. "What?"

"You need me, Molly. You just haven't realized it yet."

With a masculine nod, Marcus released her. As cool air swept between their bodies, she felt instantly bereft. She knew there was something in Marcus's statement she ought to object to. But as Molly watched him stride back to his sawhorse and go to work again, she could not for the life of her figure out what it was.

She touched her lips. Pondered the coziness she felt, with Marcus here and the two of them working side by side. Shook her head, with a dismissal she'd like to have felt more truly.

Marcus thought he wanted a helpless woman, a woman who'd need his aid time and again. He was mistaken. All he needed was to be shown the true appeal of an independent woman, Molly vowed, and promised herself she'd become that woman. For him, and for herself.

With that in mind, she watched carefully as Marcus carried his measuring instruments to her wall's wainscoting. She scrutinized his methods, committed them to memory, learned as she observed. She recalled the days' worth of such lessons she'd witnessed. Then she nodded.

For her next batch of cinnamon buns, Molly hauled out the flour and measured it. Then she measured it again, and again a third time. To her surprise, her initial measurement had been off by a few spoonfuls.

Next she grated a cone of sugar, making a pile of the sweet, sparkly stuff on her work counter. She measured it thrice as well. With an occasional pause to observe Marcus's progress on his repairs, Molly concentrated fully on the steps in making her special cinnamon buns. She consulted each step in her recipe and was surprised to realize that, although she'd thought she'd had the process committed to memory, she nearly forgot to proof the yeast.

She almost forgot to add the salt, as well. Thoughtfully, Molly stopped. She examined Marcus's work area, seeking out more hints from the man who'd fostered both a successful lumber mill business and a successful household of his own. Although the space initially looked messy to her, when she studied it more closely, Molly realized the tools and supplies looked messy because they were all laid out, ready to be used for the job at hand.

Glancing at her worktable, Molly reconsidered. Customarily she kept her baking supplies tucked away for neatness' sake. Was it possible that doing so had led her to occasionally forget an important ingredient?

On the off chance it was, she hauled out everything else she needed. Salt. Cinnamon. Butter. Milk. Then she continued. When she'd reached the kneading stage, she squeezed the dough she'd formed with amazement. It felt different. It felt good. It felt *right*.

A new encouragement filled her as she set it to rise, then later, rolled it out to form the cinnamon buns with. She buttered the dough, sprinkled it with cinnamon and sugar and her special secret ingredient, rolled it into a soft, puffy log and sliced it into sweet spirals.

Resisting the temptation to whack through the dough quickly in order to get on with the next recipe, Molly measured three times and cut carefully. Evenly. She laid the cinnamon buns aside for their final rise, then went to find more wood for the stove. In the past, she'd occasionally let her fire die too quickly, which had necessitated baking the buns at a lower temperature for a very long time.

It occurred to her that long, low temperatures also were used to produce beef jerky. Had she, without knowing it, been baking *cinnamon bun jerky?*

With a sinking feeling, Molly poked a fingertip at this morning's first batch of cinnamon buns. A hollow *thud* sounded in the shop. She picked up the sweet and rapped it on the counter.

"Someone's at your front door," Marcus said, his attention all for the wall he'd been repairing. "I heard knocking."

Appalled, Molly looked at the cinnamon bun in her hand. Tentatively she raised the thing and sniffed it. She licked it. Sweet icing tingled on her tongue. Encouraged, she took a bite.

"Ow!"

Immediately Marcus was there. "What's the matter? Did you hurt yourself? Let me see."

Looking concerned, he grasped her forearm and turned it upward. The offending cinnamon bun—without so much as a dent in its supposedly tender surface—caught his eye. He gave her a curious look.

"It's nothing. I'm fine." Molly twisted her arm, hiding the sweet. Her tooth ached fiercely, making her eyes water. "I've just realized there may be something to your philosophies, that's all."

Marcus brightened. Pleasure shone from his face. "The truth hurts, hmm?"

Molly made a face.

Too pleased to be bothered by it, he nodded. "I'm glad."

He kissed her again, then swaggered back to his work. He cast her a fond glance over his shoulder. Smiled. It occurred to Molly that Marcus looked awfully delighted for a mere...*oh*. He thought she'd decided to agree with his "I need a woman I can care for" philosophies, not his orderly work ways.

Groaning, Molly rolled her gaze to the ceiling. She didn't have the heart to correct him now, but soon she would have to. Right after she amazed him with the very best cinnamon bun he'd ever tasted.

Chapter Twelve

At the end of the workday on Friday, Marcus stood in his office with his foreman Smith, reviewing the week's timber yields. When they'd finished, he hastily drew out his cash box and counted out a stack of currency.

"For the men," he told Smith. "For next week's baked goods from Molly's supply."

As he'd done for several weeks now, Smith scooped up the money. He would take it, Marcus knew, and distribute it evenly among the lumbermen and mill hands. They, in turn, would use it to buy "delectables" from Molly.

Given his new knowledge that she was indeed the matchmaker, Marcus should have found such subterfuge unnecessary. But having helped her once, he found himself wanting to keep doing so. For Molly's sake. Being surrounded by eager customers made her so happy.

The foreman nodded his thanks, turning to leave.

"Warn the men to be more careful," Marcus said sternly. "The first one I see ramming cinnamon buns under a crooked table leg to steady it earns a week's worth of sweeping duty."

"Yes, boss."

"No using Molly's pies to prop open doors."

Smith looked pained. "Yes, boss."

Reminded of something, Marcus asked, "Has Fergus recovered from his injuries?"

"Yes, boss." Smith shuffled toward the office door, plainly eager to be gone. "He's fine now. Doc Williamson eventually pried out that apple fritter splinter."

"Good. That's all for tonight, then."

"Right, boss. Good night."

Marcus watched as Smith passed through the open doorway, then made his way slowly down the hallway beyond. He remembered something else.

"Smith?"

His foreman paused. "Yes, boss?"

"How's—" Marcus hesitated, feeling uncommonly awkward. He cleared his throat. "How's that ingrown toenail of yours?"

Smith paused, his expression befuddled. Anyone would have believed Marcus had asked him to waltz, instead of having merely asked him about his welfare. Had Marcus really been so callous a man as that?

If he had, he was no longer, thanks to Molly's example.

"Did Molly's plaster help?" he prompted. "Because if you need to spend part of the day sitting—"

A wide grin spread over his foreman's grizzled face, making his whiskers jut outward.

"Aye, I'm better now." He clomped to Marcus's side and clapped his hand heartily on his shoulder. "I begin to believe you'll be fine, also. *With Molly's care.*"

Then, with that inexplicable damned grin on his face, Smith turned and left. Marcus stared after him. With Molly's care? 'Twas he who meant to care for her, and not the other way around. What the hell had Smith meant?

Obviously Molly's remedies had addled the poor man's thinking. There was no other explanation for it.

Comforted by the notion, Marcus left the office himself, for dinner at the Crabtree household.

"Oh, Grace, no!" Molly cried. "Tell me you don't truly intend to play battle marches on the harpsichord tonight."

"Not just any battle marches," Grace said, settling

at the pianolike instrument with clear purpose. She practiced a few notes. "These are suffragette battle marches, used to work up the ladies' stamina during long marches on the capitol. With a few temperance hymns thrown in, of course."

Molly groaned. On tonight of all nights, Marcus was to be greeted at the Crabtree's front door with rousing feminist tunes. Well, it was unlikely Marcus would recognize them, she reasoned, and she had other things to worry about. Like the menu for dinner. Molly headed for the kitchen.

"Cook, is everything coming along according to plan? Are we on schedule for dinner?"

"Yes, Miss Molly. Although I can't make any promises about how this menu will turn out."

The cook wrung her hands, casting a skeptical glance toward the stove. There, several large pots bubbled and steamed. Befuddled, Molly looked in the same direction.

What *was* that unusual aroma?

Her mother passed by, obviously having overheard the conversation. "Don't worry, dear." She rearranged Molly's hair, then smiled beatifically. "Mr. Copeland will no doubt appreciate our care for his health."

"His health?" Molly asked. "What do you mean?"

But Fiona Crabtree had already drifted away, saying something about her husband's dress for the evening. Molly turned to the cook for an explanation.

"Your mama read an article in *Harper's* about Dr. Sylvester Graham's dietary reformation. She decided we were all becoming vegetarians."

"Tonight?" Molly covered her face in her hands. "We are becoming vegetarians *tonight?* Why can nothing be normal in this household?"

Fiona humphed, passing through the kitchen with two neckties and a hat in hand. "As promoted by Dr. Graham's regimen, proper and regular bowel movements are—"

"Mama!"

"—certainly normal," she said, brushing lint from the hat. "You'll thank me later, after a lovely meal of fruits, vegetables, grains and nuts."

Molly groaned. "But Marcus will be expecting a nice roast beef, with gravy and boiled potatoes."

"I daresay his bowels will be expecting the same thing," Fiona rejoined with a gleam in her eye. She thrust the hat upward, like a conquering Valkyrie with a sword in hand. "Tonight, we strike for good health!"

Before Molly could remove that disturbing notion from her mind, Adam Crabtree meandered through, wearing a rumpled shirt and an abstract expression. He held an opened book in hand. His mouth worked silently as he read.

Fiona saw him. "Adam, you're not wearing that! And where's the hair tonic I ordered for you from the apothecary? If you'd only apply a little bit of it like I told you to…"

Her voice faded as she hustled Molly's papa upstairs to get dressed. Breathing a sigh of relief, Molly leaned against a dry-goods cupboard in the kitchen. "Could you possibly prepare a small side of beef without Mama knowing about it?" she asked the cook.

"And risk another lecture on the state of my insides? No, ma'am." Cook whisked the lid from a nearby pot, releasing a burst of odorous green steam. She stirred. "If Mrs. Crabtree says we're eating bark and berries for dinner, then that's exactly what we're doing."

Molly sighed. Perhaps she could convince Marcus the strange foodstuffs were foreign in nature.

Footsteps thudded downstairs. An instant later, Sarah entered the room.

"Thank heavens. Sarah! Did you have any luck convincing Papa not to initiate his usual Friday night game of charades this evening? I doubt Marcus would take well to imitating a lovesick rhinoceros."

Her sister shook her head, not the least bit daunted by the mention of their father's unusual made-up parlor game. In it, Adam combined one adjective and one noun, drawn from slips of paper in separate hats, then compelled the players to pantomime the resulting combination. He'd always avowed that typical charades weren't challenging enough for a Crabtree.

"I forgot," Sarah said blithely. She removed one of the pots from the stove, wrapped it in a thick towel, then made to carry it out of the kitchen. "Good luck, though."

"Wait. You're not staying for dinner? Where are you going?"

"To Daniel McCabe's. He's invited me to dine with him and his nephew tonight."

"He's invited that pot of soup to dinner, you mean," Molly said, indignant on her sister's behalf. "What are you about, bringing him his meals this way? Are you his nanny, as well as his lackey?"

Sarah's eyes flashed. "Stay out of it, Molly. It's my business if I want to bring Daniel a bit of beef stew."

"Beef stew! Wait!" Molly lunged for the pot, visions of having something normal to offer Marcus dancing in her head.

Sarah proved too fast for her. In a wink, she was out the door. It slammed shut behind her, putting an end to Molly's hopes of having another ally in her quest to make a favorable impression upon Marcus.

The crashing sounds of a hymn burst from the parlor. Molly jumped. When Marcus saw the in-sanity brewing in her household, he'd no doubt run for the safety of Jack Murphy's saloon. And he'd never be back for her.

"This is an interesting meal, Mrs. Crabtree," Marcus said later, chewing thoughtfully. "I've never experienced its like."

Fiona looked pleased. So did Adam.

Across from Molly at table, Marcus beamed, handsome in a dark suit and four-in-hand necktie. His dark hair was combed neatly from his face, his jaw was clean shaven and, although the man was the very picture of charm, Molly couldn't believe her mama and papa were so gullible. During their time together, she had become wise to Marcus's double-talk.

"'Never seen its like.' Humph," she piped up, letting her spoonful of grain and vegetable stew linger over her bowl. "That's not a compliment, you know. He said the same thing about my bookkeeping system."

"Molly!" her papa objected. With an apologetic look at Marcus, he patted her hand. "She's sensitive about her lack of bookkeeping ability," he explained.

"Poor dear," her mother agreed.

They all gazed pityingly at her. Even Grace, who despite her uncanny organizing ability, everyone agreed, could hardly tally anything beyond three digits. Grace's mathematical failings weren't discussed in the family, but they were common knowledge.

As though sensing her discomfort, Grace spoke up. "Let's talk about something else, shall we?"

Molly cast her a grateful smile. No matter their disagreements, she could always count on her sister to come to her aid. Relaxing a fraction, she spooned up more stew.

In the momentary silence that followed, Grace pinned Marcus with a merciless, sham-pleasant look. "Tell me, Mr. Copeland, when will you embrace the equality required of the coming century, and hire female workers for your lumber mill?"

Molly choked on her stew. Grace the Inquisitor merely folded her hands next to her chamomile tea, waiting.

To his credit, Marcus did not so much as flinch. "When a woman can fell a fifty-foot pine as well as a man. When a woman can feed two hundred pounds of lumber into the splitter I installed, and do it safely. That's when I'll hire a woman." He savored another bite of stew. "The way I see it, equality is a matter of ability, not gender."

Grace's hand tightened on her soupspoon. Impossible as it was to believe, she seemed at an actual loss for words. Molly gawked. No one had si-

lenced her opinionated sister this thoroughly since…
well, never.

"I…I agree," Grace stammered.

"Fine," Marcus said.

A stunned moment passed. The whole family stared at the man who'd done the impossible—satisfy Grace on a point of female equality. More, she was even now gazing at him with grudging respect. Remarkable.

In the lingering silence, Fiona spoke up. "Dr. Sylvester Graham says that conversation is good for digestion," she offered. As though casting about for that good doctor's remedy, she turned to her daughter. "So in that spirit…Molly, I thought you'd decided on the blue gown for tonight?"

Oh, not this. Not tonight. Molly smoothed her pink bodice. She'd chosen this gown with Marcus in mind, hoping he'd find her appearance pleasing. "I changed my mind."

Her mama *tsk-tsked*. "You know blue suits you better."

"I prefer the pink." Likely, her cheeks were blushing to match it. Molly felt them heat and resisted an urge to fan herself with a slice of Cook's wholesome Graham flour bread. "It suits me perfectly well."

"I paid good money for the blue," Adam announced.

"I prefer the blue, also," Grace put in.

"Me, too," Cook said, bringing in another course.

Molly sank lower in her chair. Surreptitiously she sneaked a glance at Marcus. He seemed bemused... or perhaps thoughtful. At the realization of what he was witnessing, she wanted to bury her face in her bark and berries and never emerge. It was impossible that he could respect her, while viewing with his own eyes the patronizing way her family treated her.

"I find the pink delightful," Marcus announced to the table at large. His gaze swept over Molly appreciatively, proving the truth of his words. "It almost does justice to your beauty, Molly. A wise choice."

Molly could happily have kissed him for standing up for her. Despite the awkward silence that followed, a warm, grateful feeling embraced her almost as surely as did Marcus's next look, when he met her gaze over the table. He winked.

Embarrassed and relieved and thrilled, she returned her attention to her stew, dreading the rebuttals that were sure to come from her opinionated family. Molly had long been the subject of well-meant lectures in this household. That wasn't likely to change merely because of one man's interference, however heartfelt, however *wonderful,* that interference had been.

Several throats were cleared. Tension filled the

dining room, thick as the boiled barley that accompanied the stew.

"Of course," echoed around the table.

"Yes, yes. I believe you're right."

"Naturally. The pink."

Molly was thunderstruck. Hardly daring to believe her ears, she sat straighter.

"We're sorry, my dear," her mother said, reaching from her end of the table to pat Molly's hand. "Mr. Copeland is right. You look absolutely lovely. It's high time you were allowed to dress yourself without our opinions to influence you."

"I am dreaming," Molly said.

"Let's not be hasty, Fiona," her papa interrupted, looking concerned. "Molly is our youngest. We can't simply abandon our responsibilities to her."

"I have a feeling those responsibilities might soon be shared," her mama said, rising elegantly from the table. Her gentle smile seemed to rest on Marcus especially, then moved on to her eldest daughter. "Come, Grace. Let's see if Cook is ready to serve Dr. Graham's special wheat-berry porridge for dessert."

"Yes, let's," Grace agreed, also standing. She grinned, as though Fiona's smile had communicated something both meaningful and amusing. "Then I really must be off to my ladies' aid meeting. If I arrive early enough, I can waylay that dastardly Jack Murphy and his interfering nonsense."

"Wait!" Adam protested, waving one arm imperiously. "I'm not finished. What about Molly's bakeshop? What about her tendency to flit between hobbies like a hummingbird in a garden? *That* won't be cured by sugared porridge."

"Adam, give over," Fiona suggested. She paused behind his chair at the head of the table and squeezed his shoulder in a wifely gesture. "My eyes have been opened tonight. Let yours be, too."

"What? What nonsense is that? My eyes are open!"

But Fiona and Grace merely went on their way, their skirts rustling faintly as they headed for the kitchen. The lamps flickered as they passed, then settled. Molly couldn't help but feel something momentous had just occurred, but she wasn't quite sure what it was.

Obviously, neither was her father. He went right on as he'd begun, turning next to Marcus. "My daughter once professed an urge to perform on stage, in one of Shakespeare's plays. Another time, she begged me to teach her sharpshooting, so she could find a place on the range. Since she was small, she's been from one thing to another."

"Perhaps she hadn't yet found what she was looking for," Marcus interrupted with calm surety, stirring his stew. "Perhaps now she has."

Adam scoffed. "With baking? Have you *tasted* those cinnamon buns of hers?"

Molly flinched. Her papa's words hurt. Even with the knowledge that he was simply overwrought at the moment. Still she'd yet to put her new, precise baking methods, learned from Marcus's example, into widespread practice. Her papa was probably correct on this score, much as she hated to admit it.

Exactly how long had he known of her ineptitude?

"Papa, let's just finish dinner," she urged, eager to change the subject. "Afterward, we can play charades in the parlor!"

He perked up interestedly. Sweet heaven, what had she volunteered for? Molly loathed charades. It would be worth it, though, if mention of the game diverted her father from his tirade.

"An excellent idea, daughter."

Her papa patted her hand. Molly's skin was becoming nigh worn raw with the condescending gesture. She'd never noticed before just how often her family employed it with her, but now she did.

Marcus did, as well. His attention lingered for a moment on Adam's patronizing pats, then rose to Molly's face. He frowned.

"But first, I really must make clear to Mr. Copeland exactly what he's getting himself involved with," Adam insisted. "I know you two have joined into a business agreement of some sorts. He ought to know about your bookkeeping failures—"

"I understand Molly's accounting practices," Marcus said blithely, wiping his mouth with one of the linen napkins laid at each place. "I approve of them."

"You—you—*approve* of them?" As though the notion were unthinkable, her papa blinked. Quickly enough, though, he was back on course. "Mr. Copeland certainly ought to know that you've only been a baker for the past eleven months or so—"

"Longer than I've tried any other endeavor," Molly pointed out. "I will make this work, Papa. I *will*."

"Yes, but still." Another pat. "It's only a matter of time before you're off to whatever fancy grips you next. We all know that, my dear."

"There's the Chautauqua, too," she protested, desperate not to be made a fool of in front of Marcus. "If I obtain a booth there…"

"Ah, Molly." Her papa rolled his eyes good-naturedly. He tore off a piece of Graham bread, then considered its nourishing whole grains with suspicion. "If it weren't for the fact that your sister is arranging the event, I'd never have allowed you to try securing a booth of your own. Knowing Sarah will be there to oversee things, to help if you get into trouble, reassures me."

A dreadful feeling pushed through Molly, one born

of disappointment and anger alike. "No one is 'allowing' me to take part in the Chautauqua! I will earn this opportunity myself. Just see if I don't!"

"There's no call for you to make yourself upset," Adam coaxed, his graying hair gleaming in the lamplight. "I mean well, Molly. You know I only have your best interests at heart."

She did. But that didn't help when her family's constant lack of faith ground her down, time and again. Molly gave her papa a frustrated look, unwilling to go on arguing with him, but equally unwilling to back down.

Marcus threw his napkin onto the table. He fixed them both with a cocksure look. "I have tried one of Molly's cinnamon buns. Just yesterday, in fact," he informed Adam. "It was delicious. I have no doubt she'll win herself the booth she hopes for this year."

Molly turned to him in amazement. Was it her imagination, or did Marcus suddenly possess all the chivalry of a legendary knight in shining armor? His defense had come a trifle late, to be sure, but it had come. Doubtless he'd been too stunned until now to muster a reply.

Fiona and Grace returned to the dining room, bearing trays of Dr. Graham's infamous porridge. Even as they set the trays onto the table's edge and began serving, Marcus continued. To Molly's increasing delight, he looked her papa directly in the eye as he spoke firmly.

"You should also know," he said to Adam, "that the arrangement between Molly and me owes itself to *more* than business endeavors."

Gasps were heard around the table.

"I care for your daughter, Mr. Crabtree," Marcus continued, resolute and splendid. "But this—" he swept the assembly with an expression of dislike "—this is more than I can stand."

Molly's heart sank like a stone. In the space of a breath, she plummeted from giddy gratitude to grim despair, toppled by Marcus's bitten-out words. What did he mean? Being amongst her family was more than he could stand? Or being with *her* was not what he wanted?

Marcus did not meet her eyes, but the tone of his voice said much. He'd seen her as her family did, Molly realized in that painful moment. Either that, or he saw her family without the same affection that she did, and wanted no part of them, not even for the sake of winning her. Fervently Molly wished she'd never embarked on this dinner. Its cost to her had turned out to be much too high.

A moment passed. No one said a thing.

Then Adam Crabtree tossed his napkin onto the

table as Marcus had. He stood with an air of hearty cheerfulness.

"Well, now. I'd say we all know where we stand then, don't we?" He put both hands on his hips and nodded. "Perhaps a rousing game of charades in the parlor, everyone? Fiona, will the porridge keep?"

"I—I suppose so," her mama said, obviously confused as she rang the bell for Cook. In whispered tones, she instructed the woman to return everything to the kitchen, then bring coffee and tea to the parlor.

Molly and Marcus stood as well. Molly did so miserably; Marcus stiffly. He paused.

"Might I have a word with you first, Mr. Crabtree?" he asked.

Her papa hesitated. His gaze flew to Molly, then returned to Marcus. He frowned. "Very well."

Molly froze. This was it. Marcus meant to make his apologies to her papa in private, then run from their dinner like a visitor from the asylum. From here on, her dealings with Marcus would be tinged with discomfort or, worse, pity. Her spirits sank even further.

She'd so hoped Marcus would see past her family's…eccentricities, and love them as she did herself. No matter that they protected her overmuch. Molly knew they meant well.

Bravely she went to Marcus's side. She forced herself to meet his fearsome gaze, to confront his tight-pressed lips and rigid stance. She touched his sleeve.

"Thank you for coming tonight, Mr. Copeland. I fear I've…just come down with a woeful headache. I won't be able to join everyone in the parlor."

Molly delivered the lie through trembling lips, standing on quivering legs while doing so. Disappointment threatened to choke her as she swallowed hard for courage. Marcus's impassive expression told her nothing of what he felt.

"Goodnight, everyone," she said. "I'm so sorry."

Then she gathered her skirts and fled upstairs to the sanctity of her room…where no one would see her weeping for all she'd lost, between the stew and the surprises served up at table that night.

Chapter Thirteen

Morning pushed its way into Molly's chamber far too early the following day, rousing her to the remembrance of all that had passed the night before. She groaned into her pillow. What must Marcus think of her now? Things would never be the same between them. Never.

With no choice but to carry on, though, Molly did as she always did. She washed and dressed, buttoning her favorite yellow calico gown over her chemise and petticoats. She brushed her teeth and fixed her hair. Then she trod the worn stairs to the dining room, hoping to sneak through it for a piece of toasted bread and escape to her shop before anyone knew she was awake.

"Molly!" Her papa glanced up, already at the dining table with his coffee. "You look well this morning. I'm glad."

Ah. Her headache of last night. Remembering the

excuse she'd made, Molly put a hand to her forehead. "Yes, I'm fine."

"'Tis probably that yellow gown that flatters you so."

He nodded knowledgeably. Molly arched her brow.

"Per-haps," she managed, taken aback.

"Or the way she's done her hair," her mama said, breezing into the room with a bowl of oatmeal. She sat down, then nodded toward her daughter approvingly. "That chignon suits you."

Molly swept her hand from her forehead to the haphazard knot she'd pinned at her nape. As long as she could recall, her mama had never before resisted the urge to refashion her hairstyle. "It…does?"

"Indeed." Grace turned from the sideboard, her bicycling costume stained grass-green at its skirt hem. "I suppose you're up early to head to your bakeshop? Very industrious of you, Molly. I don't think I've mentioned how much I approve of your determination to succeed in business."

"No, you…haven't."

"Then I've been remiss." With characteristically brisk movements, her sister offered a cup of coffee on a saucer. She smiled as Molly accepted it. "Because I find your fortitude most impressive. I hope you *do* get your Chautauqua booth."

"Thank you." Finally! Molly had been able to utter

two words in proper succession. Marveling at the change in her family, she pulled out a chair and sank into it, setting her coffee aside. "Thank you all."

"We've been remiss," her mama said, pouring cream from an earthenware pitcher onto her oatmeal. She stirred. "Treating you as though you were a flibbertigibbet of a girl in short skirts, when by now you're a fully grown woman with ambitions of her own."

Molly's mouth dropped open in surprise.

"She's always had ambitions," Adam pointed out, nodding. "The girl's after my own heart. Remember how I started the *Pioneer Press* with a single printing press, assembled beneath an oak near the town square? I couldn't afford so much as a roof over my business."

"You erected a canvas canopy soon enough, dear," Fiona said, gazing at her husband fondly. "That was a start."

"Indeed it was. Indeed it was." Adam blinked. He shook his head, as though remembering those times before his newspaper had become Morrow Creek's largest and most popular. "But my point is, Molly takes after me! It's plain as day to me now."

Astonished, Molly gaped at them all. What had come over them? While she'd slept, her family had changed personalities entirely. Their new opinions of her would take some getting used to.

Still, she thought giddily, she was certain she could accomplish it.

Sarah bustled into the room, carrying several McGuffey readers and a few slates for her students. She said her good-mornings to all assembled, then paused beside Molly's chair.

"The Chautauqua committee will be meeting after school today, Molly. If you'll deliver me some baked goods before then, I'll take them to the meeting and put in a good word for you."

Molly gazed up at her. "You're...not angry with me? About what I said last night?"

"Pish posh." With a beatific smile, Sarah settled into her chair. She plunked down her schoolteacher supplies. Arranged her skirts in a show of feminine vanity that was utterly unlike sensible Sarah. "You don't know Daniel McCabe and his nephew as well as I do, that's all. If you did, you'd understand."

Relieved, Molly nodded. "Thank you. I'd appreciate any help you could give with the committee."

"Consider it done." Cheerily, her sister began breakfast.

So did everyone else. Their conversation resumed, roving from topic to topic in a characteristically Crabtree way. Several times, the talk turned to Molly. In each instance, someone in her family found reason to compliment her, to bolster her, to praise her efforts or encourage her. It was a completely unprecedented turn of events, nearly enough to tempt Molly into departing late for the shop, just to savor it.

She may have lost Marcus Copeland's good regard over dinner last night...but she'd definitely gained her family's. Molly hardly knew what to make of it.

"Oh, Miss Molly," the cook said, bustling into the dining room with a tray of toasted Graham flour bread. "I'm glad you're up and about. I was hoping you would help me improve my bread baking this morning. If you're willing."

Everyone gazed at Molly expectantly, pleasant smiles in place.

"That's it!" she cried, leaping to her feet. She flung her napkin to the table and faced them all with her hands on her hips. "What is the *matter* with you? I go to bed with my world all in place, and I awaken this morning to find you've gone mad, to the very last one of you!"

They gawped. Cook plunked down her toast and backed hastily from the dining room. The clatter of her burdened tray hitting the table was the only sound to be heard, save Molly's hastily drawn breath as she prepared to go on.

"Next you'll be claiming I am a genius seamstress. A songstress of renown. A certain winner for the longest line at all the Chautauqua booths!"

"Well…" her mama began. "Your special cinnamon buns *are*—"

"They are as hard as the rocks tumbled by Morrow Creek, and you all well know it!" Molly cried. "At least they have been, until now. So why, *why* have you chosen this morning to flatter me with so much kindness?"

Her parents and sisters hung their heads in apparent shame. They had a right to feel embarrassed, Molly thought in indignation. Did they think her a fool? Certainly she'd had a difficult time of it last night, with Marcus's sudden outburst at the end of dinner and his subsequent leaving. But that didn't mean…

All at once, the truth struck her.

"Are you doing this out of kindness for me?" Molly asked in a shaky voice. "Are you being especially nice today, because you feel sorry for me after last night? Because of—" she swallowed hard, searching for courage "—because of Marcus?"

Four sets of eyes guiltily averted from her gaze.

"You are, aren't you! Sweet heaven."

Molly strode to the window, needing to work off some of the emotions whirling through her. She paced back, pinning them all with a knowing look as she fisted her hands by her sides.

"Thank you," she said, striving for understanding. "Thank you for caring, and for trying to help me.

But you needn't tiptoe around me, and you needn't lie to my face in order to—"

"They weren't lies!" Grace insisted.

"They weren't," Sarah confirmed. "I meant what I said."

Waving away their protests, Molly went on. "Just because Marcus has left me…"

A fresh wave of misery swept her. Into the silence it forced upon her, Fiona spoke.

"Oh, Molly. You don't understand."

"I do understand! I understand that Marcus sped out of here as fast as his feet would carry him last night, after speaking with Papa. That he probably will never be back, and I was a fool to think he would be."

She collapsed onto her chair, burying her face against her folded forearms. Tears burned her eyes. They threatened to slide down her miserable cheeks the moment Molly let her guard down. But she did not want to let them fall now, with her family to witness her unhappiness. She shook her head.

"I have to leave," she blurted.

She rose, grabbing a shawl from one of the spare dining chairs lining the far wall. Blindly, Molly dragged its soft knit over her shoulders. She made her feet move, forcing them to carry her toward the front door, toward her escape. She meant to go to the shop and lose her troubles in the new techniques she'd learned—that, or weep in private.

"Molly, wait," her papa said. He grabbed her arm, halting her progress. "Listen to me."

"I can't." She wrenched her arm free. "Please let me go."

Her mama and both sisters urged her to stay as well. As far as Molly was concerned, that was just more proof of their intention to baby her. Right now, that overly familiar tactic was the last thing she needed.

"No, daughter," Adam said. "I won't let you go."

Molly blinked at the sternness in his voice. It was so unlike her absentminded, warmhearted papa that she quit her struggles. She blinked at him.

"Copeland did speak with me last night," he confirmed, his steely gaze locked with hers. He patted her arm gently, then released her. "But you did not stay downstairs long enough to know the truth of it. 'Twas not a prelude to escaping here, as you think."

Molly sniffled. A tiny sliver of hope struggled to life inside her. She stared at her papa, not daring to breathe.

"Last night," Adam said, sweeping everyone at the table with an oddly proud, endearingly pleased look, "Copeland spoke with me in private for a reason we might all have expected, after hearing him stand up for our Molly—"

"So chivalrously, too," her mama interrupted with clear excitement. She exchanged satisfied glances with Grace and Sarah. "Why, it certainly put all of us in our places, didn't it? Reminded us of how poorly we'd been treating our Molly May, and how we should change."

"Our eyes were opened to the truth," Grace confirmed.

Sarah and Adam nodded.

Ah. So that explained their change of heart. Marcus's interference had made an impression upon them. Funny, that one man's defense had accomplished the very thing Molly had struggled for all these years.

But she didn't want to think about that now. She wanted to know what else her papa had to say. "You were saying, Papa?"

No one heard. They were all too busy nodding to each other to heed her or to see the impatient, nudging look she threw Adam next.

"Papa!" Molly cried.

"Oh, yes. You're wondering what happened, aren't you?" Wearing a grin, her papa removed his spectacles. He took a moment to polish them. He fixed them back in place, then regarded his daughter with clear mischief. "It's simple, my dear. Last night, when

Copeland and I spoke in my study…he requested my permission to ask your hand in marriage."

Marcus found Molly outside her bakeshop that afternoon. He strode toward her from behind, admiring the swish of her skirts as she bent with a basket over one arm and something else in her opposite hand. Her muttering grew louder as he neared.

"Open up, blast you!" she said, jiggling her shop's doorknob.

It did not yield. Balling up one fist, she dropped her basket to the porch. She glared at the door. Then she kicked it. Her yelp of surprise carried clear to the street.

Marcus grinned. "That's two inches of solid pine making up your door. Nothing so dainty as your foot will have much of an impression upon it."

She whirled, her hat ribbons flying. "Marcus!"

"And my foot will likely shatter it, due to my immense size and strength." He pretended to ponder the problem as he climbed the last few steps to stand beneath her shop's hanging sign. "It looks like we're both stuck out here. Together." He gazed upward in sham consternation. "Whatever shall we do?"

"I can't imagine," she said, eyes wide.

Her lighthearted tone was a perfect imitation of his own. Hearing it, Marcus wanted to laugh aloud with pleasure. All would be fine between them. Evidently,

Molly's headache had gone, and so had any awkwardness from last night's dinner.

The dinner that had made him understand her, and her reasons for striving so hard to succeed, at long last.

Happily he drew her close on a murmured greeting. Molly came into his arms with gratifying ease, her skirts swishing around his booted feet. Face tipped upward, Molly stood in his embrace…smiling. Smiling, in fact, as though she knew a delightful secret and wasn't yet prepared to tell it. He found himself smiling as well.

Because he did have a secret. A secret to share with her. When the right time came, of course.

"That's the loveliest sight I've seen all day," Marcus told her, clasping hands with her. Her warmth reached out to him, prompting him to bend his elbows and tug her a little nearer. Their joined hands—hers gloved, his bare—rested cozily against his shirtfront. "You, smiling."

"Ah, but *you've* spent the day with lumbermen." Her nod was knowledgeable. "Doubtless they're less than lovely after chopping trees and dragging logs."

"True. But in the mornings, *before* they head into the forest, I have to admit…they're passing fair."

For his teasing, Molly gave him a playful swat.

Something glimmered as she moved, hung around her wrist on a knotted cord. Marcus grabbed it.

He turned it over in his hand. "A key?"

She ducked her head, giving him a faceful of the fabric flowers affixed to her hat brim as she tried to pull away. Bemused, Marcus tightened his grasp, not letting her leave him. He blew away a trailing ribbon.

He gave her a meaningful look.

"So you are not the only one who has changed," she muttered in reply, her words harkening to the confession Marcus had made earlier. "So I have a key. What of it?"

At her gruff admission, affection filled him. That, and a certain relief. It seemed he wasn't the only one who'd been bewitched by their time together. Molly had felt it as well. That would make everything so much easier.

Later. But for now…

"A key for the woman who never locks her doors?" he marveled, directing his gaze beneath her hat brim. He rubbed his fingers over the cord around her gloved wrist. "I can hardly believe it."

"It's nothing."

As far as Marcus was concerned, it was a confirmation that she understood him. That they shared some views in common now. "It's a key," he repeated. "*Your* key."

With clear reluctance, Molly glanced up at him. This was difficult for her, he could tell. Her indrawn breath brought their bodies closer and nearly made Marcus forget why he questioned her at all...until she answered him.

"It's for my bakeshop," she acknowledged. "Your advice was not so far off the mark. In fact, my papa had been nagging me to do the same. I only wanted to pay for the lock myself."

"Mmm. I see."

"Only now the blasted thing won't work!" She aimed a frustrated scowl at the door. "I've tried and tried to unlock it, but I can't get it to open. I can't even get into my shop!"

"Have you tried breaking a window?"

"I can't believe you'd tease me about that! You know how awful I felt about your breaking into your own house." Her chin came up. "Even though it's hardly my fault you hadn't the sense to realize a burning lamp meant someone was home."

"I'm not accustomed to having someone at home," Marcus explained, leaning in. He couldn't resist tracing the disgruntled line of her jaw with his fingertips, brushing his thumb over her soft cheek. "To having someone waiting for me. I'm a solitary man, Molly."

As though she savored his touch, her eyes had

drifted closed. Now they opened. Her gaze fixed sorrowfully upon him.

"Solitary? Oh, Marcus…"

"Let's see about opening this door." With authority, he unlooped the key from her wrist, then bent to retrieve the basket she'd set near the threshold. Carrying the wicker contraption slung over his arm, Marcus worked the key in the lock. "Sometimes new locks are stubborn."

"Perhaps that's why the two of you get on so well." Her mirth was barely suppressed. "You're stubborn, too."

He grunted. "It was stubbornness I needed to survive. Had you grown up as I did—*there*. It's open."

After a few tries, the tumblers turned. Marcus stretched to flatten his arm along the door, holding it open in a gentlemanly gesture. Molly passed by him in a sweet swoosh of yellow skirts, the scents of cinnamon and sugar trailing after her.

Marcus inhaled deeply. For all his life, he would link those spicy-sweet fragrances with Molly and the unexpected happiness he'd found with her. Closing the door behind him, he followed her inside. He set the wicker basket near his sawhorse.

"I've just been to the schoolhouse," Molly said, her high-buttoned shoes tapping briskly across the floor to her work counter. She drew off her gloves, then her hat. "The Chautauqua committee is meeting today. Sarah promised to put in a good word for me if I delivered some baked goods to her."

That explained the basket she'd carried.

"Are there any left?" Marcus nosed into the round-handled wicker, flipping aside the cloth tucked inside it. "I only came to repair your wainscoting, but I find I can't get enough of your sweets, of a sudden."

He took an enormous bite of the cinnamon bun he found. Chewing happily, he winked at Molly. He didn't know what had changed in her baking, but something most definitely had. These sweets were tender and buttery, sugary and spicy. They could not have been juggled with, used as spare baseballs in the Morrow Creek league or tamped beneath chair legs to level them.

If Molly's baking could improve, there was no telling what might happen, he thought. Surely there was magic afoot here.

On that fanciful notion, Marcus took another bite. He caught Molly watching him speculatively. Swallowed.

"Is something wrong?"

"No." Flustered, she spun to heft a sack of flour onto her work surface. Powdery whiteness puffed from the burlap's seams. "Nothing's wrong. It's just that—"

"I'll get to your repairs soon enough." He licked the sweetened icing from his fingers. "I promise."

"It's not that. I know you will. It's only…I've just remembered something my papa said to me this morning."

Her gaze flew to his. It was expectant. Anxious. Desperately hopeful, all at once.

Marcus knew exactly what that "something" she spoke of was. It was the same "something" that had kept him awake upon his pillow till all hours last night, contemplating his future.

And hers.

But now, wanting to bide his time until *he* was ready, Marcus popped the last of his cinnamon bun into his mouth and strode to his sawhorse. There he surveyed his tools. Picked up a hacksaw with all the nonchalance he could muster. Squinted. Tested its blade with his thumb.

"Marcus?"

"Hmm?"

"Did you hear me?"

He frowned. "Did you ask a question? You mentioned something about your father, but I…" He cast his palms blithely upward and shrugged. "I thought you were only reminiscing."

Molly gave a gusty sigh. She scurried around to the front of her work counter, then propped herself on one of the iron-framed stools that stood before it.

Marcus watched from the corner of his eye, pretending to measure a cut of lumber as she arranged her skirts and hair. She folded her ankles primly. Next she clasped her hands and set them serenely in her lap.

"I wasn't reminiscing," Molly blurted. "Marcus, I...know. I know what you said to my papa last night."

He paused to look at her. He'd come here with every intention of beginning as he meant to go on, of establishing that *he* was the one who would decide things between them. One look at Molly's demure posture, blushing cheeks and eager expression nearly changed his mind. He knew what she wanted. She was the very picture of a woman expecting a proposal of marriage. How could he refuse her?

How could he *not,* when doing so meant giving away his authority to this independent-minded woman from the very start?

If he was to love Molly, to have her for his own, he would need to hold steady. To do anything else was to court disaster...not to mention the ridicule of the entire Morrow Creek Men's Club.

Obstinately Marcus held his secret.

"You look beautiful," he found himself saying in its place. "I don't tell you that often enough. I look at you...and my breath stops."

She gasped. Marcus froze. How had such a mush-hearted truth slipped from his lips? Damnation! He'd only meant to avoid asking the question Molly so obviously expected. Hoping to regain some manful dignity for himself, he ducked his head and measured for certain.

"Or maybe that's the dried leaves in the air," he said gruffly, "interfering with my breathing."

She had the audacity to scoff at his tender words.

"Marcus! Didn't you hear me? I said, I know what you discussed with my papa last night."

"Ah. You mean the lecture I gave your family about how they belittle and baby you?" he asked with a knowing nod, sidestepping the issue yet again. "I know I was harsh, but damnation, Molly! They treat you poorly. You deserve better."

She squirmed on her stool.

"It was more than I could stand," he went on, marking his measurement with a pencil, "to sit there while they picked you apart. I had to say something. So I did."

"Well, whatever you said, it was magical," she admitted. "My whole family was changed this morning, even Cook."

"I'm glad."

Marcus went on working. Molly went on sitting. He'd sawed through two lengths of lumber and measured a third before she spoke again.

"Marcus, isn't there…something you wanted to say to me?"

Her soft inquiry made his heart beat faster. Ignoring it, he scraped his wood planer along a board, then squinted to check the level. He straightened. "As a matter of fact, there is."

She brightened. Patted the stool next to hers. "Then why don't you come over here and say it?"

Expectation and excitement reached clear across the room, drawing him toward her as surely as did her beautiful smile. Marcus abandoned his planer and came.

"Un-unless you'd rather not sit," she blurted, whipping her hand from the stool she'd indicated. "Unless you'd rather…stay where you are? Or perhaps *bend*…a little lower?"

Standing directly in front of her, he hid a grin. Damnation, but she was a bossy female. She'd all but grabbed his carpenter's pencil to mark out a space on the floor for him to get down on bended knee. He pictured Molly biting her lip with concentration while doing so and wanted to smile still wider.

"I'll stand," he said.

Her composure only flickered for a moment. "Oh. All right. If you like."

Her acceptance filled him with a rush of affection. Perhaps there *was* a chance they could compromise.

They would need to, he knew, if a future between them was to work.

He nodded. "Molly, I know we've been meeting at my house for my cooking and baking lessons," he began.

A slight frown creased her forehead. "Yes?"

"And, well, I know I'm not an easy pupil. Thank you for teaching me."

"You're...welcome."

Marcus nodded again, then squeezed her hand. That done, he headed back to his sawhorse.

"That's *it?*" Molly blurted from behind him.

Her tone of astonishment made him want to laugh aloud. It wasn't well done of him to tease her like this, but hell—a man had to be a man, didn't he? A *man* decided the time and place of his proposal, not the woman he meant to offer marriage to.

Even the damnable matchmaker would have agreed with that.

He glanced over his shoulder. Raised his eyebrows. "Was there something you wanted to say to *me?*" he asked.

Molly squirmed again. He could see the thoughts whirling through her ever-busy brain as surely as he could smell the cinnamon in the air. It occurred to Marcus that independent-minded Molly Crabtree might actually be bold enough to offer a marriage proposal to *him.*

The matchmaker would *definitely* have agreed with *that*.

She drew in a deep breath and opened her mouth.

"Whatever it is, we'll discuss it over dinner," he announced firmly, turning back to his work. "Tonight, at my house. After your bakeshop and my mill close."

He'd have sworn she growled in frustration. Just a tiny, feminine rumble, but a growl all the same. Truth be told, he found her lack of decorum endearing. It only showed how keen she was that they be together—a desire he shared, as well.

Still...if looks were flammable, his shoulders would have flared just then, like so much kindling.

Marcus decided a peace offering was in order. He flashed her a smile. "Oh, and Molly? Don't expect to return home early from dinner. What I have planned for us might take till midnight...or even beyond."

Chapter Fourteen

That evening, Molly ran almost all the way to Marcus's home at the edge of town. She fisted her skirts and scurried through the crisp fallen leaves and dried pine needles, let her beaded reticule bang against her dress as she hurried past darkened businesses and townspeople's homes with smoke curling from the chimneys. She'd made her excuses to her mama and papa, sidestepped Sarah and Grace's inquiries with a wave and a promise, and now she was ready—ready to see what tonight would bring.

It promised an occasion like none other, if all that Marcus had said earlier was true…an occasion that would change their lives forever.

Don't expect to return home early. What I have planned for us might take till midnight…or even beyond.

He could only mean that he *finally* meant to deliver the marriage proposal she'd expected ever since hearing her papa's startling revelation of that morning. Shivering with anticipation, Molly came to a stop just at the edge of Marcus's property. There, lamplight shone from his small house's windows. Wood smoke scented the air, along with the aroma of roasting meat. Surprised, Molly sniffed. Apparently Marcus had already started dinner. Beckoned from the chilly air by the promise of warm rooms and an even warmer man, Molly climbed the porch steps.

If Marcus wandered again around the question at hand, she promised herself as she knocked on the door, she would just have to pose it herself. Why not? Doing so was, Molly thought firmly, exactly what the matchmaker would have suggested.

Marcus opened the door on a household turned warm by the fireplace and appealing by the man who guided her past it. Just as the door thunked closed behind them, he stopped there and greeted her.

With a kiss.

And oh, what a kiss it was! Heady and sweet, passionate and surprising, it made her breath catch and her knees wobble. Caught up in the sensation of Marcus's lips against hers, Molly barely noticed when he slid her coat from her shoulders, when he untied her hat and cast it aside. She barely registered the loss of her gloves as he unbuttoned them, tugged them deftly from her hands, tossed them away with her reticule.

She knew only the murmured hello Marcus gave

her as he paused. Felt only the pleasure that un-furled inside her as his mouth returned to hers, telling her without words that she was more than welcome there. Clinging to him with bare hands and an equally bared heart, Molly kissed him back with all the fervor at her command.

"Ah, Molly," he whispered, cupping her face in his hands. "What would I do without you?"

"Don't be silly." Her smile for him felt as tender as the beating of her heart. "You'll never have to do without me."

His next kiss was fiercer, deeper. It felt changed somehow, as did Marcus's embrace when he pulled her close. He held her in his arms almost desper-ately, Molly thought. Almost as though he feared she would slip away, like the sunlight fading on her journey between her home and his.

Wanting to reassure him, Molly delved her fin-gers into his hair. She held him to her, heedless of the damage such an action might cause to the fancy dress she'd chosen for tonight. This was the man she loved. Any worry of his was a worry of hers, a worry she would do her best to vanquish.

As she hesitated on the verge of saying so, Marcus gently pulled away.

"Come into the kitchen," he said. "I have some-thing to show you."

Willingly Molly followed him. Filled with affection, she admired the masculine width of his shoulders, the steady swagger of his movements, the fine fit of his plain white shirt, dark vest and dark trousers.

All in all, she decided, his appearance befitted that of a man about to become betrothed. Giddiness whirled inside her.

Never had she thought this would happen. Never had she expected to find a man to respect, to learn from, to be challenged by and, most of all, to love. But in Marcus, Molly had found all those things... and more.

She could not have been happier. Or more eager to discover what he meant to show her next.

"What is it?" she asked, sniffing the kitchen's savory aromas. "A chicken you've trussed and roasted? A pork loin? I think I smell potatoes baking, too."

Molly glanced around the kitchen, searching for the evidence of his mealtime labor. To her surprise, there wasn't so much as a potato peel or pepper grinder in sight. The work table was spotless. The stove top boasted only a tidy saucepan, its contents simmering just enough to faintly rattle its lid.

The dining table, which until now had boasted cast-off food tins and newspapers was clean. In its center was an Indian-worked pottery bowl filled with an arrangement of brilliant autumn branches, plump pinecones and miniature acorns. Near it stood matching plates, candles, a pair of wine-colored linen napkins, gleaming cutlery and two glasses.

"I could not get flowers for you. For the table," Marcus said abruptly. "Not with cold weather already upon us."

He stood near the pantry doors, watching her. Even from the distance separating them, Molly could see the tense set of his shoulders, the uncertain angle to his jaw. He kept his arms at his sides, forearms facing her in an open, almost beseeching, position. But his gaze, when it met hers, was one-hundred percent Marcus: challenging, bold, authoritative. It almost dared her to find fault with his preparations.

"This arrangement is beautiful," she assured him, moving closer to touch one of the vivid, flame-colored oak leaves. "And very festive. As befits the occasion."

She cast him a meaningful look.

Her coquetry was wasted on Marcus. He frowned at the table settings. "The napkins are from the mercantile, just today. Luke was in the midst of refusing another ugly necktie from his matchmaker-crazed admirer, but he managed to unearth those from a box in the back." His frown deepened. "They look like my horse stomped on them. I should have tried ironing them."

"You would have burned your house down. We haven't covered flatirons and their uses yet."

Ignoring her grin, Marcus paced restlessly to the cast-iron stove. He lifted the lid of the saucepan, peered inside and gave its contents a fierce glare.

"Don't worry," Molly told him. "Whatever that is, it won't dare overcook. Not so long as you keep scaring it like that."

Marcus shook his head. "It had better not. I did not leave the lumber mill in Smith's hands today so that I could ruin this meal."

"You quit work early today?"

Marcus paused. She had the sense he hadn't meant to reveal so much, but then...

"You needn't look so astonished." Still wearing his fierce expression, Marcus grabbed a cloth from nearby and shielded his hand with it. He opened the oven door. "It wasn't as though I put Smith in charge and then came home to nap. I had things to do."

"What things?" Molly asked, bemused as she watched him spoon drippings over the chicken roasting in the oven. He may as well have been attempting something nigh impossible, so intense was the concentration he applied to the task.

"Getting the napkins." He angled his head toward the dining table, still engrossed in his cooking. "Setting the table. Collecting branches and whatnot for that bowl you see. Buying this chicken."

Marcus shook his head. "O'Neil was wearing that embroidered butcher's apron and matching neckerchief his matchmaker gal made him, poor knuck."

Molly smiled. "I'll bet he looked nice."

"He looked like a fool. Like I probably do right now."

He shut the oven door with an iron-forged clank, then straightened. The heat had reddened his face and curled the dark hair at his temples. Marcus swiped at both with his sleeve, then headed across the room, his expression grim.

"Something to drink?" he asked. "I have cider, ale—"

Molly waylaid him, grabbing both his arms. "Thank you for this," she said, wanting to ease the harsh angles in his face, wanting to reassure him. "Everything is lovely."

"The candles!" He eyeballed the two sitting on the table as though he meant to strangle them. "I forgot to light the candles."

He jerked the long tapers from the table. With decisive stomps, he carried both candles to the cast-iron stove. Seconds later, Marcus had them lit.

Molly was taken aback. "You shoved those directly into the flame."

"They're lit, aren't they?"

Marcus carried the candles, now dripping copious amounts of wax, back to the table. He arranged them beside the Indian-worked bowl, then stood back to gauge the effect. His brow furrowed. He pushed the candles an inch closer together.

He was nervous, Molly realized. Marcus was nervous about his proposal tonight, and about this meal they would share.

His concern touched her deeply. It was then that she realized exactly how much Marcus had changed. For her sake, he had set aside his work. For her sake, he had attempted cooking and cleaning and decorating. For her sake, she understood suddenly, he had forged a new openness in his life…a life that now had room to include the two of them, together.

"Hmm. That will have to do," he announced.

"It looks lovely!"

Too overwrought to hear her praise, Marcus returned to the stove. Basting spoon fisted in hand, he squinted at the clock.

"The chicken should be ready soon," he said. "I think the potatoes are already done."

He glowered at the oven door, as though his displeasure could penetrate the cast iron and compel the poultry to catch up and cook faster. Molly felt a tiny, love-filled smile come to her lips.

"Don't worry. The potatoes won't be harmed by keeping them waiting."

Marcus glanced over his shoulder. His expression

was appalled, as though he'd just recalled something important, something awful.

"You haven't become a Grahamite like your mother, have you? You still eat chicken, don't you?" He whacked himself on the forehead. "How did I forget your family's vegetarianism?"

With a growl, Marcus cast aside his spoon and paced across the kitchen. He looked so anguished, Molly couldn't stand it. She loved this man too much to see him worrying so, but all her attempts to put him at ease had come to naught. What else could she do?

"I should have known the Crabtrees would give in to faddish nonsense like Graham's preachings," Marcus muttered. "Wheat berries and bark and—"

"I like chicken."

He cast her a suspicious look. "To eat, or to keep as a pet?"

"To eat! I'm the one who taught you how to cook it, remember?" Molly went to him, spread her palms over his chest and gazed beseechingly up at him. "Please, Marcus. All will be well. We're here, together. We need nothing more. If you would only ask that question which you've been meaning to ask—"

"Ale!" He snapped his fingers. "We need ale."

Moments later, he'd opened a pint and poured a glass. He was draining his third in quick succession when Molly realized that if Marcus kept on this way, he'd never be able to form the words for his proposal, much less understand them.

"Marcus, give me that," she said, prying his glass away. The last of the ale sloshed over the rim, sending its sharp, yeasty aroma into the air between them. "You've had enough."

"Ah, you want some, too. Of course. I'm a passing poor host not to have offered you a draft."

He filled her a glass. Molly refused it.

His mournful gaze pinned her. "I can make you happy."

Was he drunk already? Molly doubted it. Nevertheless...

"Perhaps we should eat now," she suggested.

Marcus paid no attention to that sensible notion. Clearly he had something more on his mind.

"The ale, the dinner—" he flung his arms wide, swaying a little as he indicated the preparations he'd made "—they're only the beginning. If you'll let me, I can make you happy."

"I know." She'd seen her papa this way once or twice, when he'd weathered a disappointment at the newspaper, or expected bad news in a letter from the States. Molly tucked her arm around Marcus's middle, then guided him toward the kitchen table. "I know you can. I can make you happy, too."

"No!" he roared. He thumped his chest. "*I will

make you happy. Pleasing his woman is what a man is made to do."

"Grace will be happy to hear it. Sit down."

Marcus frowned. And sat. He blinked up at her, all seriousness, of a sudden. "I don't think I can do this, Molly."

A shiver of unease swept over her. Shaking it off, Molly patted his shoulder. Marcus could not be having second thoughts *now*...could he?

"The dinner will be wonderful," she said in her most comforting tone. "Would you like me to get the chicken and potatoes from the oven?"

She stepped away, intent upon doing so. Marcus stopped her with one big hand on her wrist. "I don't mean the dinner," he said gravely. "I mean *this*. I can't do it, Molly."

Miserably Marcus watched as Molly's back straightened. Her skin went cold in his grasp. He rubbed his thumb desperately over her wrist, seeking to...he didn't know. Seeking to apologize? To make himself understood? To tell her, without words, how much he'd struggled with this night?

The ale sent another wave of dizziness to his head. Hell. Maybe drinking it hadn't been such a fine idea. At the time, though, he'd needed something. Something to deaden his raging feelings, something to ease the unfamiliar uncertainty coursing through him… something to make him *not* blurt out the confession he felt himself about to make.

Molly gazed down over her shoulder at him, all sweetness and womanly confusion. He could tell he'd hurt her. The realization wounded him, as well.

"I'm not the man you think I am." Marcus cleared his throat against a sudden hoarseness there. "You don't know me."

She whirled, skirts whooshing over his knees. In a thrice, Molly was kneeling on the floor in front of his chair. Her face turned upward to his, filled with a brightness he longed to believe in.

"I *do* know you!" she cried, clasping the arms he'd left loose in his lap. She gave him a little shake. "*Don't* do this now, Marcus. Please. You've had too much ale—"

"I haven't had enough. Not for this."

"No. You're wrong." She glared at the pint bottle, as though her wish to have it gone might be enough to make it vanish. "You'll eat, you'll feel better—"

Her certainty ignited some measure of hopefulness inside him. Marcus hesitated. He drank in the sight of her, wondering if his love for Molly had come first, or his fear that this moment would arrive and damage things between them.

"There are things you don't know about me," he said.

"They cannot be so bad as your black expression

makes them seem." Her touch was a benediction. "Tell me."

He'd never thought he would. When he'd embarked on this time together with her, it had been a lark. Finding out if Molly was indeed the matchmaker had been nothing more than a task to be completed, for the satisfaction of the men's club. Marcus had never expected it to change his life.

And yet, it had.

"I never had fancy things like this, until coming here." He picked up one of the plates he'd set out, made of china so fine it sparkled in the candlelight. Catching a glimpse of himself on its pristine face, Marcus set it aside. "No china, no silver…no linen napkins or centerpieces. When you are as poor as my family was, such things are sold for food—and they were. While I was still a boy."

Molly listened, clasping his arms reassuringly, emboldening him to go on. He searched for pity or disgust in her face. Remarkably to him, he found none.

"We were so poor we lived on dandelion stew. On leavings from the butcher, and turnips that once fed us for an entire Baltimore winter. My father talked often of heading west to make a new start. But my mother was always too sick to make the journey. And so we stayed."

"Oh, Marcus. Most people aren't well-to-do," Molly protested. "I know that. My own family—"

"Eats porridge for a laugh. 'Dr. Graham's famous wheat berry porridge.'" He gave a defiant shake of his head. "Mine ate it to survive, when we couldn't finagle anything better."

Her solemn look, and the quantity of ale he'd drunk, encouraged him to go on.

"I wanted to work. But I wasn't allowed to leave school. Not till I'd mastered as much as I could without paying a university for the privilege. By the time I finished, my family had gotten used to doing without."

"Making do is nothing to be ashamed of, Marcus. I'm sure you did the best you could."

He fisted his hand, remembering. "I wanted to do more. More for my mother, more for my sisters. They suffered, and shouldn't have. That damned powerless feeling was more than I could stand."

"But it was your father's responsibility—"

"It is a *man's* responsibility to care for the people around him. Whether they're women, children, kin or strangers. A man makes sure all is well."

"But you were only a child."

"In the beginning," Marcus agreed. "But soon enough, I was a man. Old enough to head west myself. Old enough to join a logging crew and start work as a greaser." He paused, thinking of his time as the lowliest of all workers in a lumber camp. "Old enough to work my way through every damned job on that crew, until I'd mastered them all."

Her faint smile touched him. "That's why you understand me," Molly said. "Because we are equally determined."

Marcus squeezed her hand. Her acceptance was a balm to him. He couldn't look at her, though. Not yet. Molly didn't understand the whole of it.

"Once I'd mastered the lumber crew, I could see that real success came from *owning* the lumber mill. The owners weren't breaking their backs sawing and hauling and felling timber. They were prospering, enough to buy horses and houses and land. That's what I wanted. That's what I got."

He swept his household with a savage glance. Seeing the results of his success reassured him. He had done what he'd set out to do, and he'd done it well.

"And your family? What about them?"

Marcus turned a hardened gaze on her. "What about them?"

"You helped them, of course."

Deliberately he remained silent.

"I won't believe otherwise! Marcus, you are too good a man, with too strong a sense of duty, to see them struggle while you prosper. Tell me what you did for them."

"No one has ever asked me that before."

"Then no one knows you as I do."

"The whole of Morrow Creek thinks me a miser," Marcus said. "Even you did, once."

Molly shook her head. She held his hand between both of hers, cradling it. "Tell me," she urged. "I won't be deterred. You know I am as stubborn as the lock on my bakeshop door, and twice as talkative. I'll have the truth from you."

A smile touched his lips. Marcus felt his heart ease. 'Twas a mere fraction, but it was enough.

With her heart in her eyes, Molly continued to gaze up at him. Waiting. He could not disappoint her, any more than she had *not* disappointed him. She had seen through his ruse, after all. That was a first, in his experience.

Marcus relented. "I bought them a house, outside of the city. Land, and livestock. My father is a gentle-man farmer these days, and my mother a farmer's wife. My sisters live nearby. Those dark days are behind them."

Her smile proved triumphant. "See? I am right about you."

Fiercely he went on. "Once I had given them a better start, my world seemed to turn upright again. That much is true."

"Because you are a good man."

"No. You don't understand." Marcus raked a hand

through his hair, dreading this moment. "I did it to make *myself* feel better. To this day I help them because I need to, the same way I need to fill my pantry to bursting. The same way I need to tuck bread in my pockets and tally all my ledgers twice."

Molly did not so much as glance across the room at his telltale pantry. Instead, she shook her head. "You did it because you care for them. You help your family because you love them. It is as plain as that."

He stared at her, wanting to believe.

Stubbornly he could not.

"You have it turned around," Marcus insisted. "They care for me *because* I help them. I know it."

"Then you are a fool," Molly said gently. She rose higher on her knees, releasing his hand to lay both palms against his chest. She pressed her lips to his, once. "A fool who must be loved well, in order to be taught the error of his judgment."

"I bought their house!" Marcus insisted. "The very land they farm on! Without me—"

"Shh." Her kiss cut short his words. "I believe in you, Marcus. I won't listen to anyone berate you. Not even yourself."

"I am right," he grumbled. "About myself, and everything else."

Molly merely smiled, as though his talk were all bluster, without basis in fact.

Beneath the tender persuasion of her touch, Marcus felt himself weakening. He wanted to believe her… yet he knew the truth with everything inside him. The most he had to offer was the labor of his own two hands and the results of that labor. The most he could give was caretaking and protection. The woman before him needed neither of those things. The realization of that fact was what knifed through him still.

"If you like to stock your pantry," Molly observed into the silence, "then it's only because you are caring for yourself as well as you care for your family. If you like to carry bread in your pockets, then it's only to have it on hand, to offer to a lady who needs some."

At her words, Marcus recalled their first shared meal at this table, remembered the tin of beans he'd pressed in her hand and the leftover bread he'd been so pleased to offer. All at once, a measure of relief pushed inside him.

"You have the right of it there," he agreed.

"And if you must tally your ledgers twice," she went on, "then it's only because you haven't an excellent system like mine, to help you keep track of things."

"Indeed." He couldn't help but smile.

"So you see, I do understand you, Marcus," Molly said as she walked her fingers up his shirtfront. "I told you once that I have no illusions about you. That remains true to this night." She cupped the nape of his neck in her hand, then kissed him chastely once more. "You are an excellent man. A man I will be proud to have a certain…*question* from."

Her eyebrows flared meaningfully. Her expression turned expectant, even excited. They were back to this, then.

"Question?" Marcus repeated. He pretended to ponder it. "Do you mean…are you hungry?"

"Marcus!"

"Thirsty, then? There's still some ale—"

"Grr…"

He leaned back to examine her face. It was the most beloved sight he thought he'd ever seen, even scrunched as it was in feminine consternation.

"Or I have cider—"

"You are doing this apurpose!"

"Doing what?" Given the relief and good cheer burbling inside him, it was hard to keep an innocent expression. Molly did not think less of him. She wanted him still. "I am asking you questions. Are you not proud to have them?"

"That's it." With a distinct huff and a businesslike flutter of her skirts, Molly rearranged her position. Before he'd even realized what she was about, she'd propped herself on bended knee at his feet and was

reaching for his hand. She cleared her throat, then gazed up at him nervously.

"Marcus, we've known each other for quite some time now. I've come to care for you very much."

"I care for you also." He regarded her in puzzlement, wondering at her anxiety. Their sentiments were hardly unknown to each other. So why, now, had she...*oh, hell.*

"When the kind of caring we share comes to its natural fruition," Molly went on, "it's only fitting and right that we should pledge to each other a lifetime of—"

She was proposing to him. She, a woman, was proposing to him. A man.

Matchmaker or not, this would never do.

"—fidelity and companionship—"

He had nothing to offer her that she couldn't obtain for her own. Nothing...save himself.

"—no matter what we might face together," Molly was rambling, her cheeks pinkening, "I think it's only correct and proper that we—aah!"

Her words were cut short as Marcus leaped desperately from his chair, not so much thinking as acting on instinct. He caught her in his arms as they both fell to the floor. There, atop the round rag rug, Molly glared at him.

"What are you *doing?* I was in the middle of something."

"Yes. And you were coming uncomfortably close to the end of it. I had to stop you somehow."

"By dragging me to the floor? Marcus, that was a prop—"

"Here. This will be more comfortable." Marcus rearranged his arms, using one of them to pillow her head and shoulders. He gazed down at her urgently. "Better?"

She blinked in confusion. "Yes."

"Good. Then marry me, Molly."

"Marcus! I—"

He kissed her once, just to be sure she understood he meant it. When their lips parted again, her eyes were still widened in shock, but at least she wasn't protesting now.

"Marry me," he begged, his heart pounding wildly with the fear that she might, after all this, say no—possibly out of sheer contrariness that he'd foiled her proposal. That would be like her, Marcus thought wildly, and knew he had to press on. "You might not think you need me. But you'll never find a man who loves you the way I do—"

"On the floor?"

"—no matter how hard you try."

"I haven't tried. I—"

"I need you, Molly. I need you more than I ever knew." With a trembling hand, Marcus touched her face. Love swelled within him, making him feel both humble and afraid. Humble that he'd gotten this far…afraid that she'd say no. "Please," he said hoarsely. "Say you'll be my wife, and make me the happiest man in Morrow Creek. I love you, Molly. So much."

"Oh, Marcus." Her eyes turned moist with unshed tears. She reached for him there, on the floor. "I am already yours. I was yours from the moment you brought me to your mill, and from the moment you regarded me with such seriousness. I was yours from the moment you treated me as a business equal, *and* a woman to be courted. No man had ever treated me as such—no man was exceptional enough for that, save you. I may as well say it now, before we go on…your good opinion of my work meant so much to me."

Her shining gaze captured his, stirred guilty discomfort within him. If Molly ever discovered the truth of the machinations that had brought her to his lumber mill…the subterfuge that still went on as he paid his men to buy her sweets…Lord, he could not stand it.

"I think that quality in you may well have turned the tide between us," she was saying, cheerfully. "That is why I know we can be happy together. Ours will be a union of equals."

A union of equals. To his surprise, Marcus wanted that, too. But not if it was based on a lie. That, indeed, was what his initial encouragement of her bakeshop had been.

He tried to turn the subject. "A union of equals? Your sister Grace has been evangelizing her beliefs at home, as well as on the street."

Molly smiled. "Only you would be so accepting of her."

"Jack Murphy is not. That is for certain."

"I know. You are a unique man. Encouraging me at my bakeshop was only the beginning of it. So tonight, as far as your question goes—"

"Wait! Don't tell me your answer now."

Desperately Marcus stopped Molly with a kiss. He felt ashamed of having deceived her as much as he had, woefully fearful that if she continued as she'd begun, she would talk herself into marrying him for all the wrong reasons. For his false support, his sham encouragement, his pretended good opinion of her baking. He should at least, he told himself, give her other reasons to care for him.

"Let me show you the dinner we're to share," he coaxed, hitting upon the strategy in just that moment. "Before you decide."

"But—"

"Please, Molly." He stroked her hair away from her face, trying not to show the bullheaded need he felt to make her love him for *himself*...not for a thing he'd done in an attempt to uncover the secret matchmaker in as unobtrusive a manner as possible. For that, precisely, was what bringing Molly to his lumber mill had been.

At first.

He pressed further, willing to appear as foolish as necessary in order to win her. "Or did you think," he asked, "that you are the only one who wants encouragement in your endeavors?"

Molly's expression, initially confused, turned canny...then teasing. "Encouragement, my eye! You simply want me sated and pleased before I give you my answer. You think to influence me with roasted chicken and potatoes."

"And boiled carrots. Don't forget those."

"Very well." Laughing, Molly pushed his chest as though to move him so they could get to their feet. "Let's have this great feast of yours. But I warn you, it won't change my mind a bit. My answer is formed. Despite my past, I'm more decisive than you or anyone else in Morrow Creek really knows."

He hoped she was wrong about that.

"Hmm," was all he said.

Marcus rolled aside. He helped Molly to a seated position, then leaped up to help her stand. She shrieked with surprise when he pulled her immediately into his arms again.

"Perhaps dinner won't change your mind," he agreed, pausing to press a leisurely kiss to her lips. "But I'd be willing to bet that what I have planned for afterward…might."

Chapter Fifteen

That evening, Molly was swept off her feet.

First, quite literally as Marcus tumbled them both to the floor for his sudden proposal. Then, figuratively as he proceeded to shower her with attention, ply her with delicious food and drink, tease her with laughter and good humor. As it happened, Marcus Copeland could make himself nigh irresistible when he chose to…and tonight, he most definitely chose to.

They finished dinner unhurriedly, lingering over the succulent chicken. They sat together in the candlelight, Molly exclaiming over Marcus's newly learned talents in the kitchen. They talked and laughed, occasionally kissed. Molly, emboldened, even dared to try a sip of ale.

"Bah! How can you drink the stuff?" she exclaimed afterward, covering her mouth in horror. "It tastes awful!"

But then a pleasant wooziness stole over her, and

Molly understood. Ale gave a sensation similar to the feeling that newfound love engendered—tingling fingers, and all. Under its influence, the room seemed cozier, the lamplight brighter, the company wittier.

"No wonder all those men linger at Jack Murphy's saloon," Molly marveled, nodding toward the pint. "They're looking for the experience of love! I wonder if they know it."

She explained her theory to Marcus, who only laughed. He did not agree with her that this revelation only proved what Molly had known all along—there was a *need* for the matchmaker in Morrow Creek. The men's very actions proved it.

"I don't want to talk about the matchmaker tonight," Marcus said. "And two sips is more than enough ale for you." He held out his hand. "Come. I want to show you my home."

"I've already seen it. When I—" *Invaded it, had the locks changed, mistook you for a burglar and threatened to bludgeon you with a ledger.* No, that would never do. "Lovely! Let's."

They wandered through the place hand in hand, Marcus showing the things he'd bought to furnish his home and also pointing out the things he'd built himself. While a lantern's light enclosed them in a moving circle of brightness, he entertained her with stories of the house's construction, and made sure she saw all the most newfangled features.

"Any woman who chooses to become mistress of this household," he said with a meaningful squeeze of her hand, "will enjoy all of this. I keep the roof repaired, the wood box full and all the mattresses stuffed. Outside there's room for a vegetable garden, too. Even flowers might grow there."

Thoughtfully Molly merely nodded.

They moved onward, stopping in the room Marcus used for an office. He indicated his shelves of ledgers with a wave of the lantern. "One look through those would tell the new mistress of this household that she'd joined futures with a man of business. A man who'd built a lumber mill from nothing, and made it one of the top timber suppliers in the territory."

Thoughtful, Molly merely smiled.

They climbed the stairs, emerging in a hallway with a paneled alcove bordering it. Marcus tugged her inside the small space. He cleared his throat, frowning slightly.

"I'm told this will make a good sewing area," he said. "I can bring in a chair and a machine, and there's good light from that window for fancywork. A woman who liked to sew—or knit—would enjoy it."

He raised his eyebrows hopefully at her. Molly gave a small "hmm."

Next they traversed the hallway, peeking into two sparsely furnished rooms before entering the largest bedroom. There, a massive carved-pine bedstead occupied most of the space. It was covered in a thick burgundy coverlet and several pillows, and looked fluffy enough to bounce upon.

Molly and Marcus stared at it. Molly was suddenly aware of exactly where they were: in Marcus's bedroom. In his private space, a room which only Marcus and his beloved ought to share. Being there felt dangerous, in a way…but it also felt, somehow, right. In the lamplight, a seeming loss for words fell upon them both. Marcus released her hand to rub the back of his neck in an uncomfortable gesture.

Almost defiantly, he spoke. "This is my bedroom. It will be the mistress of this household's chamber, as well. I keep it warm and clean, and the bed is of the newest design."

Marcus strode farther inside the room. He set down the lamp on a bureau nearby and tested the mattress with his hand. "The way I constructed this bed makes it very sturdy."

Molly merely smiled. Then, she spoke.

"Why does it need to be so sturdy?" She followed him, thinking of her initial impression of the bed. She paused beside it, her heartbeat quickening at finding herself in so intimate a space with a man. With Marcus. "I wonder…do you bounce on it?"

She raised her eyebrows.

He stared back, looking momentarily befuddled.

"It might be fun to bounce on it," Molly added.

"Yes." He sounded slightly strangled. "It might."

The moment stretched between them, fraught with unspoken questions. Unvoiced desires. Unpracticed longing. Marcus's dark gaze held hers, promising love and protection...and something more. Something heady and wonderful.

Abruptly he grabbed the lantern. Its circle of light bobbed crazily as he shifted it to his opposite hand. "We should look at the outbuildings now. I have a small carriage house. Although it only holds a wagon at the moment."

Molly touched his arm and felt the strength emanating from him as surely as she sensed the tension within him, as surely as she wanted to ease it. "Let's stay here."

"I keep the wagon in good repair," he went on, still fixed on his mission. "I have two good horses. No mistress of this house would ever need to worry about making a long journey."

"I know I would be safe with you."

His jaw tightened. His gaze swept her face. Then, as though he wasn't sure she'd understood him, he tried again.

"Those linens are the finest I could buy," Marcus blurted, swinging the lantern to illuminate the bed again. "Goose down pillows, fine cotton sheets, warm woolen blankets."

Molly stepped nearer. She lay her hand on his chest, then gave him a solemn look. "The mistress of this house will doubtless enjoy them…perhaps sooner than you think."

His whole being stilled. With an expression torn between raw male need and a fierce wish to show her everything else he'd intended to, Marcus regarded her. His eyebrow rose.

"She will?"

She nodded, feeling as though she might laugh aloud with joy—that, or let the tears in her eyes fall at last. "*I* will, of course. Me. Did you think I'd changed my mind? Marcus, I accept your proposal."

He looked dumbstruck. "I haven't even shown you my root cellar yet. I keep it very thoroughly stocked, with—"

"You don't need to show me anything." Gently Molly pried the lantern from his hand. She set it on the bureau, then stepped still nearer to Marcus again. "You never did. I love you, Marcus. I love your smile and your wit, your intelligence and your caring. I love your kisses. I love the way you touch me, and I love the way you make me laugh. I love *you*."

He still looked mystified. Molly knew why. She knew Marcus believed he could only be loved when he was giving to someone. Caring for someone. Protecting someone. His words before dinner—and his actions during his household tour—had told her that much.

They love me because *I help them. I know it.*

For as long as it took, she would prove to him that he was wrong about that heartbreaking notion. That he could be loved merely for who he was, not for what he had to give. Not for what she might or might not need from him.

"So if you have not changed your mind between my arrival and this moment...yes, Mr. Copeland." Molly drew in a deep, jubilant breath, fixing her gaze upon his face. "I will marry you. And I will do my best, my *very* best, to make you happy."

"Ahh, Molly." He blinked, seeming to return to himself. A wide smile spread across his face, making him twice as handsome to her...twice as beloved. "Just seeing you smile makes me happier than I've ever been."

He touched her, his hands trembling, with relief or passion, Molly didn't know. All she knew was that Marcus tilted her face within the masculine planes of his palms, that his warmth penetrated all the way to her heart as he stepped nearer, that he lowered his mouth to hers and sealed their engagement with a wonderful kiss. His lips met hers in a union so true it was all she could do to hang on... to give herself to him as freely as she already had surrendered her heart.

Wanting him, delighting in the rugged feel of his broad shoulders beneath her hands, Molly edged closer. Their bodies met, sharing heat even as their kiss went on and on. To Molly, it felt as though they'd been meant to enjoy such togetherness, as though Marcus had been meant for *her,* all along.

Between kisses, he murmured sweet words to her. Molly loved them all. She reciprocated with compliments and gestures, with shy touches and tentative whispers. Being with Marcus was surprisingly easy, she found. Somehow he removed all awkwardness from their encounter; bridged her lack of knowledge with understanding and care. His caressing hands were a celebration of their betrothal, and so were the kisses he lavished on her, over and over again.

Before long, Molly felt breathless with excitement. Nearly undone with anticipation. And positively overflowing with love. 'Twas something Marcus felt, as well. Molly knew he did, because his love showed in the reverent way he slipped his hands to her breasts, in the awestruck angles of his face as he marveled at her helpless reaction to his touch.

"Molly, you are so beautiful to me," he said hoarsely. "To know you'll soon be mine..."

"I am yours already," she answered. "Yours forever."

With a moan of pleasure, Marcus carried them both down onto the bed's soft coverlet. Its texture embraced them, cozy and warm. Caught within it, Molly relaxed even further. This was Marcus, the man she loved. The man she would marry. Whatever happened between them this night was right, and good.

"I have dreamed of this," he said, raising himself on his forearms above her. Tousled dark hair framed his features, giving him the look of a rascal, but in his face, she glimpsed only affection and caring. "Of being together like this, with you."

"I…have also," she confessed. She ran her hands over the taut muscles of his arms, meandered her way to the solid strength of his chest. "My upbringing was liberal, as you know, and…well, I cannot pretend I never wondered what your embrace would feel like."

Truly, it was more than an embrace they shared. Marcus's body pressed hers into the plush mattress beneath them. He felt more muscular than she could have imagined, and far more remarkable. His heat surrounded her. His smile rewarded her.

"Does it meet your expectations?"

She nodded. "It—*you*—exceed them."

Looking boyishly pleased, Marcus ducked his head. Then he kissed her neck, her earlobe, her jaw… before long, Molly forgot they'd been speaking at all, much less what they'd been speaking of. She writhed beneath his touch, urging him as much as she dared to continue, to go on, *please*. She thought she might faint if he did not.

"Truly, I feel quite giddy," she told him. "I don't even dare get up from this bed."

"I hope you don't," he returned, his next touch a bold sweep of his hand from her waist to her thigh. "Stay with me, Molly. Stay…and love me."

"Oh, Marcus. I will."

His was a request she could not deny. Did not *want* to deny. And so, when Marcus's fingers deftly slipped her dress's buttons through their holes, Molly helped. When his hands delved between the resulting gap to caress the bare skin he'd revealed, she arched herself upward to meet him. When his mouth lowered to her throat for a newer, more seductive kind of kiss, she gasped…and then begged him for more of the same.

Long moments later, Marcus drew her dress fully from her shoulders. He pushed away its unbuttoned length, kissed her as he worked at her corset's fastenings, whispered how beautiful she was as he let her undergarments fall beside the bed. Clad only in her chemise, Molly might have felt vulnerable, even frightened. Instead, she merely felt beautiful and adored. Marcus made her feel that way. Because of it, she loved him all the more.

He cupped her breasts in his hands, stroking her through the delicate fabric of her chemise. He kissed her mouth, making her writhe in pleasure. He loved her and caressed her, praised her and admired her, and just when Molly thought she might die of newly discovered ecstasy, Marcus rapidly shed all his clothes and introduced her to a new level of wonder.

His body was perfectly made, wide at the shoulder and lean at the hip. His limbs were formed of corded muscle; his chest was broad, made for her hands to press against. Unable to do so while Marcus stood beside the bed, Molly instead let her gaze follow the short dark hair on his chest. It trailed lower, passing over his flat belly to join the remarkable sight at the junction of his thighs.

At her first glimpse of his…Molly couldn't bring herself to even think the word, but the part of him it described was incredible…she thought she might swoon. She swallowed hard, unable to pull her gaze away.

Marcus closed her mouth with a brush of his knuckles beneath her chin. He grinned fondly as he kicked away the last of his clothes. He swaggered to the bed and joined her there.

She jerked as his body settled intimately against her thigh. He felt so huge. So hot. So…hard.

"This cannot work between us," she blurted. "You are much too large. And I…I am untried.

Marcus, you've made a mistake! You must choose another—"

"Shh," he murmured, stopping her babbling with a kiss. With soothing strokes of his hands, he cuddled her close, then kissed her once more. "I know what I'm doing."

"What? What are you doing?" She tried to bolt upright, but his arms held her still. A thin edge of panic gripped her. "I thought I knew what this was about, but perhaps I've misunderstood all this time. I've been wrong before."

"Infrequently, I'm sure."

"Of course. But still—"

"Trust me," Marcus urged.

When next his hands touched her, Molly knew that she would. She would trust him, because this was the man she loved. And so she bravely offered herself to him.

Her reward was a new level of intimacy…a new pleasure. Marcus stripped away her chemise, leaving her bared for his obvious appreciation. His dark gaze swept over her nakedness, then he pulled her close. To Molly's relief, their bodies felt right together— even better, she realized, unclothed.

His mouth found her breast, kissed its sensitive tip. Overcome by the enjoyment of it all, Molly grasped his head and held him to her, brazen in her passion. She reveled in pleasure as Marcus kissed his way down her body, then acquiesced when he asked her to open herself to him.

With an expression of wonder, Marcus trailed his gaze upward, from the feminine secrets she'd revealed to her face. He entwined his fingers with hers. He smiled, acknowledging the gift she meant to share with him.

Molly felt her cheeks heat as she blushed. But the love in Marcus's face was too real to be denied. Made stronger by it, she opened her arms to him. Tonight she would show Marcus that he needn't doubt her, and he needn't worry over *doing* things for her. She would, as best as she was able, actively love him herself.

In that spirit, Molly kissed him when he came to her. But before she'd gotten very far, Marcus gave her a lopsided, loving smile and took control of everything.

Their coming together was tender and magical, revelatory and loving. In Marcus's arms, Molly discovered what it meant to be a woman in love and felt herself swept away by the care with which Marcus insured her pleasure. Heat rose between them, urging them onward…love surged within them, compelling them to even greater heights.

'Twas more moving than Molly could ever have imagined, to be joined with Marcus that way. He showed her what it meant to be a woman, taught her what bliss could be coaxed from her body. And then, only then, he took his satisfaction as well. He gazed into her eyes as ecstasy shook him, moaned her name as he relaxed against her...stroked her hair tenderly as they lay together afterward, united in that most intimate of ways.

Gradually, awareness of their surroundings returned to her, reminding Molly of the soft linens against her skin, the enormous bedstead they lay upon, the flickering lamplight and faint autumn chill in the bedroom beyond them. Although the chamber held a fireplace, it was unlit.

As though sensing her thoughts, Marcus cuddled her close to keep her warm. He drew the woolen coverlet over them both.

"I will care for you always," he promised, touching her cheek as he gazed at her in wonder. "You must know that."

"I will care for you, as well," Molly told him.

He frowned, appearing to consider it. "Fair enough."

His concession meant much, given all he'd told her that night. Perhaps they *would* be able to compromise, Molly thought. They would need to, she knew, if a future between them was to work.

"Then it's settled. We shall care for each other," she agreed, heartened by Marcus's words. "And we shall be married!"

"The sooner the better."

Molly nodded. "It will be such fun to plan all the baking! The wedding cake, the groom's cake, petits fours for each place at our reception, sweets for an engagement party. I wonder, do you prefer chocolate, or vanilla? I make an excellent Lady Baltimore cake, as well."

She paused in the midst of her excited planning, feeling nearly breathless. She gazed at Marcus expectantly.

"I enjoy all your sweets. Make what you wish."

"Oh, but you must have a say! And we'll have a wedding dinner of all the dishes you enjoy the most, and I'll wear my nicest dress—you haven't seen it yet, fortunately—and I'll enlist Grace and Sarah to help me write invitations to all our friends!"

Molly sat upright, feeling so filled with happiness she could hardly stand it. Considering the sensation, she stopped. She gave Marcus a puzzled look.

"I do believe you've changed me somehow. I feel quite as though I could fly." She hadn't expected that.

He smiled. "I could fly as well. So long as you were by my side."

"Ooh. Oh, Marcus." Giddily Molly flopped downward onto the bed again. She turned her head to look at him. "I love you so very much."

"I love you. Even more."

"Then everything will be wonderful from here on, won't it?"

"Yes." He drew her into his arms, kissing the top of her head as he hugged her close. A sigh escaped him. For an instant, Molly wondered at it. But all Marcus did was give her a squeeze, one that meant he never intended to let her go.

"I think it will," he told her. "I hope…it will."

Chapter Sixteen

The next day, the Sabbath, flew by for Marcus in a happy blur. He attended church services with Molly and her family, stood beside her in a pew as they sang hymns together. He joined the Crabtrees for another Grahamite meal afterward, choking down several slices of hearty Graham flour bread and a stew he'd swear had been brewed of pine bark, acorns and assorted weeds. He played billiards with Adam, discussed presidential gossip with Fiona, listened to Sarah read poetry aloud and debated the temperance movement with Grace.

All the while, Molly stayed by his side. She held his hand, smiled at him, welcomed his words and his laughter. Unlikely as it had once seemed, it felt to Marcus as though they belonged together. Forever.

It was good, he thought, to be so welcomed into a family. If only he could have brought his own parents and sisters to the territory, he felt sure they and the Crabtrees would have fit together remarkably. But the Copelands liked their new life too well to leave it now. Marcus decided he'd have to take Molly on a rail journey eastward to visit them. Perhaps for a wedding trip…

The planning for that wedding proceeded apace, begun in Molly's busy head and encouraged by her mother and sisters. To a woman, they were atwitter. Truthfully, though, Marcus enjoyed seeing Molly so excited. Her eyes shone, her cheeks glowed…her very being seemed filled to the brim with vigor and plans and chatter. He took to kissing her at unexpected moments, just to witness the blush on her cheeks and to be ambushed with nuptial-related decisions.

He'd never forget the look on Molly's face when he'd suggested saying their vows over ale at Jack Murphy's saloon. Keeping a sober expression while doing so had been passing difficult, but he'd done it. Despite the wallop he'd endured for his troubles, it had been worth it to see her searching for a tactful way to extinguish his idea.

"Perhaps we'll serve ale *after* the ceremony?" Molly had suggested, and he'd loved her even more for being willing to try to see things the way she thought he wanted them.

The coming week passed as Sunday had, with planning and chattering and decisions to be made right and left. Between doing so, Marcus and Molly met privately whenever they could. He still found it hard to believe she would soon be his.

The members of the Morrow Creek Men's Club, however, found the news of Marcus's engagement not nearly so difficult to accept. To a man, they thought Marcus beaten. Brought to heel beneath the matchmaker's scheming, they said with frowns of disgust. Knuckled under by the matchmaker's plan to have every last free man in the town—in the territory!—locked up in wedding shackles before the frost even lifted. They shook their heads when they saw him, grumbled about "another good man gone bad."

But Marcus did not care; nor did he reveal what he suspected of the matchmaker's identity. Of a certain, the handwriting sample in Molly's ledger had matched the script in Jack Murphy's purloined note, but did that really prove anything? When he had time, Marcus promised himself, he would meet again with Jack and with Daniel McCabe, and they would form their conclusions about the matchmaker's identity. But for now…it could wait.

It could wait until after he'd made Molly his own.

His days at the lumber mill drifted past, with Marcus hardly able to concentrate on timber yields and bookkeeping and railway shipments. His men elbowed each other knowingly when he passed. Smith even remarked that Marcus looked "cheerful as a june bug dipped in whiskey." But Marcus didn't care. Molly would be his, they would be happy together, and all would be well.

He hoped.

By the time another Sabbath rolled around, Marcus found himself ready to have things settled between him and Molly. Their wedding date was set for the Saturday morn eleven days hence, but that didn't stop Marcus from trying to hasten the process.

"Let's elope," he suggested, sitting with her on the Crabtrees' front porch in the twilight that Sunday. "We can be off to the train depot and on our way to a wedding trip by this time tomorrow."

Molly smiled. "If you think to avoid wearing that fancy wedding suit my mama's stitching for you, you'd better think again," she said placidly. "She'd be heartbroken! Especially after having embroidered all that elegant stitchery on the shirt collar and cuffs for you."

"I hadn't even thought of that suit." He did now, and pulled at his collar in uncomfortable remembrance of his last, hurried fitting. "I only want to make you mine."

Before everything falls apart. Before you discover what I've done. He needed to settle things between them, Marcus knew, feeling an urgency he couldn't quite hide. Before it was too late. If he went to his lumber mill early tomorrow, spoke with Smith about ending the delectables payments to his men…

"And I want to be yours." Molly looped her arm at his elbow and hugged him close to her. "Especially while you're in that, er, magnificent suit."

"Humph. Are you laughing?" he demanded.

Vigorously she shook her head, lips pressed tight together.

"You're turning suspiciously purple," he observed.

She burst into guffaws. "All right, all right. So Mama's suit is a little much," Molly agreed. "She means well."

"So did the matchmaker, when she suggested those gals give away ugly neckties, rifle cozies and matching kerchiefs and aprons with embroidery on them," Marcus grumbled. "That meddlesome woman has a distinct fondness for hideous stitching projects."

"I have a distinct fondness for *you,*" Molly purred… then she tilted her head, closed her eyes and beckoned him nearer beneath the starlight. "I'm also wondering if you might, perhaps…kiss me tonight?"

Marcus could not refuse. Being with Molly was too precious to him. So it wasn't until later that he began wondering, himself. However pleasurable kissing Molly had been, he couldn't help but harbor a few lingering suspicions. Had she been distracting him from their talk of the matchmaker?

Was it possible that Molly was not, in fact, the matchmaker—and Fiona Crabtree was? Fiona

Crabtree, who had a fondness for both outlandish sewing *and* meddlesome matchmaking?

Marcus didn't know. And his curiosity about it was dampened the following morning, when Molly visited his lumber mill shortly after the break of dawn…and the disaster he'd feared finally struck.

She was going to get her Chautauqua booth.

Filled with excitement at the thought, Molly lifted her skirts and raced down the rutted road to Marcus's lumber mill, intent on telling him her good news.

She'd finally done it!

Sarah had shared the committee's final decision with her that very morning over breakfast. It seemed the committee members had been impressed with Molly's improved baking skills, her sister had told her. And Marcus's patronage of her bakeshop had helped a great deal, too. As a respectable business-man, his willingness to take a chance on Molly's skills had carried her Chautauqua application to the top of the pile.

He would be so proud of her, Molly knew. Of everyone in her life, Marcus was the one who most encouraged her business aspirations. He was the one who most understood her, who most *believed* in her. It was only fitting that he should hear this happy news first thing this morning.

As she approached his lumber mill, Molly pictured

Marcus's delighted expression upon hearing of her triumph. She imagined him twirling her in his arms for a celebratory embrace, and almost sighed aloud. She loved him so. There was no one she would rather share this news with than the man who had helped make it happen, through his faith in her alone.

With rapid footsteps, Molly crossed the yard. By now she recognized most of the lumbermen. She waved at the few who greeted her, too intent on her mission to stop and chat. This news would not wait. She blinked as she left behind the bright sunshine to step into the lumber mill's interior, then gained her bearings and headed toward Marcus's office.

Before she'd quite reached the partly opened door at the end of the hallway, Marcus's voice carried from within the small room.

"Damn it, Smith! I'm telling you, something has got to be done about this. If anyone else finds out about it—"

"There's no call for anybody to find out a thing," Smith said calmly. "'Sides, you ain't heard what I been telling you. The men don't want your money anymore."

In the hallway, Molly paused. If Marcus was conducting business with his foreman, she didn't want to interrupt. Quietly she began edging away. He'd probably only be a few minutes, and then she could—

"They won't even buy Molly's baked goods with

my money anymore?" Marcus asked, disbelief and aggravation in his voice. "Hell, Smith! Her sweets aren't that bad."

At the sound of her own name, Molly stopped. Frozen in place, she felt her heart begin to beat faster. *Why were they talking about her? And her baked goods?*

"I know, boss. They ain't that bad anymore," Mr. Smith agreed. "I had one of them cinnamon buns o' hers just a few days ago. It was a sight better than them doorstops she used to bring in here."

"She has improved," Marcus agreed in a calmer voice.

Molly cringed. She wanted to sink into the mill hallway behind her, to creep away and hear no more of this. But something held her there. She had to know what this was about.

"So why the hell won't the men take my money?" Marcus demanded. "If they stop buying from Molly just because they have to pay their own coin, I'll—"

"It's not that, boss," Mr. Smith interrupted. "I been telling ya'"

He went on talking, but Molly couldn't listen anymore. The truth crashed around her, laid out in plain talk that she couldn't deny. Marcus had been *paying* his men to buy her baked goods, all along.

He'd never believed in her. Had never believed she

could make a success of her bakery on her own. Had never wanted to help her.

Instead, he'd made a fool of her. He'd paraded her in front of his men—had allowed them to build a sales stall for her!—just as though she might succeed. He'd talked about her talent, had even repaired her bakeshop...but all the while, he'd been forcing his men to buy "doorstops" from her.

Humiliation washed over her. *She* hadn't made a success of her bakery—Marcus had. *She* hadn't won her much-coveted booth at the Chautauqua—Marcus had. *She* hadn't found someone who believed in her—Marcus had. He'd found someone gullible enough, foolhardy enough, to believe his lies.

He'd found Molly. Silly Molly Crabtree, the joke of Morrow Creek.

Well, now she'd be more of a joke than ever, Molly realized. When word of Marcus's charade got out, there'd be no end to the pitying glances and the gossip. She'd been worried that Sarah would make herself a fool over Daniel McCabe, or that Grace would cause a ruckus by feuding with Jack Murphy, but the person Molly should have been worrying about was herself. Just as her sisters had expected, she'd proved to be the most foolish of all.

You haven't the experience or the critical nature to recognize when you're being led astray, Grace had told her all those weeks ago, while warning her to be wary of Marcus. *Be careful,* Sarah had urged. But Molly had impetuously ignored them both. She had only herself to blame for this.

"You have to listen to me, boss," Mr. Smith said.

"No. I've heard enough." Marcus's voice was firm. Decisive. "I'll talk to the men myself."

A chair scraped. Marcus's heavy footfalls sounded. *He was coming this way!* She had to leave before he saw her there. The only thing worse than hearing this news would be seeing the pity on Marcus's face when he realized she knew the truth.

Molly whirled to run. Her reticule smacked into a nearby doorjamb, its beaded length wrenched from her wrist. She heard it plop to the floor but couldn't take the time to fetch it. There was a creak as Marcus's office door swung open. Glancing back once, she glimpsed his shocked expression as he saw her.

His face paled. "Molly!"

She couldn't stop. She hurried onward, too tightly laced for a full run. Darting around a surprised-looking mill hand, she dared another glance over her shoulder.

Marcus had retrieved her reticule from the floor. Holding it in his hands, he started after her.

No. He couldn't follow her. She couldn't stand it. He could not love her as he'd claimed, Molly realized sadly. No man who could deceive her so could also love her as he'd professed to. Miserably, half-blinded by tears, she rushed forward.

"Molly! Stop!"

His shouted words followed her out the door. Desperate to get away, Molly found her way to the road. Her breath hitched as she hurried along it, swiping the tears from her cheeks.

Before long, she couldn't go on. Molly stopped beneath a pine tree, laboring for breath. A quick glance behind told her no one had followed her. *Why should he?* a heartsick part of her demanded. Doubtless, as soon as Marcus had realized exactly what she'd overheard, he'd understood the futility of trying to continue his lie.

With a small cry, Molly sank to a crouch, her back against the rough pine bark. Pain filled her. Heartache was, she realized in that moment, a real physical ache. It made her heart hurt, her insides feel hollow, her mind scream for relief.

Marcus had never loved her. He couldn't have loved her.

But she had loved him. And the worst part was, no matter how she tried to deny it…she loved him still.

Marcus stood in the hallway beyond his office, sick with shock. It had finally happened. Molly had finally realized what he'd done and she would clearly never forgive him for it.

She was right not to, he told himself savagely. He had used her from the beginning. Trying to explain now would not change that truth. He'd used Molly to uncover the damned matchmaker's identity—no matter that doing so now was a task he cared nothing for, and hadn't for weeks.

The fact of his deception remained.

Tightening his fist on her reticule, Marcus exhaled. For another several moments, he stared at the passageway where Molly had disappeared. Ridiculous hope surged inside him. Maybe she would return. Maybe, somehow, she would be stronger than he was. Maybe she would be able to forgive him, even for the thing he could not forgive himself for.

No sign of Molly came. No fluttering of skirts, no laughter, no cinnamon and sugar sweetness. She had gone, and she clearly was not coming back.

'Twas only right, Marcus figured, feeling his expression settle into stony disregard. After all, Molly did not need him. He was the one who needed *her*… who had needed her, all along. By the time he'd realized it, it had been too late to take another course.

"Boss?" Smith asked. "You hear me?"

"No." Resigned, Marcus faced his foreman. The man blanched at the sight of him. Still fisting Molly's reticule, Marcus returned to his office. "Our business here is done for now. I have other work to do."

It was a lie. The notion of work was laughable to him. But Marcus could think of no other way to get the solitude he craved. He longed to shut the door, to close his gritty eyes, to work past the damnable lump in his throat whenever he recalled Molly's pain-filled eyes.

"Can't leave," Smith said stoically. "I ain't showed you this yet."

"Later." Marcus gestured impatiently toward the door.

"Now." With a grunt, Smith hefted the wooden barrel he'd carried inside the office from its place on the floor to the top of Marcus's desk. "It's waited long enough. There's something here you've got to see."

"A nail barrel?" Marcus eyed the thing with annoyance. He recognized the metallic clang of the fasteners inside as the barrel struck his desk. "I don't have—"

"If only that little gal had stuck around for another minute, she might've heard what I been tryin' to tell you all along." Biting his lip, Smith worked at the barrel's lid. He popped it free, then removed it with a flourish. He reached inside. "Some of this trouble might've been got 'round right clean."

"Smith—"

"It's the delectables money," the foreman said. He grabbed Marcus's hand and poured coins into his palm. "It didn't seem right, the men told me, to get paid for somethin' they all enjoyed doing."

Marcus stared in amazement at the money in his hand. He levered upward and gaped into the barrel. It was filled near to the brim with coins. "There must be weeks' worth of payments here."

Smith scratched his head. His face shone with pride. "'Bout six weeks, I think. The men all want you to have it back. They're happy to spend their own coin on Miss Molly's baked goods, from here on out."

It couldn't be. Marcus fisted the coins, then used his other hand to tip the barrel toward himself. Inside, coins of every denomination shifted and rattled, speckled with occasional bits of paper currency.

"Most of 'em paid you back for them first few weeks, too," Smith explained. He grinned as Marcus lifted his gaze from the astonishing sight. "Ever since then, they been taking your money every week—"

"And giving it straight back to you, to keep in this barrel." The realization came quickly. "Damn it, Smith! Why didn't you tell me?"

His foreman shrugged. "You seemed so happy to be helpin' Miss Molly. None of us had the heart to stop you."

Marcus shook his head. Smith didn't understand.

He *had* enjoyed helping Molly. It was his way. But in the end, that hadn't mattered a damned bit. He'd still hurt her.

He frowned downward, regret pouring through him. If only Molly had stayed long enough to hear the rattle of that money-filled barrel hitting the desk. Then she would have understood exactly what she'd accomplished. Instead, it had been plain from the hurt look on her face that she'd overheard everything—and drawn all the wrong conclusions from it.

"*Somebody* should've stopped me," Marcus said, disgustedly throwing his coins back into the barrel, "before it came to this."

"Came to what?"

"Molly. Finding out. Misunderstanding." He gestured toward the hallway, and the lumber mill door beyond. An ache filled him as he remembered. "Leaving."

"What's to misunderstand?" Smith asked, looking genuinely mystified. "You helped her. She oughtta be glad. Till you came along, that gal couldn't have sold them petrified pies to a living soul—leastwise, not one that had all its wits about it. You done her a favor."

"She doesn't want my help. She never did."

"Well, now, that's just plain foolish." His foreman settled in the chair opposite Marcus's desk. He gave him a matter-of-fact look. "Everybody needs help now and again."

"Not Molly Crabtree."

"Pshaw. She might be a mite prickly about getting it, but she needs help. Same as you."

"Me?" Marcus scoffed. "The last time anybody helped me, I was a babe. Maybe not even then."

"So you changed your nappies all by yourself, did you? Got yourself off to the schoolhouse every day, and tucked yourself in at night?"

With a grunt, Marcus settled into his chair. His foreman's nonsense didn't deserve an answer.

"Got yourself west all on your own, eh? Started up this here lumber mill all by your lonesome, did you?"

"Shut up, Smith. You know damned well how much you helped start up this place."

Smith's grin was knowing. "And I know damned well the way things sit today, *boss*. Molly Crabtree changed you. She *helped* you. Whether you see it or not."

"Humph."

"The way I see it, the two of you needed each other." Smith folded his arms across his chest. "Still do, I reckon."

Marcus's scowl deepened. "Don't you have work to do?"

"Sure do. Right now, it's right here." His finger

jabbed downward, indicating the floorboards. "In this office."

"You're dismissed. Take the day off. Soak your ingrown toenail."

"Can't. I have to look after things here."

"I'll look after things here."

Smith shook his head. Had Marcus only imagined it, or did his foreman look vaguely smug about something? Damn it all! The man was insufferable.

"I *said*," Marcus muttered through clenched teeth, "you're dismissed. Go soak your—"

"Go on. I'll look after the mill," Smith urged, waving toward the door. "Git after her."

Marcus stared across his desk, his throat tight with misery. He wanted to believe Smith was right…

"Go on. Make her understand what them payments were all about, afore it's too late."

Frowning, Marcus shook his head. He *knew* what those payments had been about. That was the trouble. "It's already too late. She's gone."

"She's only gone if you let her go."

Despite everything, a flicker of hope came to life inside Marcus. Warily he agreed. "She ought to know the whole truth."

Smith nodded.

"I never wanted to hurt her."

"What're you telling me for?" His foreman gave

a horror-struck sound. "I ain't near so pretty. Nor so likely to marry you next week. Now am I?"

Marcus couldn't help it. A smile came to his lips, a small one that restored even more of the hope in his heart. "God help me."

Suddenly decisive, he grabbed Molly's lost reticule. He stood. "I'm going after her. Before *you* get to jawing about sharing a damned wedding night with you and your hairy old knees."

Chapter Seventeen

Molly trudged onward toward town, her heart heavy. She didn't know how long she'd spent weeping beneath that lone pine tree. It had felt like days. Eventually, though, she'd found herself longing for the solitude of her own chamber in which to cry. So she'd gotten up, dusted herself off and headed as far from the scene of her heartbreak as she could.

Every step reminded her of Marcus. She recalled how often they'd trod this path together. How he'd carried her over his shoulder that day, all masculine dominance and steadfast surety. How he'd set her down outside of town, so she could stride into Morrow Creek on her own two feet, with her dignity intact.

Today her dignity was too badly bruised for anything but a slow plodding. With her skirts dragging at her ankles, Molly doggedly moved onward, trying to push thoughts of Marcus from her mind.

It was no use, though. She seemed to hear his

footsteps as though they ghosted her very own, fancied she heard his voice calling out in the wind. Tears prickled her eyes. Was there no escape from her thoughts of him?

At this rate, she would need to leave Morrow Creek behind her in order to avoid these constant reminders of Marcus. Blazes! She even thought she sensed the bay rum aroma of his hair pomade, brought to her on the same breeze that dragged strands of long hair from her chignon.

Tucking them back, she continued on.

"Molly!" came Marcus's voice again. "Wait!"

Heavens, but her imagination had a fierceness to it. It almost had her convinced she heard a certain hoarseness to Marcus's voice, detected a distinct regret in his called-out words. Most likely, she only wished he felt that way.

"Molly!" floated toward her, louder this time. "Wait!"

Sucking in a deep breath, she glanced over her shoulder. She would prove to her poor run-amok mind that these imaginings were nonsense, and then—

Marcus loomed at the top of the last distant rise she'd trudged over, his hair blown back and his suit coat flapping as he ran. While she watched, he wrenched the garment from his sleeves. He threw it aside. He came on, faster now that he'd shed the impeding wool.

His suit coat hit the dust and Molly's heart skipped a beat. *He'd followed her!* Followed her, and without a heed for his fancy clothes *or* his reputation, either. Truly, Marcus risked looking utterly daft, speeding along as he was. Surely that meant he still wanted her, still needed her…still loved her. Didn't it?

For one buoyant instant, she paused.

Then she remembered. Remembered that he was not, after all, the man she'd believed in. Remembered that he'd deceived her, made a fool of her, probably even laughed at her. Just as her family and the whole of Morrow Creek had been laughing at her and her grand aspirations for all these years. Long-overdue anger sparked inside her. Molly turned on her heel and strode faster.

"Molly! Wait!"

His words spurred her to an even faster pace. If Marcus Copeland thought he was better than silly Molly Crabtree…well, he could just think again. Chin held high, jaw set, fists pumping in time with her steps, Molly ignored her gouging stays and climbed the next rise.

The kicked-up dust blowing from behind her alerted her that Marcus had nearly caught up. Filled with dismay, Molly forced her legs to carry her faster. Hurt and indignation powered every stride.

If it was the last thing she did, she would get away from Marcus, and she would stay away, too.

Suddenly he grabbed her arm. Startled, Molly glanced sideways to glimpse his flashing eyes and determined jaw. She remembered kissing that jaw just yesterday, recalled feeling its scratchy beard stubble against her cheek. Helpless love for him nearly brought her to her knees. Through force of will alone, Molly kept her reaction to a stumble.

"Listen to me," he demanded, still holding her. "You don't understand what happened back there."

He wasn't even winded, she observed with an odd sense of detachment. It was the shock she'd experienced making her feel that way, Molly supposed. The shock of that, and of seeing Marcus chase after her the way he had. His dramatic pursuit had looked a grand if addled gesture, but it clearly had cost him nothing. The realization gave her the courage to go on.

"I understand *everything*." She wrenched her arm to get free. Pointlessly, as it turned out, for he did not let her go. "And at long last, too."

"You don't. You don't understand. Molly, listen."

"And be made a fool of again? No, thank you."

Fiercely she stomped his boot. Marcus's eyes widened in surprise. He hopped on one foot, automatically releasing her. With a righteous huff, Molly grabbed her reticule from his free hand and began walking again. Her breath wheezed from her lungs as she forced a faster pace. Keeping her back as straight as the soldiers' posture at Camp Verde, Molly hurried onward.

Marcus did, too, his shirtsleeves flapping in the breeze. He limped a little, but he obstinately kept pace. "I never meant to hurt you."

Stubbornly she remained silent.

"I was looking for a way to spend time with you," he went on, "so I could learn what you knew of the matchmaker's identity. Bringing you to my lumber mill each day seemed an expedient way to do that."

"Hmmph." Molly swerved around a rocky place in the road. So she'd been right from the beginning about his motivations. He *had* wanted to uncover the matchmaker's identity. But knowing that now was small comfort to her, as was the realization that she, at least, had held up her part of the secret.

She hitched her chin still higher. "You sound almost as though that's a reasonable explanation," she observed.

"It's what I promised to the men's club. My honor was at stake."

"Your honor? You mean you possess some honor? What does your 'honor' say about lying? About continuing to lie, over and over again? About making a fool—" Her throat shut tight with unshed tears, closing off her words. Molly struggled to continue. "About making a fool of the woman who loved you?"

"'Loved'? Molly, no."

Marcus caught hold of her hand, hauling her to a stop at the road's edge. In the distance, the storefronts and households of Morrow Creek stood within the trees…but here, now, Marcus's desperate gaze met hers. It was all she could see.

"*Loves,*" he urged. "The woman who loves me. Please. That hasn't changed. We're to be married."

Married. How she'd wanted that. How she'd wanted to share her life with him. But how could she, now, given what she knew of him? Marcus was not the man she'd thought he was at all.

"No. Despite your efforts—" Molly drew herself up, desperate to ignore the familiar feel of his hand cradling hers "—I will not be made a fool of twice."

Marcus felt his features harden. Clearly this woman meant to push him to the edge of his patience and beyond with her stubbornness. He'd already chased her willy-nilly through the woods. He'd already nearly fallen to his knees and begged her forgiveness. What more did she want?

"I never meant to hurt you," he repeated tightly, as angry now as she was. "Or to make you look foolish.

I did not think I'd be required to pay my men to buy your baked goods more than once or twice. After that, I assumed they would use their own coin. When I saw that they would not, I continued my scheme. How was I to know your sweets were that bad?"

"'That bad'?" Molly whirled, trembling visibly as she confronted him. "I'll have you know, they were good enough to earn me the Chautauqua booth I wanted!"

"The committee approved it?"

Reluctant triumph filled her face. She nodded.

"Ah, Molly." Marcus moved forward to embrace her, their current troubles momentarily forgotten. Now, surely, she would feel happy again. "You deserve this," he said, hugging her board-stiff shoulders. "Your booth will have the longest lines, the happiest customers—"

"I don't want you to visit it."

He felt his smile falter. "Of course I will visit it. Hell, I'll build it for you."

"No. I'll not have it." Molly stepped from his embrace, then faced him with her shoulders squared. "I don't need you there, Marcus. As difficult as this may be for you to believe, I can succeed on my own, and I plan to. Without you."

He could not speak. What had gone wrong with his explanations? Marcus recalled what he'd said, tried desperately to discover where he'd stumbled.

"I don't need your help." Molly looked downward, seemed to draw in a deep breath. When she again raised her gaze to his, her eyes were filled with hurt, but her expression bespoke nothing save determination. "And I don't need you."

Her words struck him, each one a fresh blow. This was everything Marcus had feared, happening before his eyes. Molly did not need him. She did not want him. And if she did love him, those feelings were not enough to change the truth.

He'd fallen in love with a woman who didn't need his protection, didn't need his strength or his money or his business knowledge...didn't need, as she'd so plainly put it, *him*.

Stricken by the painful irony of it, Marcus took a step backward. His fists clenched uselessly at his sides. His insides hurt. He'd have sworn there was something wrong with his chest, something wrong with his heart; otherwise, why did he feel such emptiness there?

"Our engagement is ended," Molly said.

"No! Molly, hear me. Damnation! Your baked goods are fine now. My men have not taken my money for them for weeks. I did not know it until today."

"Marcus—"

"In the beginning, I was wrong. But later...later it

made you so happy, to see them clamoring for your sweets. It made *me* happy, to see you that way. How could I put an end to that? 'Twas only that I wanted to help you. I swear it."

Her voice softened, just for a moment. "I—I think it's wisest we don't see each other."

No. This could not be happening. He would explain. He would make her see the truth.

"We live in this same small town," Marcus told her gruffly. "Morrow Creek is less than a mile from end to end. We'll see each other."

"No." Hesitantly Molly placed her palm over the empty-feeling place in his chest. She gazed up at him. "I could not bear it if we did. Please, Marcus. Please leave me alone."

With a desperate gesture, he reached for her hand. At the same instant, she whisked it away. *This was the last time she would touch him,* Marcus realized with a sense of disbelief. The last time he would ever touch her, and know the softness and light that had made him a better man...for however short a while.

Their fingers grazed each other, a heartbeat's brief embrace. Then Molly turned and hurried into town—her final gift to him a backward glance that told him he was not the only one who wept over all they'd lost.

* * *

In her meeting room at the top of Jack Murphy's saloon, Grace sighed. "You are not meant for this work, Molly. Look at that sign you just lettered."

Dispiritedly Molly glanced downward, pencil in hand. For the whole afternoon, she'd been sitting on the floor helping her sister make signs, meant for use by her women's group members as they paraded throughout the Chautauqua.

"Fight For Female Stufferage," she read, voice wooden. She clapped her hand over her mouth. "Oh, Grace, I'm sorry. This sounds as though I mean for all women to stuff balled-up stockings into their corset tops, or some such."

"*Not* a tactic all of us have need for," Grace agreed, giving a nod toward Molly's generous bosoms. She leaned forward on hands and knees, then prosaically flipped over the signboard. "Why don't you try again on the other side?"

Molly stared at it, nearly moved to tears. These days, she found herself frightfully close to bawling at the oddest moments. She sniffled. "You're being very understanding."

Her sister shrugged. "We women must stick together, through good times and bad. That philosophy is at the root of all my dealings, you know."

"Even your dealings with Jack Murphy?"

"Shh!" Grace hissed. She rolled her eyes meaningfully toward the floorboards. "He might hear you. He's right downstairs."

"I'm sorry." Morosely, Molly traced three ruler lines onto the clean side of her sign, forming guides for the slogan letters to come. "I'm the last person who should be nosing into your relationship with Mr. Murphy. Or into anyone's relationship with a man, in general. Clearly, I know nothing of the species."

She recalled the disaster her dalliance with Marcus had become, and a lump rose to her throat. She fought back tears again. When last she'd seen him, reaching for her hand on the road, he had looked… broken. Lost, almost. But how could that be, when he was the one who'd broken *her* heart?

"They are incomprehensible at times," Grace agreed with a breezy wave. "High-handed. Domineering. Stupidly opinionated."

Helplessly Molly thought again of Marcus, and was forced to stifle a sigh. Yes, at times he'd been all those things. But he had been so much more, too. It had been days since she'd last seen him. He had done as she asked and stayed away. But the pain of losing him—of missing him—had not lessened.

What she needed, Molly decided, was to move on. Otherwise, she might be miserable forever.

"Too true," she said to Grace, hoping to goad her sister into detailing more of the faults of men. Ordinarily, she could be counted on for a good suffragette-spirited discourse, something that Molly figured might help ease her broken heart.

"Why, one pass through Murphy's saloon to get here," Molly went on, "made it plain as day that men in general are sloppy, often foulmouthed—"

"True, true. But when they smile at you…" Grace crossed her arms in her lap, her paintbrush at serious risk of dripping green paint onto the floor. She did not notice, though, so dreamy was her expression. "Oh, *then* they are magnificent."

Molly was dumbfounded.

Her sister's faraway gaze drifted sideways. Caught Molly's aghast expression. Grace cleared her throat and got back to work. "Overall, though, they are useless creatures."

In astonishment, Molly observed Grace's awkward movements as she sketched. She took in the blush on her sister's cheeks, the rose cameo pinned un-characteristically at the throat of her high-necked dress, the slight fragrance of lavender that clung to her sister's person. Ordinarily Grace could not be bothered with feminine modesty, did not care for fripperies like jewelry, and smelled of nothing more exotic than commonsense castile soap.

"If I did not know better," Molly marveled, scrutinizing her further, "I would swear that the matchmaker has been at it again. With you…and Jack Murphy."

"Nonsense."

"You are smitten! It's plain in your face!"

"Jack Murphy wants me to yield my portion of this building," Grace replied staunchly. "He wants to know the identity of the matchmaker. If he seeks to charm me to gain what he wishes, then I—"

"Oh, Grace." Molly eyed her elder sister's trembling hands, her facade of serenity. "I pray that this ends more happily for you than it did for me. I truly do."

A moment's silence fell between them. They shared a telling glance, one filled with understanding. Over the past days, while Molly had suffered, Grace had listened. She had listened, and she'd been there to commiserate while Molly cried, as only a sister could.

Grace reached out and squeezed Molly's hand. For a moment, she looked strangely uncertain. She bit her lip in thought. Then she turned to Molly decisively.

"You can change this, Moll!" she said. "Don't let what you've had with Mr. Copeland slip away. If you still love him…"

Shocked, Molly stared. Was this truly her female suffrage-minded sister advocating true love?

"Loving him does not matter," she managed, "when—"

"It is the *only* thing that matters!" Grace insisted.

"Apologize to him, and move past this. Men are proud. You've always been too stubborn for your own good. For once in your life, don't let your pride stand in your way."

"My pride? 'For once in my life'?" Piqued, Molly threw down her pencil. "What are you accusing me of? How *dare* you?"

"I dare because you're my sister. I want you to be happy."

"Fine." Stiffly, Molly stood. "Because I must tell you—making these signs with you no longer makes me happy."

"Moll, wait. You are stiff-necked at times, you must admit that. When you think someone has no faith in you, you are driven to extremes. We've all seen it."

"I am in no mood for this babying." She grabbed her things.

"It is not babying! What does it matter what anyone else believes, so long as *you* believe in yourself?"

Molly faced her, trembling. "Such a thing is easy for you to say. You are the eldest. No one has ever doubted you."

Sadly, Grace shook her head. "That is where you are wrong. Everyone has doubted me. But I...I have never doubted *myself.*"

In disbelief, Molly stared at her sister. Then

she pulled on her gloves. "Good luck with your signs," she said, and left.

The men of Morrow Creek gathered together late of night, pints of lager and bottles of whiskey at hand. Grousing raised the rafters at Jack Murphy's saloon, all of it related to one woman. One mysterious, troublesome woman.

"The matchmaker has struck again!" someone said.

"Ruined another perfectly good bachelor," added another.

"A toast, to Marcus Copeland!" yelled the butcher. "Sorriest son of a bitch in the territory. He set out to corral the matchmaker, and nearly got himself hitched for his trouble."

A chorus of hoots and hollers rang out.

"Barely escaped with his manhood intact," a miner chortled. "Glad to have you back, Copeland!"

From his customary chair at the back of the room, Marcus frowned. He raised his whiskey glass in a halfhearted salute, then slugged its contents down. More and more these days, liquor seemed a good solution to the god-awful ache inside him. In the days since he'd last seen Molly, he'd finished more than his share of strong spirits.

Oddly enough, though, they never provided the

relief he sought. Only being with Molly might do that, Marcus knew. And that was impossible now.

I don't need your help. I don't need you.

With a cynical arch of his brow, Marcus raised his whiskey glass again—to himself. He drank. He'd set out to find the matchmaker...and wound up losing his heart to the one woman who was most wrong for him. What were the odds?

What were the odds he would ever forget her, when day after day he longed to see her smile, to touch her cheek, to hear her voice as she called his name?

A rail worker stood with his ale in hand, weaving a bit. "It's up to Murphy and McCabe to uncover the blasted matchmaker now," he said, saluting them with his pint. "Good luck, boys."

"Good luck!" came other shouts.

Marcus shook his head. Perhaps Jack and Daniel *would* find the matchmaker, he thought. To be certain, the meddlesome creature could not be Molly, despite the scant evidence he'd gleaned of her handwriting. No woman who could savagely stomp on his heart like this could truly be the marriage-minded matchmaker they all sought.

Later that night, Marcus told Jack Murphy exactly that.

"I am ready to have done with this," Marcus added. "More than ready." He'd lingered in his chair after the men's club meeting had ended, then wandered to the bar for another slug of Old Orchard. "I'm sorry I ever set out to uncover that damnable woman in the first place."

"Between the two of us," Jack said as he slapped his cloth onto the bar, then leaned forward, "I'm sorry, too. Grace Crabtree eludes me at every turn. If I told that woman the sky was blue, she'd argue it for green just to aggravate me."

Beside them, Daniel McCabe finished his ale. "Her sister's not like that. You've never seen a more amenable woman than Sarah Crabtree. She hasn't given me a lick of trouble."

Marcus and Jack raised their eyebrows at him.

"What? It's true." He wiped his mouth, then picked up his flat-brimmed black hat. He fitted it onto his head, giving them both a cocky look. "You just have to know how to handle women, is all. Like I do."

Daniel slapped Marcus heartily on the back. He prepared to leave.

"Hang on, McCabe."

"Yeah. Hang on."

The blacksmith turned, a hint of apprehension on his face. He hid it beneath a blustery smile. "You two wanting pointers on handling females?"

Jack shared a glance with Marcus. "She's gone and snared him, too," the saloonkeeper said.

Marcus nodded. "I guess you're right."

"What the hell are you two talking about? Nobody's snared me."

"The matchmaker has," Marcus and Jack said in unison. They shook their heads. Marcus tipped back a little more whiskey.

"You might as well surrender, McCabe," he told the blacksmith. "No use fighting it."

"You two are crazy!"

"We're right," Jack told him blithely, wiping the bar. "Don't fret, though. If I were a different kind of man—a weaker man—I might've succumbed, too."

This time, it was Marcus and Daniel who shared a disbelieving look. They shook their heads at Jack.

"Only a matter of time, Murphy," Daniel assured him.

"Just give in now," Marcus advised. "I've met Grace Crabtree. If she's set her sights on something, you don't stand a snowball's chance in hell of changing her mind."

Murphy's jaw tightened. The three men fell silent, each lost in his own thoughts.

Despite his own troubles, in that moment Marcus experienced a sort of shared kinship between them, a bond forged by the muddle he and Daniel and Jack seemed to have made of their matchmaker search. Feeling relieved to be in good company, he looked at both men.

"I guess we're in a fix," he said. "What do we do about it now?"

Murphy's jaw dropped. "Not a thing! I'm not beaten yet."

"Don't look at me." McCabe raised his broad palms, obviously aghast. "I'm not giving up. Beaten, by a woman? Hell, no!"

So much for kinship, Marcus thought wryly. It looked as though he was on his own. He finished his whiskey and stood.

"I've got ledgers to see to," he said, pulling on his coat. "Best of luck to you both. You'll need it."

Outside, the autumn night made Marcus clutch his coat tighter. Holding it in one fist, he turned. Thoughtfully, he regarded the saloon, the place where his decision to meet with Molly had begun. It was shuttered now, quiet and mostly dark, but upstairs…was that lamplight in the window?

He squinted. Two feminine faces showed clearly there, and they were faces he recognized, too. Hardly able to believe his eyes, Marcus stepped nearer.

They saw him. Rapidly they clapped the shutters closed.

Marcus frowned, distracted now from his plans to walk home and lose himself in work. Exactly what had Grace and Sarah Crabtree overheard from upstairs? he wondered. And exactly what, he wondered further, would they do about it?

* * *

Upstairs in Grace's meeting room, Grace and Sarah clapped the shutters closed with a small shriek. Arms fluttering, Sarah paced across the room.

"He's seen us," she blurted.

"I know." Grace crossed her arms over her chest. "Plain as day. Why did you have to breathe so noisily, Sarah?"

"Me? You were the one who gasped when he emerged from the saloon."

"Only because you whooshed the shutters open so quickly. It's cold outside!"

"How else were we to see where he was going?"

Calmly Fiona Crabtree halted her sewing needle in mid-stitch. "I told you he would see you, girls."

"We had to do something, Mama," Sarah insisted, still pacing. She paused for an instant, staring at the signs they'd spent the evening painting. "You know what Molly is like. And Marcus Copeland seems to match her for stubbornness!"

"The two of them are obviously miserable," Grace agreed. She cast her mother a pleading look. "Something *must* be done."

"You may be right," Fiona said. She began stitching again, her work on the embroidered shirt cuffs she'd been sewing nearly at an end. "At this rate, Molly and Mr. Copeland will never make amends with each other. Especially not in time for the wedding date they'd set. They so clearly belong together, too."

She raised her head, sharing a conspiratorial glance with her daughters. "It may be time, girls, to pay a special visit to the *Pioneer Press.*"

Chapter Eighteen

The day began as any other in the Crabtree household. Molly came downstairs to the sight of her family bustling around the dining table, pouring coffee or tea and sitting down to bowls of porridge with apples. Conversation carried throughout the room, amiable and frequent. Cook hurried in and out with fresh plates and napkins, her face flushed with the heat of the kitchen's cookstove.

Molly slid into her place. With a sideways glance at Grace, she arranged a napkin atop her skirts. Her sister may have been right about her, Molly had decided after much thought. Perhaps she *was* overly prideful at times. Perhaps she *did* react overmuch to any perceived lack of faith. Perhaps it *was* necessary to believe in herself, first of all.

But that didn't mean Molly meant to give Grace the satisfaction of knowing she'd been right. Chin high, she reached for a teacup.

"Molly, have you seen the newspaper?" Sarah

asked. She pushed the folded issue across the table. "It's this morning's edition."

"Thank you." Leaving it for now, Molly accepted a slice of toasted Graham flour bread from Cook. "Are there any strawberry preserves?"

She glanced around the table, looking for them. As she raised her eyes, she glimpsed something curious—her entire family was staring at her.

Molly frowned. As one, they studiously returned to what they'd been doing. Her papa raised his book. Her mama stirred cream into her porridge. Her sisters buttered their bread, sneaking a shared glance.

Molly shrugged. Most likely, they were merely worried about her. She *had* been miserable lately. She could hardly fault her family for caring about her.

"The preserves are right there," Grace said. "Beside your newspaper."

"Oh. Thank you." Molly grabbed them.

A collective sigh issued.

She cocked her head, examining her family inquisitively. Again they returned to their tasks.

Molly had finished two-thirds of her toasted bread when her papa cleared his throat. He nodded toward her place at table. "I am finished with that newspaper, you know. If you'd like to read it."

Her mama, Sarah and Grace looked on eagerly.

"Yes," Fiona urged. "There are some interesting features in your father's newspaper this morning."

They all beamed at her with bright, expectant smiles.

Slowly Molly reached out her free hand for the newspaper. She may as well humor them, she reasoned. "If it would make all of you feel better about my well-being…"

"It would!" Grace urged, her eyes shining. "Taking an interest in current events is the duty of every forward-thinking woman, you know."

"Then I'll read it first thing after I finish breakfast." Molly placed the newspaper beside her plate. Warmed by her family's concern, she took another bite of bread.

"Read it now!" her sisters shouted.

"Grace! Sarah!" Fiona admonished. "Control yourselves."

More and more intrigued, Molly examined all of them. "What is going on?" she asked. "Why are you all behaving so peculiarly?"

"Read the newspaper!" Fiona and Adam shouted.

"Mama! Papa!"

They flushed like guilty children. Her mama twisted her hands in her lap, her gaze fixed on the *Pioneer Press*. "It's only that we believe we've spotted something…special for you in the newspaper today."

"Next to the last page," her papa instructed gruffly.

Bemused, Molly reached for it. The newsprint rattled as she turned pages, examining the vertical columns crowded with all manner of news, advertisements and fancy typefaces. At last, she found the portion her papa had indicated.

Suspiciously she gazed into their impatient faces. "The personal advertisements?"

Nods were seen all around. "Yes!" Sarah said.

With a dawning sensation of nervousness, Molly smoothed out the newspaper. A part of her did not want to read this, whatever it was, at all. A part of her most desperately did.

"Is there some kind of problem with the advertisements sent to the matchmaker?" she inquired, still skimming. "I *knew* those would only stir up trouble. Some people in this family might not agree, but—oh, my."

Molly stopped. The newsprint shook in her grasp. Forcing herself to draw in a steadying breath, she located the item she'd just passed over.

Personal: Would the beautiful lady—whose affections I held so close until recently—please meet this sorrowful gentleman at the steps of M.C.'s bakery? I was grievously wrong, and must make amends. I will wear a forget-me-not, today and on every other day until I see you again. Please come.

With a gasp, Molly read it again. It had to be Marcus! Who else could possibly want to meet her at "the steps of M.C.'s bakery," *her* bakery?

Stunned, she touched her fingers to the type.

A forget-me-not. So appropriate. She had not, for an instant, begun to forget him.

This sorrowful gentleman. Molly sighed.

He was sorry.

So was she. But she'd never have expected Marcus to come forward like this, to be the first to make amends. Grace had had the right of it—men *were* proud, and Marcus among the proudest of them all. But this...well, it was a start. A new start, for them both.

This time, she could not be too stubborn to seize it. For once in her life, Molly vowed, she would believe the best of the people around her, and of herself. Why hadn't she done so before? This would be perfect!

Glancing upward, she could not prevent a silly smile from coming to her lips. Bedazzled, she gazed at the advertisement again.

"It is from Marcus," she said, hearing the excitement in her own voice as she tossed down the newspaper. "He wants to meet me."

His bed was spinning.
Marcus awoke to that disturbing realization, along with a pounding on his front door. Groggily he raised his head.

Immediately he lowered it again, putting a careful hand to his throbbing forehead. Even his hair seemed to complain at the movement. Damnation. What had possessed him to drink so much last night? It was not as though he might find Molly at the bottom of a whiskey bottle.

The pounding continued. Suddenly reminded of the time Molly had visited him here for his first lesson, awakening him in much the same way, Marcus found the stamina to rise. He discovered himself wearing the same clothes from last night, down to his boots. His mouth tasted as though he'd swished afore bed with his hair pomade.

Ugh. He made his way downstairs, hoping against hope that when he'd navigated to the front door, Molly would be there as she used to be—a basket over her arm, a smile for him on her face, a loving look in her eyes. He missed her.

Holding his breath, he opened his door. The burst of sunlight streaming through it sent him staggering backward. Squinting, Marcus leaned against the doorjamb for support.

Clearly he was a mess without Molly.

Just as clearly, she was not now standing on his threshold. Molly did not possess britches, bristly hair or an unshaven beard. Moreover, there was only *one* of the woman he loved—and there were *two* of the invaders on his steps.

Unless he was seeing double. He blinked. *No such luck.*

"It's gotten worse," Jack Murphy said, shouldering his way inside. He hurled a newspaper at Marcus's chest.

"*Dangerously* worse," Daniel McCabe growled. Likewise, he entered the house, shoving a newspaper toward Marcus.

Mystified, Marcus held the identical issues of the *Pioneer Press* against his chest. He yawned. He watched as both men trudged around the room, looking aggravated.

"What are you going to do about *that?*" McCabe asked, his nod indicating the newspapers. "'Cause you've gotta do something."

Murphy nodded. "It's true. If you knuckle under to that blasted advertisement, the matchmaker will think she can ride roughshod over all of us."

They both stared at him expectantly. Marcus

blinked once more, trying to clear his head. The last thing he remembered was coming home last night, then staring distractedly at his ledgers while thoughts of Molly ran through his mind. Rummaging through his pantry, while a fierce cinnamon-bun craving took hold of him. Falling into bed with a whiskey bottle for company, just in case he woke up thirsty, and… *wait a minute.*

He recalled seeing Grace and Sarah Crabtree in the saloon's upstairs window. More than anyone else, Marcus understood that two Crabtree women—especially two Crabtree women in cahoots with each other—boded no good. With dawning suspicion, he grabbed one of the newspapers. The other he threw onto a nearby chair.

He paced, reading, turning newsprint pages. It wasn't long before Marcus spotted it: the matchmaker's advertisement he should have expected but had not.

Personal: Would M.C., the wondrous gentleman—whose heartfelt aid I so unfortunately spurned—please meet this sorrowful lady at the steps of M.C.'s bakery? I was grievously wrong, and must make amends. I will wear a forget-me-not, today and on every other day until I see you again. Please come.

Slowly Marcus traced his fingers over the advertisement's expert typeface. Mixed emotions jumbled
together inside him, coming so quickly he could not
keep up.

"He's smiling!" Murphy observed, plainly disgruntled.

"Aww, hell," McCabe complained. "We're too
damned late."

It was Molly, Marcus realized, feeling his grin
broaden. *Molly had done this.* Not her sisters. Molly
had struck upon a way to reach out to him, by placing
a notice through the matchmaker. Who else could
want to meet him at "the steps of M.C.'s bakery,"
Molly's bakery?

Stunned, he read the advertisement again.

A forget-me-not. A perfect flower, he acknowledged. Marcus didn't know much of fripperies,
wasn't versed in the language of flowers, but he did
know one thing. He had not, for an instant, begun
to forget Molly.

This sorrowful lady. Marcus sighed.

She was sorry.

So was he. But he'd never have expected Molly
to come forward like this, to be the first to make
amends. He'd had the right of it last night. Grace was
not the only stubborn Crabtree woman. Molly was

perhaps the most bullheaded of them all. But this…
well, it was a start. A new start, for them both.

This time, he could not stumble over what he
meant to tell her. This time, he would make himself
understood.

"Copeland? Copeland!" Murphy waved a hand
in front of Marcus's face. Disgustedly he let it fall.
"He's a goner."

McCabe agreed. "We're on our own."

"It is from Molly Crabtree," Marcus told them,
hearing the excitement in his own voice as he hurled
the newspaper back to Jack. "She wants to meet
me."

Both men scoffed. "Lord help us."

"Look. He's considering it. Why, why, why?"

McCabe looked fit to tear into the *Pioneer Press*
with his teeth. Stepping nearer to him, Marcus looked
the blacksmith up and down. Then, he broadened his
perusal to Murphy.

"Damn right, I'm considering it. I'm doing more
than that. I'm going. But first, there's something I've
got to know."

Suspiciously they glared at him. Marcus took their
combined grunts for agreement.

"Exactly what," he asked with a grin, "were the
two of *you* doing reading the matchmaker's personal
advertisements in the first place?"

They remained silent. Marcus, feeling immensely

better, slapped them both jovially on the back. "Time to head out, you two. I've got myself an appointment to keep."

Chapter Nineteen

The sun had just barely cleared the rooftops of the buildings in the heart of Morrow Creek when Marcus made his way to Molly's bakeshop. Freshly shaved, washed and dressed, he strode down the street in the same shirt and britches he'd been wearing during his first baking lesson with her. Truth be told, plain clothes like these took less time to jump into than a highfalutin suit did.

With every step Marcus took, his heart lightened. Soon he would see Molly. He pictured her on the steps of her shop, wearing one of her brightly colored dresses and a smile made just for him. He would take her in his arms, and everything would be right between them again.

He rounded the corner of the millinery shop, then passed the book and news depot. Molly's bakery came into view, outfitted with its fancy siding and gingerbread trim. His heartbeat quickening, Marcus squinted toward the steps.

No one waited there.

For an instant, he faltered. Then, reasoning that Molly must have decided to wait inside, safe from the autumn chill in the air, he hastened onward. The picture in his head shifted, becoming a vision of the two of them amid her fancy wirework chairs and pastel-painted wainscoting. He'd pull Molly into his arms, and then—

The front door was locked. All was quiet. Feeling the barest nudge of consternation, Marcus cupped his hands around his temples and peered through the window. Empty.

Nonplussed, he scratched his head. Surely she should be there. The *Pioneer Press* printed its morning edition at dawn. By now, Molly must have known he'd have read her advertisement.

Marcus waited. Nervousness and anticipation thrummed through him. He couldn't help but pace across the front porch, his boots ringing out in the stillness. What if he'd misread the matchmaker's advertisement somehow? What if he'd mistaken Molly's plans?

What if she did not intend to meet him at all?

By the time a few minutes had passed, Marcus was as wound up as could be. He continued to pace, stopping now and then to straighten his clothes and finger-comb his hair. He wanted to look fine for

Molly, wanted to please her in any way he could. If only she would—

He turned around, and there she was, rounding the corner to the bakeshop dressed all in blue.

At her first glimpse of Marcus, waiting there at her bakeshop's threshold, Molly knew she had been without him for too long. She wanted to run to him, to throw her arms around him and whoop with gladness that he'd made this meeting possible between them…without the awkwardness that might have ensued, save his deft use of the matchmaker's tactics. But, wanting to make a fine impression on the man she meant to spend her life with, Molly forced herself to walk calmly.

She fixed her gaze on his face. A trembling smile came to her lips, pushed there by a mixture of happiness and nervousness she could hardly deny. Her heart felt truly in her throat. Inhaling deeply for courage, she ascended the two short steps to her bakery. There, she pulled the personal advertisement from her reticule, and held it toward Marcus with quivering fingers.

"Does this mean," she asked, "that you want to put things right between us?"

Marcus accepted the scrap of newsprint. He frowned, seeming surprised at the message appearing there. Molly would have sworn—oddly enough—that she saw his lips move as he read "grievously wrong." Next, Marcus paused. He shook his head as though to clear it, glanced up at her and continued on.

All but wringing her hands with sudden apprehension, Molly watched him. Had she somehow misread the matchmaker's advertisement? she wondered. Had she mistaken Marcus's plans? Dismay rolled through her as another thought struck her.

Had he not intended to meet with her at all?

It was possible, Molly realized in a dither, that Marcus had merely chosen today to complete his repairs on her bakeshop. That he hadn't missed her, hadn't needed to be with her, hadn't *loved* her the same way that she did *him.* And yet here he was, just as the advertisement had foretold, wearing a forget-me-not and—

Molly glanced at his shirtfront. No telltale flower adorned the fabric. Crestfallen, she looked up at him.

At the very same moment, Marcus lifted his gaze from her dress bodice. His expression, Molly saw, appeared very much as she imagined hers did—disappointed.

"I—I'm very sorry. I've made a mistake." Swallowing past the lump in her throat, she reached for the advertisement.

Marcus held it away. "No. This *does* mean everything will be right between us again," he said urgently. His dark-eyed gaze pulled her closer as he spoke. He reached out a hand for her, too. "It will… if we let it. Oh, Molly. I've missed you so much."

"I've missed you, too!" Relief burbled inside her. Molly felt like laughing aloud with the happiness she'd held inside. "Oh, Marcus. These past days without you…I never want anything like them to happen again."

"I was wrong," he said. "Wrong to meddle in your business, wrong to deceive you. Most of all, I was wrong to let you get away. Please, Molly. Say you'll forgive me."

"Forgive you?" Joyful tears prickled her eyes. Molly sniffled. "Only if you can forgive *me,* for being so bullheaded, so stupidly stubborn. I learned so much from you, Marcus! My cinnamon buns aren't like rocks anymore. My pies won't work as doorstops, and my cookies are more suited for eating than for shingling a roof with. I owe it all to you."

He shook his head, disagreeing. "You did that on your own. You have a talent, Molly. And it's a talent for more than simply baking. It's a talent for bringing people to life. Before you, I was only half a man."

"A charming half," she teased, letting him draw her into his arms. There, she felt warm and beloved and protected. As protected as she always would be, with Marcus, so long as she trusted enough to allow it. "A half that might combine with me, and make a brand-new whole."

Seriously Marcus gazed at her. He caressed her cheek with his fingertips, as though assuring himself she was really there, with him, at last. Molly understood. After the days they'd spent apart, she felt much the same.

"Marry me, Molly," he said, his gaze never swerving from hers. "Marry me, as we'd planned, and make us both whole like this forever. I love you more than I can say, more than I can even understand. But I know now that the need for you will never leave me."

"Oh, Marcus…" Blinking back her tears, Molly smiled at him. "Yes. Yes, I will!"

"You might not think you need me," he said, tilting her face upward to his, "but by God, I swear I need you. I thought I needed to *do* for you, too. But it turns out, all I need is for you to let me love you."

"That turns out fine." How could she be smiling, even through the tears that had turned her whole world sparkly and wet? Never mind, Molly decided. She was, and that was that. "Because all I really need is to love you in return."

Finally smiling back, Marcus gazed at her for a long moment. Happiness stretched between them, a little hard-won, and all the more precious for it. Together, they had changed just enough to make a perfect match, Molly realized. Between the two of them, there was nothing they could not do.

"Molly," Marcus breathed. "I love you."

"And I love you," she said.

He cupped her face in his hands and lowered his mouth to hers. The kiss they shared next was more tender, more certain, more wonderful than any they had experienced so far. Molly felt her heart fill with joy. She spread her palms over Marcus's shirtfront, sensing the steady beat of his heart. Fittingly enough, it seemed to match hers perfectly.

When their kiss ended, Marcus grinned again. He pulled something from his pocket—a scrap of newsprint, Molly saw—and crumpled it in his fist. He made to toss it away.

"Even without forget-me-nots," he said, "we did right fine, I'd say."

"Forget-me-nots?" Puzzled, Molly stayed his hand. "*You* were supposed to be wearing a forget-me-not, but I—"

"You were supposed to be wearing one, too."

Suddenly comprehension dawned. "May I see that?"

Marcus complied. Rapidly Molly skimmed the personal advertisement he'd brought, torn from the pages of the *Pioneer Press*. She nodded, her suspicions confirmed. She recognized those signature matchmaker touches as well as anyone…perhaps even better.

"Humph. We have been matched," she announced.

"You did not place that advertisement?" Obviously bemused, Marcus glanced around them, as though looking for the culprit.

Molly did, as well. "I did not. But I *think* I know who did."

"Right you are, daughter!" came a voice from around the corner of the bakeshop. "Right you are."

Marcus was stunned. He'd never expected—

"I must be getting slow in my old age, though," Adam Crabtree said. "I nearly forgot to bring you *these* from Fiona's greenhouse."

Wearing a proud smile, the Crabtree patriarch offered Marcus and Molly each a stem of pale blue flowers with brilliant yellow centers. *Forget-me-nots,* Marcus assumed. He reached for his, only to stop as Molly gasped.

"Papa! You mustn't be seen here like this!" Fumbling with her key, she finally opened the door to her shop and hustled them all inside. She flattened her hand over her heart. "And after all the care we've taken to guard your secret, too. Do you want the whole town to know what you're up to?"

"Actually…I hardly wanted the two of you to

know," Adam admitted. "But since you do, you might as well have these."

Cheerfully he offered the flowers again. Marcus took his, finding their delicate blossoms strange in his big hand. With a fond shake of her head, Molly accepted her nosegay as well. She lifted it to inhale its sweet fragrance, then twirled the blooms as she gazed over their colorful tops at Marcus.

"So, now you know the truth," she said.

He nodded. "I'd never have guessed it." He probably should not reveal this now, but Marcus couldn't help it. His curiosity was too strong. "Especially since the matchmaker's handwriting matched the script in your account books, Molly."

It was her turn to look enlightened. "Aha. No wonder you were so certain about me! But you were wrong. Papa tried to help me with my accounting methods, remember? That is why you saw his handwriting there, while you were snooping."

Marcus accepted her teasing, knowing he deserved it and knowing they'd settled things between them at last. "That makes sense. But how…why—"

"Oh, Copeland. If you were the father of three daughters, you would understand." Adam gave a long, weary sigh as he settled into one of the wirework chairs. "I told them they could marry for love. But when year after year passes with no daughters leaving the house, a man gets a tad desperate. You'd do the same, for a little peace and quiet."

"Papa!" Molly gave him a mock-censorious shake of her head. "You know there's more to it than that."

With a shrug, Adam gazed at the pair of them. "I only want to see my daughters happy. Truth be told—"

"Truth be told, he *likes* matchmaking," Molly assured Marcus. "He likes to meddle, he likes to stir up trouble, and he likes to have a hand in everything. Isn't that right, Papa?"

"Truth be told," Adam repeated with genial patience, directing his answer at Marcus, "I think you just might be the man to make this particular daughter happy. Welcome to the family, son."

"You may live to regret it," Molly warned.

Adam harumphed. "Aside from the bark and berries dinners and the excess of hair ribbons in my parlor…it's not so bad."

"I welcome it all," Marcus said. "So long as Molly comes with it."

Giving him a sweet smile, Molly moved to stand beside him. They joined hands, comfortable together now. "Thank you, Marcus." She paused. "But I *insist* upon making our home at your house."

They all laughed. Moments later, a knocking at

the bakery door surprised them. Grunting, Adam Crabtree went to answer it.

"I'll get that. I'd better be off to the newspaper office anyway." He stopped beside Marcus and gave him a no-nonsense look. "You can have my daughter, Copeland. But I'll need one thing from you in exchange."

"Anything." Marcus squeezed Molly's hand, filled with joy.

"You'll have to keep my secret, like my daughters do. No one can know I'm the matchmaker. Not even the Morrow Creek Men's Club."

Silently, Marcus considered it. For the entire space of a hairbreadth. "Agreed. You have my word. Your secret is safe with me."

"Fair enough." Adam nodded, then opened the door. As he left, Marcus and Molly stepped backward, surprised to see several more men filing in after him.

First was Smith, rolling in a familiar-looking barrel. He upended it as several more lumbermen followed behind him. The rattle of coins inside it was music to Marcus's ears. He sneaked a glance at Molly.

She stared, dumbfounded, as more and more lumbermen made their way into her small bakeshop. They occupied all the chairs, crowded into the corners, filled the place near to bursting. A hubbub rose as they shuffled their feet and whispered to each other, several men wearing wide grins.

His foreman met Marcus's eye. In that single glance, Marcus understood. He nodded his agreement to Smith.

"Shouldn't you men all be at work?" Marcus demanded. "What are you about, heading into town during a workday? There's timber to be felled, lumber to be hauled! Get your sorry selves out of this bakery and get to work."

Beside him, Molly tensed. She shot him a worried glance.

Smith shook his head. "The men are on strike, boss."

"On strike? That's outrageous."

His foreman gave an apologetic shrug. "It seems they won't work without having their conditions met."

Marcus narrowed his eyes, enjoying his role. He tried to appear as menacing as possible. "What conditions?"

"Well, first…" Smith loosened his shirt collar as though desperately afraid of what might happen next. The man always had been a bit of a show-off. "First, you have to agree to take back this here delectables money. The men have been paying for their own sweets for weeks now, and you know it."

Molly gasped. Marcus made a small show of grumbling, even kicked his foot a little. "Fine. What else?"

"Cinnamon buns!" came the roar of the assembled men. "We won't work without cinnamon buns!"

"And snickerdoodles!"

"Lemon tarts!"

"Apple tea cakes!"

Amid the shouting out of sweets, Marcus turned to Molly. She seemed truly flabbergasted. She laid her hand over her heart and looked out over the rough-hewn lumbermen clamoring for her baked goods. A wide smile broke across her face.

She met his gaze. "Thank you," she mouthed.

"My pleasure."

Marcus shooed a man from a nearby chair. Spanning Molly's waist with his hands, Marcus lifted her onto it. Standing there, she addressed his men.

"I'll get to baking right away," she promised.

"Hurrah!"

The lumbermen's roar of approval was deafening. As one, they pushed forward with money in hand. Molly burst out laughing.

"She can't very well bake if you won't give her room to breathe," Marcus said, commanding quiet from the men. "Head on out, now. Miss Crabtree will make an appearance at the mill soon enough."

Still talking and cheering, the men obediently filed out again, their wishes fulfilled. Smith was the last to leave. He thumped the money-filled barrel with a satisfied motion, then offered a salute to Marcus and Molly.

"Happy things worked out for you two," he said with a smile. "I knew I had the right of it, boss."

They watched the foreman leave. Then, alone in the shop, Marcus lowered Molly from her perch on the chair.

He pulled her into his arms once more. "Finally. I thought they'd never leave."

She smiled up at him. "I know. I need to get baking! Can you imagine the orders I'll have? It will be wonderful. With steady customers, I'll be free to try new recipes, to invest in supplies, to buy new baking pans! In a few years, I might even have the where-withal to enlarge the bakeshop. Oh, Marcus! Isn't this exciting? I'd better get started right away."

"In a minute," he assured her, delighting in her nearness, her excitement, her happiness. No one could chatter like Molly, but now, he loved her for it. "First, there's something I have to show you."

"Oh?" Her nose scrunched adorably. "What is it?"

"This," Marcus said, and lowered his head for

another, lingering kiss. "Because in all this world, the only thing sweeter than those cinnamon buns of yours is the two of us, together."

"Forever," she agreed.

And when their lips met again, Marcus knew that she was right. However it had come about, he and Molly were a match made in magic. A match that would last...forever.

Discover Pure Reading Pleasure with

Visit the Mills & Boon website for all the latest in romance

Buy all the latest releases, backlist and eBooks

Find out more about our authors and their books

Join our community and chat to authors and other readers

Free online reads from your favourite authors

Win with our fantastic online competitions

Sign up for our free monthly eNewsletter

Tell us what you think by signing up to our reader panel

Rate and review books with our star system

www.millsandboon.co.uk

 Follow us at twitter.com/millsandboonuk

 Become a fan at facebook.com/romancehq